WOLF TRIALS

THE SHADOWMATE SERIES

M. YOUNG

R. A. JOHNS

CONTENTS

The Shadowmate Series   vii
Wolf Trials   ix
Prophecy of the Deep   xi

Chapter 1   1
Chapter 2   21
Chapter 3   40
Chapter 4   55
Chapter 5   75
Chapter 6   95
Chapter 7   106
Chapter 8   123
Chapter 9   139
Chapter 10   154
Chapter 11   176
Chapter 12   191
Chapter 13   206
Chapter 14   219
Chapter 15   240
Chapter 16   248
Chapter 17   268
Chapter 18   294

Appendix One   305
Appendix Two   307
About M. Young   309
About R.A. Johns   311

Finding my fated mate just took a deadly twist.

When Dad dies, I'm shocked to discover my family's lies in the secret town of Fable. It sucks to return to the Sun pack that I fled. It sucks worse to be thrown into a dangerous game, which will end in my official wolf mating with the winner...unless *I'm* the victor.

Of course, I refuse. I'm 17, for wolf's sake. But wolf politics are savage, and Mom gives me two commands as cold as the snowstorm hitting town.

#1 Join the Wolf Games

#2 Win

But then, I meet *them*. The two gorgeous shifters from rival packs, who are entering the games. Are they with or against me?

Hunter, the scorching-hot, mysterious Moon Wolf and my first crush.

And Ri, the brooding Irish Shadow Wolf and my enemy.

They're as ruthless as Mom and fiercely determined to win for their packs. I've found myself in the middle of a war that could tear me apart, body and soul.

Except, what if my greatest secret is the wolf inside me?

PROPHECY OF THE DEEP

Every wolf has a shadow, and every shadow must find its mate.
Prophecy of the Deep, Book One

CHAPTER 1
WYNTER

he world is dying. All that matters is how you live and who dies first.

Those were my mom's words... words I haven't heard in over four years since I moved to New York with Dad and away from the wolf world into the human one. But now they play on my mind, as the bus I'm on takes me back to her wolf pack in the town of Fable.

When I left, I was only a weak kid, known as Wyn. But now I'm seventeen, been through so much, and if there's strength in pain, then I'm strong now. I've earned the name Wynter.

Living with the humans and being away from Mom's ruthless Sun Wolves has been like putting my life on pause.

There are three moments in my life, however, when I'm certain that the world actually *did* pause.

The moment I found out that I was so sick, I might never heal.

When my parents broke up.

And then, when Dad died.

I miss him like an aching bruise.

It's been thirty-seven days since his death, which is the reason I'm on this bus, returning to my old life.

It was a traffic accident on a rainy day. *His tires slid,* the cops told me, *and the semi-truck he collided into took him quickly. He went fast and felt no pain.*

But how do they truly know what he felt?

I blink back tears.

Many of the wolves in Fable didn't believe that love between a human and a wolf could last. They were shocked when my parents gave birth to me: *a hybrid.* They were less shocked when I grew weak and sick. They were vindicated in their beliefs, when my parents broke up.

Was it my fault?

Maybe I haven't dealt with the grief, or maybe I haven't cried enough, but it feels like ever since Dad's death, I've been endlessly trapped in his accident with him.

Dad took me to the city for access to doctors, yet it's him who was taken from the world. Now, the past four years are stolen from me as well, along with the few friends I made at school, the freedom of living away from wolves, even the addiction I developed for Nacho Doritos.

All right, I haven't had much experience in life yet, with being sick and all. But having spent too much time suffering in bed with an illness not even the doctors can diagnose makes you crave things other people take for granted. Parties. Boyfriends. That sort of thing.

Rain hits the bus window, while the flat land stretches outward like it goes on forever and we could be anywhere. The sky is bruised with storm clouds, as my mind floods with memories of Dad.

A crack of thunder booms overhead, shaking the bus, while the engine grunts in its struggle to climb the steep hill. When the bus suddenly lurches to a halt, the next thing I know, we're sliding backward. The screech of tires pierces my ears.

Panic rises through me as I grip the seat in front of me and look around. The bus struggles for traction on the road. My heart beats faster at how quickly the driver's lost control.

Someone's hollering, and our driver's swearing, as the rear of the bus sways right and then directly off the road. There are no cars behind us to slam into, but that doesn't help us.

The tires screech even louder again, and this time, my stomach drops that we're going to end up in a crash.

Was it like this for Dad?

The driver swerves us too fast, as the bus careens across the slippery road. There are no guardrails either, between the woods and us. I frantically look left and right for a way out.

But everything happens too fast. The entire bus tilts up on its side on two tires, throwing me against the window, shoulder first. The side of my head whacks into the glass. Pain bursts across my skull. I find myself staring outside at the ground, which rushes up toward me.

Panic slams into me, and I scream.

Everyone's screaming now.

Sure, death's been on my thoughts a lot, but that doesn't mean I want to die.

Please, let me live...

The world slows down to a heartbeat. My mind fills with tumbling images of all us passengers endlessly trapped in the overturned bus, never able to escape: *that I'll die in a traffic accident just like Dad.*

"Hold on," the bus driver yells.

A backpack flies across the bus, slamming into my shoulder, and I groan.

It's chaos.

Breathless, my hands and face are pressed flat to the window, but by some miracle, the bus crashes back down onto all its wheels.

Midnight Goddess, save us.

I'm jostled backward. The impact throws me sideways and right out of my seat. Agony flares in my hip, as I land on my side.

Yet survival is all I can think about. Adrenaline pumps through me. I need to get the hell out of this tin can prison.

The side-to-side rocking of the bus flings me back against the edge of my seat.

My pulse races, throbbing with my thunderous heart. The world outside seems to be moving... *except it's us.* We're still sliding down the street.

Shit!

I scramble to get back into my seat, when I notice that a woman with graying hair and smeared cherry lipstick has fallen to the floor too. My startled gaze meets hers, and I reach for her hand to help her.

But then, the bus slams into something with a hideous crunching sound. I'm thrown back, away from the woman with the cherry lipstick, onto the aisle between the seats.

I let out an *oomph*, as the wind's knocked out of me.

Finally, the bus shudders to a stop.

I don't move at first, not believing it's safe yet. I catch the faint smell of burning rubber and something else metallic. Then I lift my head and twist around. My neck hurts. A plume of black smoke wafts outside from the rear of the bus, where we've crashed into a pine tree.

Quickly, I scramble to my feet, rushing to the woman, who's still on her hands and knees. I help her back up, noting that there are no cuts on her hands, just terror lingering in her eyes. I can smell the perspiration and fear on her.

"You'll be okay," I murmur.

She's nodding, too scared to talk, as she dabs at her mouth like she can unsmear her lipstick.

"Everyone all right?" The bus driver calls out.

The driver is a thickset man, who's so pale that he looks like he's been turned into a ghost by the crash. He pulls the latch to the doors, which screech as they slide open. He scans the passengers and then hurries outside.

I follow him. I'm desperate to get off the bus. A wall of freezing wind collides into me, and I tug my jacket tighter around myself to shield against the cold.

The smoke from the rear of the bus is thick, curling up into the darkening clouds. The air stinks.

My heart is still thumping too fast at how close I came to dying.

The bus isn't going anywhere anytime soon: the whole backside is wrapped around a tall pine tree.

I scan the steep road and woodland.

Wait, I know this place.

I know exactly where I am. It's not far from my pack home in the national park. I can walk the rest of the way. I'd have got off at the next stop anyway.

I rub the back of my neck, where the muscles still twinge. My head and hip hurt, but I'll survive.

Surviving's what matters. Always has and always will.

My legs are unsteady, but I approach the bus driver, only to find that he's on his mobile, calling for help.

I can't wait for the authorities to arrive. It's too much: *paramedics...cops...sirens...*

Just, too much.

And Mom is expecting me in Sun House, which is the manor house in Fable, where I was raised. I don't need to play by human rules any longer, only those of the wolf. It's strange to be caught between worlds like this.

I rush into the bus, pushing aside the strewn luggage, to collect my backpack and bag on wheels. Everything I own is in these two cases.

I square my shoulders and set off up the hill.

"Hey," the driver shouts after me, "where are you going? Are you hurt? You should wait for a paramedic to check you over."

"My home's close," I reply, without looking around.

It's weird to say *home* about Sun Wolf territory. *About Fable.* Is it my home anymore? "I'm going to go on foot from here."

Why am I shivering? Shock, probably.

But I've had my fill of human doctors. It's why half my bag is filled with vitamins and meds.

When I reach the top of the hill, I glance back to where the bus remains wrapped around the tree. Most of the passengers now spill out onto the road.

Will they be the last humans that I see for years? *Victims of a crash?*

"Great start to your home-coming, Wynter," I whisper.

Over the hill, the pines are tightly packed together, but I spy the dirt track, which leads into the forest up ahead. I draw in a long breath, savoring the heady blend of earthy smells, along with the crispness of rain.

When I was a kid, I used this path as a shortcut to explore the woods. Now, I feel like a stranger here.

The ground is pebbly and wet. I drag my bag behind me, and the wheels jump about; it's not exactly made for tracking through the woods.

Somewhere behind me, a twig snaps.

I pause and look back, half expecting someone from the bus to have followed me. But there's no one there.

Humans aren't welcome in Fable and they're rarely seen. But they *are* tolerated, which is code for not being savaged on sight, since the lands are protected as a national park and permission given to us to live here. Most humans, however, have no clue that our kind exists.

My human dad was unusual because he was embraced out of respect for Mom, who's the Alpha of all the three wolf packs: Sun, Moon, and Shadow. Mom's the *only* Alpha in the territory, and a Sun Wolf has held the honored position of Alpha for generations. Because Mom is the Alpha, every Sun Wolf is respected over the other wolves, I remember that.

Only dense fir and pine trees surround me, while the forest is filled with the soft tapping of rain hitting the trees. The chill in the air sinks into my bones, and my teeth chatter.

"It's only animals." I'm still shaking from almost being crushed in the bus. "Racoons, a stag, or…"

Another snap, this one closer and *definitely* someone's footstep.

I turn around. My stomach churns at the thought of meeting anyone from the pack. Of course, it's inevitable eventually, but tell that to my brain.

No one's there. Except, I know that I'm not alone.

Why are even the birds silent?

I freeze.

"Stop watching me," I call out, gripping the handlebar of my bag and pushing the strap of the backpack higher up on my shoulder, turning on the spot to scan the woods. "Or is the whole stalker act your thing?"

It's what I don't miss about Fable: that there's always someone keeping an eye on you, whether you know it or not.

Wolves are always watching from the shadows.

"My *thing*?" a deep male voice responds with a lilting

Irish accent. "My thing is to tell you that you shouldn't be here." He speaks with authority like he's used to others obeying him. *Good luck trying that with me.* "Turn around and leave. You're in the wrong place."

I bristle, peering through the shadowy woods to spot him. "Maybe *you're* in the wrong place."

He huffs. "I'm exactly where I should be. And brilliant comeback, by the way."

Asshole.

He steps out from behind a giant pine. Shadows conceal him, until he moves forward into the light.

He's a wolf; I know it, before the breeze brings me his woodsy wolven scent. Yet I don't recognize him from Fable.

I don't back away, however, because I came here to join the pack, not run from them.

Okay, so he's tall. I have to tilt my head to look up at him, and why does that do funny things to my insides, when I stare into his emerald eyes?

His lashes are longer and darker than should be legal. His hair is a tumble of black curls, shorter at the sides and longer on the top, and it's soaking wet. His skin is almost translucently pale and perfect, just like his full kissable lips, sharp cheekbones, and powerful body.

I shouldn't be staring, but Emerald Eyes is the kind of guy who'd easily cause my panties to catch on fire with a single look.

Now *that* would be a talent.

His black Henley top is plastered to his chest from the rain. He's ripped, the fabric following every curve of his chest and biceps. These aren't the type of muscles I expect on someone who looks only a couple of years older than me. No human guy had them back at my school in the city. And none of them wore jeans so low on their hips, that the V-line at the sides of their hip bones made warmth flood through me. Even through his wet shirt, it's clear that he's strong.

And he holds himself like he thinks he's an Alpha.

Who is he?

My breath races at the sight of him; my heart thuds equally as fast.

My attention slides back up to his face, which is dripping with rain. I pretend not to notice the way his gaze studies me as well: my almost violet eyes, waist-length brunette hair, skinny jeans, and tatty Converse.

How long has he been out in *my* woods, anyway? And who said that he was the only one who got to be possessive about them?

Something flickers in his eyes: a fire that screams *predator*.

And just as quickly, my wolf stirs within, pressing against me. My muscles tense, and every breath is a struggle. I stumble, as I use the bag on wheels to catch myself.

My wolf... she hasn't shown herself for the last four years. Now, I've barely entered the woods, and she's making a show in response to this guy of all people...?

The pull between us startles, *scares* me.

Is it possible to be so addictively attracted to someone after just meeting them? Being away from the pack made me forget just how gorgeous wolf shifters are.

But the sudden swell of desire is distracting me from the danger this new wolf poses. I straighten, shocked.

Mom told me once, when I was too young to understand, that Alphas use their unique gifts over the opposite sex to conquer and control them. She'd laughed softly and said it was how she'd mated with Dad.

What did she mean?

Well, Mom's meant to be the only Alpha in the territory. But the guy in front of me is every inch an Alpha.

Mom will tear out his throat if she finds him in her woods. Unless she already knows that he's here…?

"Who the hell are you?" I demand, struggling to calm the wave of heat that's swallowing me. "You're the one who shouldn't be lurking in the Sun Wolves' woods. It's not safe."

Why am I warning Emerald Eyes? Except, he's far too handsome to end up savaged.

His head tilts back, and he inhales deeply; his nostrils flare.

He's sniffing me: is that polite?

I guess that I *did* sniff him first.

"The Sun Wolves' wood…? We appear to be the only ones here. Are you scared that the big, bad Alpha is going to jump out and eat us up?" His intense gaze rests on me again. "Where are you from, wolf?"

Why does he make the *wolf* sound like a question? *Is it because I'm a hybrid?*

Jerk.

I flush.

When he runs a hand through his damp hair, my gaze settles on the way that his bicep flexes.

He notices.

Fire blazes across my cheeks, reddening them. "If you're not going to answer my question, then get out of my way," I bluster, when I finally find my voice, gripping the strap of my backpack harder.

"Like I said, you don't belong here." He hesitates, and I wonder if he's debating saying *human, wolf, hybrid,* or something else entirely. "So, you're going the wrong way, right?"

His brow furrows, broodily.

Why does it sound like *he's* warning *me*?

I give him a mock laugh, pushing myself to swagger forward, so I can stop making a fool of myself by blushing. My stomach twists, as I stroll past him, and I can't help the way my breath hitches.

I keep my chin high, however, refusing to show him how easily he's affected me.

It doesn't matter how handsome a shifter is, all wolves are dangerous, especially when they're from an opposing pack. And I'm convinced that Emerald Eyes must be. No Sun Wolf would dare talk about Mom like he has because they *would* be scared of the big, bad Alpha.

"Look, you probably won't listen to me, but I have to try. You're making a mistake joining this pack," Emerald Eyes warns.

Then to my surprise, he flashes a leisurely grin that'll imprint on my mind for eternity.

Somehow, I'm having trouble focusing on anything

but his smile, and the way he stands there, nonchalantly, confirms he knows the impact he has.

I narrow my gaze at him.

His persistence chases away my earlier embarrassment. "And if I were you, I'd get out of here before my mom, *the Alpha*, has you hunted down for talking like that."

Instantly, I cringe.

Relying on the crutch of Mom's power is something that I always promised myself I'd never do.

He watches me from behind hooded eyes, before he smirks. "Big words from such a pretty, little wolf."

Okay, twice my size or not, I will find a way to kick his ass for that. Just not right now.

I glare at him as I hurry down the sloped hill. I sense his gaze on my back, but I don't stop. Yet I can tell by the heavy footsteps behind me that he's following.

"So, you're the Alpha's sick daughter, who was sent to heal with the humans," Emerald Eyes says almost conversationally.

What, can he not tell by the literal fact that I'm walking away that the conversation is over?

"You don't know anything about it." I don't look around. Perhaps, if I ignore him, he'll go away. "Don't pretend that you do."

He laughs. *Why does the sound have to be so delicious?* "I know more than you realize. In the name of the Great Shadow Wolf, I guess that I simply know more than you, period."

A surge of adrenaline pours through me.

I stop, whipping around to face him. "No, you don't."

He arches an eyebrow at me. He's now standing a couple of feet away, protected by a canopy of branches from the rain. This close, I see the golden flecks in his green eyes, the faint shade of growth across his strong jawline.

How can one person be so easy on the eyes and a douche at the same time?

He folds his arms across his chest, and an amused expression washes across his face. "Aye, I know that you were born with wealth and power, that you have no understanding of what it's like to be at the bottom of the pack hierarchy, unlike the Moon Wolves. And everything must come easy, when you have others serving you. Here's the thing of it, I know all that too. But there's a difference. You've been protected from the brutal truth of the wolf world. Tell me, how much blood have you spilled to retain the high position of your family's pack status? I'm guessing not much, but do you bat an eye at those who have?"

I'm shaking with anger, and I curl my hands into fists. "Don't you dare talk to me about not under-standing sorrow and suffering."

"Right, you were sick."

It shouldn't hurt. But it does.

I narrow my eyes at him. "Take your personal issues elsewhere and stay the hell out of mine. Trust me, if I have anything to do with it, we won't be crossing paths again."

A smile curls his lips like he's succeeded in getting the reaction out of me that he intended. Then he moves toward me so fast that I barely have time to react. He's right in my space. He leans in, and I can't help but breathe in deeply, taking in his addictive masculine scent that makes my knees almost buckle.

"I sensed the way your wolf reacted to me, Sun Girl." His gaze searches mine, as if for answers.

Then he steps back, stalking into the shadows of the woods.

I stumble, gasping for air, needing a moment to catch myself.

"Asshole," I mutter.

The sound of his laugh echoes from deep in the woods.

What a psychopath!

A deliciously *sexy* psychopath, but that doesn't make him any less dangerous.

I'm shaking as I march away. I keep looking over my shoulder, but he's not coming after me.

I remind myself why I didn't want to return to my pack in the first place. I'd forgotten about the underlying rivalry between the different types of wolves within the pack, and whoever this new pack member is, he's already got on Mom's bad side, that's clear.

Then again, she does a fantastic job of upsetting anyone she meets.

The rain picks up, and I'm completely drenched, so I hurry.

Maybe the bus accident and clashing with Emerald Eyes were all signs that I should just leave. But then what? Live on the streets?

When I finally step out of the woods and into an expansive clearing, I pause. To my right, towers the monstrous mountains and at their base, huddles the town of Fable. Beyond the houses and stores, lies a winding river, a bridge, and the field on the other side often used for pack rituals.

I make quick work of reaching the main part of town, the wet ground splashing with each step. Two enormous oaks mark the entry into the village, their sloped branches arching over the entry path like this is a joyful, old-fashioned town but that's the farthest from the truth. It's a mask. There may be no guards in sight, but they're always on watch in Fable, hidden in the woods, in the trees...anywhere.

With different packs calling the location home, Fable has long been divided into three quadrants—Sun, Moon, and Shadow—with the main road slicing through the village shared by all as neutral grounds.

I rush past storefronts: the local coffee shop, the Storm Moon store that carries everything, and even a bakery. *My favorite.* It's like a small human town in the middle of nowhere, except everyone here goes furry.

Like Mom used to say, *just because we live in the woods, doesn't mean we're savages.*

Head low, I stride past a couple on the sidewalk, who stare at me strangely. Once I reach the end of the road, I turn right and dart through open gates and into the Sun district. It's a part of Fable where every home is a three-story mansion made of light stone and the gardens out the front are perfectly manicured with shrubs cut into the shape of wolves.

At the end of the street stands my family home, Sun House, like an overbearing giant backing onto the

mountain and encased by lofty pines. It's also positioned on the highest platform in town, giving it the
best vantage point to look out across Fable. White stone
walls glint from the sunlight peeking out from behind
the clouds. Bronze sun faces are attached onto each
wall, looking down on Fable from every side.

I make my way up the sloped street.

The ruling pack takes the best homes, Mom once
explained. *Our family won the right to be their Alpha, and
so our pack won the right to the best of everything within
Fable.*

I cross the lawn of my home, and the front door
opens for me, before I can reach for the handle.

Faith, Mom's housekeeper, stands in the doorway,
staring at me with huge, startled eyes. She examines me
like she's seeing a ghost.

Hasn't Mom told her that I was returning? Perhaps,
she's just taking in the new me? There are things about
me that've changed over the past four years, like my
longer hair and fuller lips, not to mention that I've
now filled out and have tits I'd have killed for back
then.

Faith is shorter than me but so maternal that I spent
my life as a kid, being either cuddled or scolded to do
my homework. She's one of the kindest Moon Wolves
who works for the Sun pack as a servant. She cared for
me growing up, as Mom didn't have time. The Moon
pack have only a low status in the territory and most
work as servants or in manual labour.

My heart clenches at the thought, but who am I to
make the rules?

"Wyn, you're back." Faith smiles warmly, and joy rushes through me at her welcome.

Somebody does want me here.

She hurries forward to embrace me but stops short when heavy steps sound behind her. She looks over her shoulder, pulling back, as a figure emerges from within the house.

"My sweet daughter, you've finally arrived," Mom's voice is cool.

I swallow hard, as Faith withdraws, vanishing into the house as meekly as a mouse.

Mom steps outside, straightening her back. Her silk dress, the color of a sunset, spills down to her ankles. A thin belt cinches in around her waist, and the buttons go all the way up to the base of her throat. Her dark hair is impeccably styled and shiny, pulled off her face by diamante pins.

"Why are you still outside in the rain?" Mom scowls, taking my hand and squeezing. She drags me inside. I stumble in, before dumping my bags near the door. Faith hurries to collect them for me. "You're wet and a mess."

Mom still holds my hand but doesn't hug me. She studies me up and down, then looks at my face. Her brow furrows.

Yet she's smiling, even if it's a rare stretching of her mouth that looks uncomfortable on her.

"Well, it's raining, and I had to walk here. But I'm back, I guess. Maybe not for long," I say, my voice cracking.

Why am I babbling?

I accepted that Mom had kept her distance from Dad and me in the city, and I stopped crying about her not attending his funeral, but now standing in front of her, a storm of emotions batter me. They batter the wind out of me. Batter my confidence. Batter the perfect wall I set up before I left the city, knowing with wolves you never show weakness because the moment you do, others will walk all over you... especially my mom.

"Whatever do you mean? You're here to stay with us. I've missed you so much." She cups the sides of my face with two hands, and when I look deep into her pale eyes, I don't see the love that should match her words. But she always knows the right things to say, even if they aren't true. "You should've come straight home. People are already talking about you roaming the woods like a wild girl. Why didn't you use the main track into town?"

I blink at her; tiredness swallows me. "What people?"

She simply shakes her head.

All I want is to go to my room, have a scalding hot shower to chase away the cold, and sleep.

"You've grown so much. You're a woman now. Blessed sun, it's time you caught up. Let's hope you're simply a late bloomer. You were always so skinny."

I roll my eyes. "If you'd visited Dad and me in the city, you'd have seen that I changed."

Mom sighs, her gaze lowering momentarily, and I almost believe her. "Dear, you were on my mind every single day. But you know being in charge of Fable is a responsibility that I can't walk away from. So many people rely on me."

And I don't?

"I get it," I say with difficulty.

A shadow flares in Mom's pale eyes, darkening them. "I know it was hard to lose your father, and I'm sorry you had to go through that. Having you back will help, I promise, even if it doesn't seem like it now."

When she embraces me, it catches me by surprise. The lump in my throat thickens, while tears form in my eyes: tears that I promised myself to leave behind in New York.

Next thing I know, Mom is ushering me upstairs. "Quickly, go and get changed. Put your clothes away, before you make me all soppy, then we can properly catch up."

My stomach tightens, and I find myself reverting back to the girl from four years ago, who couldn't tell if Mom's kindness was sincere. Her emotions have always flared to polar opposites within the span of a second.

The thing is, I grew up in a house of lies.

In the Sun House, every word spoken or heard could come back to bite you.

CHAPTER 2
WYNTER

First comes the darkness in the woods, stealing the light.

I'm stumbling, turning on the spot, lost, unsure where I am. Shivers race down my spine, along with the foreboding feeling that I'm being watched.

Then comes the panic.

Shadows surrounding me give nothing away, only the trepidation from being alone.

So... I run.

Branches whip against me, shrubs snag on my jeans, while my emotions are sucked through me like a black hole, draining me.

Why can't I remember how I got here?

Or where here is?

Sweat rolls down my neck. My insides are like a supernova with heat, flaming through me.

When up ahead, I spot a light bleeding in oranges and reds through the darkness, it's my salvation. I sprint faster.

When I burst free from the forest, I pause at the edge of a

lookout. I'm standing on a mountain and before me lies a city, blinking to life from windows in apartments, skyscrapers, and the Empire State Building.

New York!

Staring at it fills me with a yearning, as well as with memories of what was taken from me.

Then I gasp.

What's that scraping sound?

I glance around me.

Someone's hunched over with their back to me. They're dressed all in black, and they're digging madly into the earth using only their bare hands.

Scrape, scrape, scrape.

"Hello, are you okay?" My words echo around us like we're in a cave, and the sounds cause a murder of crows to burst out from the trees.

I duck.

There are so many crows. They circle the reddish sky, watching us with beady, black eyes.

I turn to study the guy again. Then I sidestep him, keeping my distance and sink to my knees.

The moment that I do, he lifts his head.

My breath hitches, as our gazes meet. His eyes are as dark as obsidian stones. His pale face, and the way that he looks at me, leaves me feeling vulnerable, as though he can see the shadow deep inside me.

"Wynter," he groans, startling me. "Your return will bring death. But there's a way out, if you dare."

"W-what do you mean?" A chill encases me, and I want to know more, but I don't at the same time.

"Be mine," he whispers into the darkness, before lifting his

dirt-covered hands, palms upward. "You must give yourself first. Are you ready, Wynter?"

And with that single question, his face twitches, and his eyes blink.

In a heartbeat, a familiar face with emerald eyes stares back at me.

I lurch backward and fall onto my ass.

It's the guy from the woods: Emerald Eyes.

The crows sweep over us, and I'm swallowed completely by their shadows.

I wake up abruptly like my body has been electrocuted, and my mind races to place where I am.

Memories flood me—the bus accident, the guy in the woods, and the freaky dream. I'm breathing hard, and sweat coats my nape.

The dream's nothing more than my anxiety, right? I chew on my lower lip. Anxiety mixed with stalker vibes and a healthy dose of crushing on bad boys.

I climb out from beneath the blankets. The morning light pours into my bedroom, and I'm still in yesterday's jeans and black tee. My bare feet touch the cold floorboards.

Yesterday, I came up to my room to rest after arriving, but I must've fallen asleep. The meds I'm on sometimes do that to me.

When I hear the *click-clack* of claws on the floorboards, I glance over to a grey and white Huskie, who's poking his head happily around the side of the bed. A giddy excitement fills me, and I leap to my feet at seeing my dog.

"Hades!" I throw myself across the bed and embrace him, while he rests his chin on my shoulder, making grunting sounds. "I know boy, I missed you so much too. I'm sorry I couldn't come and see you earlier."

He used to sleep on my bed with me, and to leave him behind four years ago destroyed me. Dad tried to bring him with us to New York, but Mom wouldn't allow it.

There are a lot of things on Mom's *not allowed* list.

I ruffle Hades' fur and kiss him on his head, loving how soft he feels. "So, what's been going on here? Are you keeping everyone in check? Have you been staying in my room?"

Hades tilts his head to the side, making another throaty sound.

I laugh and hug him again. "You're the best thing to return to, you know that?" I furrow my brow. "I wish you'd been with me last night. You could've bitten a certain psycho shifter every time that he called me *wolf*."

Hades barks enthusiastically.

Except, I don't mean it. Yesterday, warmth tingled across my skin at the way the word rolled off his tongue in his lilting accent.

Perhaps, Hades could just give Emerald Eyes a little nip for the *pretty, little wolf* comment?

I push myself up, moving across the familiar room that I grew up in, studying the white walls, my desk against the wall, the mahogany dresser and matching wardrobe. The fairy lights I had draped around the furniture have all been removed, but it still feels like my room.

My bags remain in the corner, unpacked. Hades is on my heels though, headbutting my legs for more scratches.

"Not much has changed. You're still the biggest cry baby for pats." I laugh at him.

I turn to the large window across from the bed and look out over the grounds past the river. Feather-soft snow is falling, explaining the chill in the air that sinks its teeth into my flesh, and I rub my arms free of goosebumps.

It's always on the brink of snowing nowadays like it needs only the lightest push to tip into the permanent winter that everyone's fearing.

Blossom trees dot the slumbering earth, blooming despite everything else, fading in color from the wintery days consuming every season. Bright green leaves and red silky-petals spread across the branches, while the petals flourish across the ground like the magic of cherry blossom trees. Though, when snow comes, the ruby-red petals always remind me of bloody footprints in the snow.

Ancient Wolf Magic is what keeps them blooming during the cold months, which takes a lot of effort to maintain, instead of allowing them the normal cycle of sleeping. But as a symbol of elite pack power, Mom insists on them eternally flowering.

Only the Alpha's family wear their fragrant flowers as symbols of our power.

Beyond the trees, are two people out in the field, and it's too hard to tell who they are from this distance.

Are they Sun Wolves?

It's weird to be home and yet not know who's in my own territory.

Something glints, as the sunlight catches on it. The people in the field are holding something metallic. I press closer to the window to make out what it is. Swords? Axes?

Panic winds through me. *Are they chopping down the trees?*

By the Blessed Sun, they wouldn't. Mom would have them driven from the pack, if she didn't savage them herself, wouldn't she?

Maybe a lot more has changed over the past four years than I expected. Nature has always been respected, so this is new.

I wet my dry lips, before I glance down at Hades. "Wanna go for a walk?"

He breaks into an ear-piercing howl, and I cringe. "I'll take that as a yes. But first, I need a shower. So, do you wanna hear all about New York?"

Hades trails after me into the bathroom, making himself comfortable on the fluffy floor mat.

Once I'm finished with my shower and all talked out, I dress in black jeans, thick, knee-length boots, and a long-sleeve top.

Then I pat my thigh for Hades to follow me, before I stumble down the stairs.

"Breakfast is ready," Mom calls out, as I attempt to

sneak for the front door. *Damn, nearly made it.* "Eat something."

"I'm no longer a kid, you know."

"You're seventeen, so that makes you under my authority. In fact, everyone in Fable is under mine."

I sigh.

Only a couple more weeks to go, until I turn eighteen. Then under the rules of Fable, I'm an independent wolf. I can leave here if I want to...not that I have anywhere to go.

And if I stay within Fable, Mom will still be my Alpha.

"Come and join us," Mom says.

Us? I blink and twist around, peering into the dining hall, where I catch Mom staring at me from the edge of the table, her lips tight.

Hades groans, and I rub his head. "Sorry, Hades. Just give me a sec."

I cross the room and enter the dining hall. Mom is at one end of the long oak table, her partner, Addison, on the opposite end.

I glance between them in surprise. Are they deliberately sitting as far away from each other as possible or is this some weird wolf hierarchy thing about second partners?

Mom and Dad always sat as close as possible at all times. They'd been like best friends, until, well, they *weren't*.

But then, Dad was a human.

After Mom and Dad split up, she matched with Addison from a neighboring Sun family to help her run

Fable. He's a wolf of stature when it comes to power and wealth, and Mom only insists on the best. I wonder whether he had to pass some kind of inspection or written test.

Mom apparently had a lot of making up to do to the Sun Wolves for taking a human husband in the first place. I'd heard the secret conversations: the pack hadn't been happy with that arrangement.

It's another reason that I'm nervous about coming back here now. After all, I'm half-human, half-wolf, making me just as much an outcast as Dad had been.

Addison's dark hair is parted just over his temple and peppered white. He has a dimpled chin and flaring nostrils. I bet he was one of the handsomest bachelors when he was young.

I take the seat at the side of the table, a sense of awkwardness settling over me. Now the three of us are at the long table, and all eyes are on me, but no one says anything.

Mom's gaze is impatient, reminding me of growing up in Fable and how nothing I did was good enough. Addison's eyes, on the other hand, are pale grey and distant, like his thoughts are miles away, while pretending he's here with us.

Maybe that's *his* way of surviving.

There are no photos in the dining hall, only floor to ceiling windows on one side adorned by heavy velvet curtains, golden candelabras, and a complete contradiction to the notion of wolves living in the wilderness.

"Well, this is...awkward," I say.

"I'm so sorry, child, to hear about your father." Addison's gaze finally focuses on me. "But it's wonderful to have you back with us."

I can't help but feel like his comforting words stem from a place that has nothing to do with me but more of a response to a power struggle he had with Mom before I entered the room.

I offer him a weak smile, which feels unnatural on my lips, then I turn to my empty plate. In front of me lies a buffet: scones, scrambled eggs and bacon, blood sausages, fried tomatoes, and fruit. Fable has a plethora of foods for those who can afford it, of course, grown in greenhouses, and everything they serve in town is made from scratch. Anything processed is forbidden, though I have snuck in a few packets of Doritos no one needs to know about.

"So, tell us what New York is like," Addison says politely, before taking a savage bite of a muffin and looking like he can hardly restrain himself from moaning.

The muffins in Fable *are* delicious.

It's weird though. Dad worked three jobs, just to pay for my medical bills and keep food on the table. It tugs at something inside me that here Mom can provide all this stuff for me like it's nothing. But really, it didn't matter that Dad and I were poor because we had each other.

I bite my lip, hard.

"Don't be so insensitive," Mom fires back. "She's left all that behind; it's going to be hard for her to talk about it. It's best we catch her up on the status of the Deep and how much closer it is than most people realize."

The Deep.

Two words I haven't heard in so long.

The Deep refers to a deep winter, a continual winter that's been prophesied to take us all into an Ice Age and wipe out all existence.

The world has been in a perpetual cold streak for at least a decade, not to mention the floods and extreme storms. The humans blame global warming and the polar vortex, while the wolves blame The Deep.

Animals sense danger, and I've picked up on it too… *an unease.*

Something is definitely broken with the world.

"My treasured Alpha, now's not the time. Let her settle in." Addison tilts up his chin.

So, her partner isn't some meek wolf. Perhaps, there's a reason that they're sitting so far apart.

I duck my head, as I serve myself eggs on toast.

"Of course, it's the time," Mom snarls. "We've been in winter for years. There are no more denials or excuses to be made."

I've seen a lot of discussions on TV about fears of a big freeze coming, but many people dismiss it as conspiracy theories or that it's a natural weather cycle. Except, what if the wolf prophecies are correct and this is the end of life as we know it in our lifetime?

Flashes of my dream come to me, but that was just a stress dream, nothing more, right?

"No one's denying it," Addison says, softly. "But she's only just arrived. Things are overwhelming, and you can be intense, my treasure, you know you can. I'm sure she'll prefer to talk about New York, right Wynter?" he asks, drawing me out of my thoughts.

I shoot him a relieved glance. I already like him for getting Mom off my back.

I hated him when he first got together with Mom, but that had everything to do with my parents splitting up and nothing to do with him.

His mating with Mom was a political arrangement: an alliance. I can't blame him for that.

I shudder. Will Mom try and arrange who I mate with?

Midnight Goddess, save me from that. It'd wreck me.

I don't think matchings should be like that. They didn't used to be. Once, they were fated mates who you loved with all your Soul: *shadowmates.*

But then the long, slow march toward the Deep began, and no one knows what happened. Our biology became messed up or something broke inside us, but now we can no longer sense our shadowmates.

Sometimes, I think that shadowmates are only a fairy tale, and matchings like this cold one between Mom and Addison are the only reality us wolves will ever know.

Mom huffs in frustration.

"I don't mind talking about the city." I grab a glass and fill it with orange juice. Two maids hurry into the room to top up plates with more food... more food than three people could ever eat in one sitting.

What a waste.

"Tell me, have you climbed to the top of The Statue

of Liberty?" Addison distracts me. "The view from up there must be spectacular."

He sounds excited, wistful. He's never left pack territory. Does he wish that he could?

Mom scrapes her plate hard, as she cuts her sausage; her lips thin. She glares at Addison, and I hurriedly tell him about living in New York because I want to see him smile.

And I realize that maybe I was lucky to have seen New York in the first place.

I suspect the way Mom and Addison are together has everything to do with wolves no longer having the ability to sense their shadowmates. Are they truly that different to humans now?

When I reach for another slice of toast, Addison wipes his mouth with the napkin and stands from the table.

"I need to go and summon the Fearless," he tells Mom, then glances my way. "Now that your precious Wynter has returned, we can begin."

"Begin?" I tilt my head to the side.

Plus, *precious Wynter*? What the hell!

"Well, then off you go." Mom shoos Addison away like he's Hades.

Addison nods curtly, striding out of the room.

"Why is he gathering the Fearless council? What's he beginning?" I ask.

I may have been gone for four years, but I still know that nothing good ever comes of summoning the Fearless. The council is made up of representatives of each pack and come together in emergencies, to settle disputes, or hand out punishments.

"Oh, it's nothing to worry about." Mom doesn't meet my eye. "What are your plans today, dear?"

I blink at her, knowing she won't tell me until she decides I deserve to know.

Yeah, this is still the house of lies.

So, I change the topic before she interrogates me about what I intend to do, which in truth, has only gone so far as heading outside to see who's in the field and what they're doing.

Hades sits impatiently by my seat, glancing up at me with a, *are-you-finished*, look.

"How's everything going with you and Addison?" I ask, carefully.

Mom arches a manicured eyebrow. "Why in the wild wolves' name would you ask that?"

I take a big gulp of my juice, seeing the defenses rising in her gaze. "I was just thinking how things may be different, if we were able to feel our fated bonds. You know, if our wolves could find their shadowmates. If you didn't meet Dad, then I might not exist. And with Addison, you don't know if he really *is* your shadowmate."

"I never took you for being sentimental," Mom's response is clipped. "None of us will ever find our true shadowmates anymore. Sometimes, the loss of our ability to find our fated mates feels like a bad nightmare." She pauses, studying me as if trying to work me out. "Anyway, you're too young to be jaded about things that happened before you were even born."

But not too young to bury my dad.

I jerk, as the thought hits me: agonizing and unexpected.

Instantly, I lose my appetite.

Wiping my mouth, I leap up. "I'm going for a walk with Hades."

Mom sighs and calls out, before I can leave, "Don't forget your snow jacket. It feels like it'll never be summer again. Maybe it won't."

She falls silent.

Without a word, I grab my jacket, slip it on, and head out of the front door. Hades bursts right past me and darts across the yard, as I zip up my polar jacket, which is the color of snow. He jumps about crazily, trying to snap at the descending snow.

Pushing the hood over my head, with my hands tucked into my pockets, I stride out onto the sidewalk and make my way down the long street, through the Sun pack gates, and avoid the main road. More people are roaming about in town, but my sights are set on the wooden, arched bridge that only spans ten feet across the river.

Hades charges ahead toward the bridge, and I speed up after him. We may be wolves, but not everyone appreciates a dog as our pet.

I bolt after him. My boots slap the bridge with each fast footstep. The river gurgles underneath us, its banks already icing over, and I wonder how long before it's all solid ice.

I loved ice skating over the river with my best friend Hunter, when I was a kid. I didn't have many friends because I was a hybrid, but Hunter made up for that. He always protected me and made sure that I didn't feel left out, even though he was from the Moon pack, and his Mom, Faith, was our housekeeper. We stayed out for hours ice skating, until I could no longer feel my toes, and we were forced back inside.

I finally catch up to Hades, who's thrown himself into a fresh patch of snow near a blossom tree and is rubbing his back into it with his legs in the air. He's groaning, having way too much fun.

The field is just as I remember it: it's enormous and accessible from all edges of the surrounding woods. I'm certain that Fable guards protect it aggressively. My gaze darts to where the clank of metal clashing against metal drifts over.

I'm standing about sixty-feet away silently, and I watch as two people battle. A guy and a girl. They aren't actually chopping wood with their axes, but training with them.

My eyes widen.

The guy's wearing black pants and no shirt. His powerful muscles are distinct and move easily beneath his skin. But there are silvery scars across his muscled back like savage claw marks. They should've healed. What happened to him? Why haven't they?

They glimmer in the light. They're strangely beautiful.

He's fluid in his actions against his opponent, using the handle of the axe in defense against the axe coming straight for his head.

He blocks the attack and kicks his heel into the girl's thigh, sending her reeling.

"Stop cheating, Ri," she calls out, her voice carrying over on the breeze.

Then she attacks him with a war cry and a fierceness that takes away my breath.

He only chuckles, ducking out of her reach, then whips around. He recoils a few steps and raises his axe.

And that's when I catch a glimpse of his face.

I freeze: It's *Emerald Eyes*.

Except, now I know his name. He's called Ri.

I roll his name over my tongue...*Ri*.

It's different. He sounds Irish, but if he's from the Irish packs, why is he in Fable?

"And you've got to be kidding me," I mutter. "Why him of all people? Is he stalking the blossom trees now as well? And who takes off their shirt in the snow?"

I should look away but I'm half mesmerized by the badass fighting of the girl, who looks around my age.

She's dressed in a black bodysuit and has fiery red hair. She's curvy and moves fast. She's terrifyingly agile with the axe.

Who in the world are these two?

My gaze shifts over Ri, who pivots just out of reach of her axe. Its sharp blade sweeps inches from slashing his chest.

I hold my breath. Their deadly dance is spellbinding. Each swing is precise, each duck and maneuver to avoid being sliced in half, is elegant.

I've never seen anything like it, and especially nothing like this has ever been around wolves. We're primal animals, we hunt, we transform into our beast forms, and attack. At least, that's what I was taught growing up at Fable School. We trained with teeth, using our senses and our strength.

When I look at this pair battling, however, I'm in awe. It seems like the opposite of what a wolf does, yet it's as dangerous and lethal.

On his next defensive move, Ri whips around, but this time, his gaze meets mine.

We lock eyes.

I'm paralyzed, imprisoned by his green irises.

Wait, didn't I promise that I'd never cross paths with him again? And now I'm playing the stalker, spying on him.

I blush. What a reversal.

My heart thunders in my chest, and my cheeks are burning up. A shiver slides up my arms. Ri may be alluring and addictive to look at, especially with his chest and muscles on show, but under his gaze, I don't feel safe. Everything about him screams danger and power, and I don't want to be around a wolf who dominates others.

I don't want him, right?

I hate wolves who want to be Alphas.

The girl smirks, seeing Ri's distracted by me, and sneakily kicks Ri in the side. Startled, he stumbles.

"I win," she crows.

Our connection breaks, and panic climbs through me. I shouldn't be out here near him. I want to run and never look back. So, I twist, and turn to leave, but instead, I crash right into Hades, who's suddenly in front of me.

I tumble over Hades. Of course, he scrambles out of my way, leaving me to fall like a clumsy fool who can't even stand on two legs.

But then, Ri fell first, distracted by *me...*

It's not much comfort, as I hit the cold floor. The snow is wet against my hands. Quickly, I scramble back up, embarrassment chewing on me.

"Hades," I scold, but in fact, I'm the one to blame for letting myself fall under that guy's spell again.

I chance a quick glance over at the pair of wolves, who are both staring at me. They stand next to each other, looking like the perfect couple.

Goddess, what if she's his mate?

I feel a sickness in my gut at how love-struck I've been acting around him. And with it comes a sliver of jealousy at how much more beautiful and *fierce* she is than me.

Hades' head jerks up, his eyes on them, and my stomach somersaults that he'll run up to them. He should be growling or acting out my *nipping* daydream, but he's soft and loves attention.

And I want to be a million miles away from *him!*

"Don't you dare, Hades." I scratch his ear to snap his attention back to me.

"Wynter," Mom's voice calls, and I flinch, confused.

Then I spot her standing by the bridge, waving at me to go join her.

I sigh heavily, flushing. I can't believe that she's done this in front of wolves who've been battling with axes.

Hades could've at least snarled at them to make it look like I had a badass fighter dog.

Instead, he hangs his head like Mom is scolding him.

The look Mom gives me is definitely one that she used to give, when I was in trouble. But I'm no longer the young teenager that I was four years ago.

I start running toward her, Hades on my heels, and the whole time I can feel Ri and the beautiful girl's gaze on me, probably laughing at my mom coming to collect me.

Unless of course something bad has happened.

Reaching the bridge, I'm gasping for air. "What's wrong?"

"It's the initiation." Mom's eyes are wide. Is she frightened or excited? "They're starting it early because the snow's come, and you aren't even ready."

My thoughts spiral.

Initiation?

What in the name of the Midnight Goddess am I being initiated into? And why does the way that Mom's hand shakes, as she grips my hand to pull me after her, fill me with terror?

Nobody's born an Alpha.

You fight for the title with claws and fangs.

Yet, the difference is, in Fable the heart of the wolf has been forgotten. For a century, the title's been passed like a crown down a single line of Sun Wolves.

How screwed is that?

The humans once had a despot called the Sun King. Yeah, Fable has its Alpha Sun Queen, instead.

In Ireland, which is where I lived until a year ago, my da was the Alpha because he fought for that right. So, the Alpha in *this* pack had better watch her back. I'm the wolf who's going to break her crown.

I growl. As soon as I stop making an idiot of myself in front of her daughter, of course.

Nothing makes an idiot faster out of a man, than a call to his inner wolf, Da would say with a wink.

Great Shadow Wolf, my inner wolf is a growly, possessive idiot.

I throw myself back onto the bed, dragging my leather jacket tighter around myself against the cold. My bedroom is plain, obsessively neat (I have a fierce desire to control where things should be), and built of pine like the rest of my Uncle Jack's house, which is built on the edges of the park.

Jack may be the pack leader of the Shadow Wolves here in America but he's also pack Healer, and is as independent from the screwed-up politics and dodgy pack rivalries as he can be.

If he could be a lone wolf, he would be. Only, he cares too much about helping people, even if they bring him trouble. After all, he took my sis and me in.

I pull out the photo of Da, which I always carry in my pocket. It's faded and creased, but I thumb over his green eyes and coal black curls. The pack were fond of saying that I looked like him. He was the most powerful wolf of his generation.

My gaze swings to my axe, which rests in the corner of the room. It's ancient, passed down through my family, and its mighty steel head and obsidian handle gleam.

My axe's name is Crown Breaker. Once, it belonged to Da. How many hours will I need to practise to live up to his name?

Because I will.

I survived...I'm alive...but for how long? And survival isn't enough. It never is.

Yet how many wolves understand that with the storm howling at their door, they must *adapt*?

I smile as I smooth out the photo. It's the only one

that I have: a simple snapshot. It was the single photo that I could snatch, when I escaped with my sister, Brey, from Ireland.

Nothing else from that life exists any longer.

I clench my jaw. A cold ball of homesickness forms in my stomach. Can you be sick for a home that no longer exists?

By the shadows, I'm missing ghosts.

I know that I shouldn't lose myself in the memories but sometimes, when I'm alone, I do because Brey won't talk about it...*them*...any of it. It's like the trauma's too much, so she can't even mention our family or friend's names. Yet I don't stop wanting to remember what we've lost: the castle on the coast with the crashing waves beneath, the blue sky above with cawing crows, and the emerald fields stretching like life to the village.

The ancient seat of the Shadow Wolves in Ireland, our pack, and family are gone.

And so is Da.

"What are you doing, pup? Still crying your wee heart out because you lost?" Brey strolls into my bedroom (without knocking, as usual).

I hurriedly push Da's photo into my pocket, since Brey never wants to see it. I let the ghosts haunt me, but if Brey needs to see our new home in America as a fresh start, then I'll give her that.

Darkest shadows, I'd give my sister the world if I could.

Except, *pup...?* Okay, wee sis, you're not getting away with that.

I swing my legs around, until I'm sitting on the edge

of the bed. "Nay, but are you still doing your victory dance that makes you look like a demented fox?"

Her grin is sharp (note to self: never forget how dangerous Brey is), "Oh, you mean the one that goes like *this*?"

She runs her hand through her fiery hair with a smirk, before throwing herself into her enthusiastic victory dance that makes her look *exactly* like a demented fox.

When she stops, panting, she raises her eyebrow.

"Aye, that'll be the one." I push myself up with a frustrated snarl. "And lay off, you only won because I was distracted by…"

I snap my mouth shut.

Don't think about the Sun Girl who blazed so brightly that she could melt me with a look...

Too late.

Brey pats my cheek. "Aw, it's cute. I know *what* you were distracted by bro, and it's between your legs. Is your bad bastard inner wolf getting all horny and…?" Her eyes light up, and she snatches me by the shoulders. "Wait, are we talking about shadowmates?"

I pull away from her. "Chance would be a fine thing. That doesn't work anymore."

Da once sat Brey and me down underneath the stars on the beach and told us the Shadowmate Legend.

I remember the lulling sound of the waves and the crackle of the bonfire. The moment had felt magical: lit only by fire and stars.

In hushed tones, Da explained that wolves' Souls are

truly shadows. And that a wolf is fated to find their Soul Bond – shadowmate – and merge into one with them.

Wolves' shadows began with the first wolf: the Great Shadow Wolf, who was born in Ireland, in my own pack. Protecting the ancestral seat and lineage of my home, therefore, was the most important duty any of us would have.

Yet I'd failed because now I was in America.

Forgive me, Great Shadow Wolf, forgive me, forgive...

"The Alpha's daughter isn't my shadowmate and she never will be," I snarl.

"Well, that's great to hear." Uncle Jack stands in the doorway with crossed arms.

I swallow, taking a careful breath. The trouble with getting lost in the past, is that you're not alert enough in the present. I need to be more aware. How can I keep my sis safe otherwise?

The Alpha promises that everyone's safe in this territory, but only if they *know their place.*

I've always been bad at that.

Who doesn't love a rebel? Apart from the Alpha and her Sun Wolf goons, of course.

Jack's dressed in jeans and a dark denim shirt; his thick black hair is only beginning to be threaded with silver at the sides, and his eyes are equally as silver. He's tall and rugged, in a different way to my da was, who spent hours on his appearance.

The spectacle.

Jack used to live in this house with my aunt, but she died in an extreme snowstorm two years ago. Sometimes, it feels like the Deep is slowly coming for us all.

With the long, dark nights, the shortening days with blindingly white snow…this constant winter…I ache with the sense that if I don't fight…screw…*do something*…right now, then I'll never be able to.

Because there won't be a future.

Jack's also pack leader, and if he tells me something, then I have enough respect to listen.

At least, to *pretend* to.

My expression hardens. "I'm not daft enough to make a move on a Sun Wolf. Let alone a brat like her."

Even if Wynter has spellbinding violet eyes and kissable lips.

She should be my enemy. Yet even drenched, shivering, and looking pissed as hell, she'd been gorgeous. Plus, most wolves would've bared their necks in submission, but she stood up to me, and my wolf howled for her.

So, I *may* get hot for women who are as strong as me. Warriors. Funny thing about this one though, I don't think that she knows she's powerful. She's not like Brey who sleeps with a knife under her pillow. But I can smell it on her: the *potential*.

Enemy or not, I crave to bring her darkness out to meet mine.

Jack fixes me with a level stare; he's not buying my innocent act. "You can't touch her. I mean it. You're only safe in this territory because you're in my house but even then, you need to keep quiet and conceal who you truly are."

"*Know our place?*" Brey huffs.

Jack points at me. "Don't challenge the Alpha."

It's like he can read minds.

I run my hand through my tumble of hair. "Would I do a foolish thing like that?"

Jack attempts to look stern, but I can tell he's smothering a smile. "In a heartbeat. Just stay away from Wynter, that's the girl who's come back from the human world. The Alpha's made it clear that no one can mate with her, and drawing the attention of the Alpha's the last thing that you want. How about you don't get your ass kicked by Sun Wolves?"

I smirk. "It could be fun." When Brey growls, I laugh and hold up my hands in defeat. "Okay, okay, no touching."

But looking's still fine, right?

Yesterday, I'd been patrolling the woods around the Healer's Cottage like I do most days and nights to keep my family safe, and then this Wynter wolf had just been there, acting like *I* was the one who shouldn't be there.

Like she owned the whole bastard world...like she didn't understand anything that was going on in Fable.

A Shadow Wolf can only transform on a full moon, but we have wolf-like strength all the time, even in human form. The other packs don't have that. It'd taken all my restraint not to show her last night why she didn't have the power to boss me around, but then, I smelled her scent of pine forest.

And it made my wolf howl.

My wolf rose then, in a way that shouldn't have been possible. It'd been desperate to connect with her wolf. What in the name of the great shadows did it mean?

I hadn't wanted to let Wynter out of my sight.

I *am* possessively protective of those I…well, my pack. But then, I'm also like that with my guitar. So, wanting to keep her safe doesn't mean I care for her more than that, right?

Still, she said I was stalking her. But she stalked *me* during my training.

My heart clenches at the memory because honestly, it's kind of hot to think of someone watching me. On the other hand, she made me lose to Brey, which led to the Demented Fox victory dance and endless teasing.

It was worth it to see her again.

I grit my teeth. That's just my wolf talking. I tried to warn Wynter, and she threatened to have me hunted down.

Fair play to her, in the olden days that was how most relationships started (but am I kind of damaged that I find that hot too?).

But she doesn't know who I am. Perhaps, she thinks that I'm one of the cowed Moon Wolves, who've spent too long working as servants.

Right, like I'd last five minutes as a servant without taking a bite out of someone.

I glance out of the wide window that runs by my bed into the shadows of the wood; great oaks arch over the house.

Brey feels safe here, but I know that we're not. The thing is, Fable's not safe from *me*.

When you've fallen from the heights and hit the bottom, you're the most dangerous monster of all, and I have the scars to prove it.

Feral. Primal. Wild.

Jack gives me a final, long look, before nodding toward the hall. "Come on, I have some new herbs you can help me with, if you want."

I grin. "Fine by me."

Jack's teaching me his skills, which is an honor. Back in Ireland, Da would drill Brey and me on the rules of wolven civilization, etiquette, and hierarchy for hours each day. Yet none of those saved him. His wolven civilization was torn apart by claws and fangs.

Brey rolls her eyes, distracting me. I know she'd rather be training, running, hunting, pretty much anything other than working on healing. "I can chop, as long as I get to hold a knife."

Jack laughs. "You get the sharpest one."

"Deal."

I follow them both through into the large kitchen, which has a vast oak table in the center, a counter along the side, and shelves that are crammed with potions and pastes. I wrinkle my nose at the scent of lavender and sage, which are the two strongest herbs for healing. A roaring fire crackles and spits on the far wall, and I sigh at its warmth.

Jack points at the mint that's laid in the pestle and mortar on the counter, waiting to be crushed.

Brey dives past me to the knives that hang from a rack, claiming the largest one and cradling it to her chest. "Overcompensator, I've missed you!"

I shoot her an unimpressed look.

She smirks. "When you get some pet knives of your own, you can name them."

I laugh.

"Thanks for helping out." Jack opens a pungent scented bottle, which contains the strongest healing paste. "You're a hard worker, Ryan. And neither of you have acted like any of your chores in this pack are beneath you."

I concentrate on crushing the mint. "You took us in."

Jack leans on the counter. "That's what pack does."

I glance at him. "Not all pack."

"A good one." He stirs the paste. "This is Lunar Salve. They say our ancestors discovered how to draw on the power of the moon to heal themselves. The truth is that us wolves don't get sick like humans, but we still hurt if we're injured: broken bones or wounds in battle." I shift my shoulders. The scars are still tight on my back. I can feel the ghost claws, raking at my skin even now. Jack's expression gentles. "But we also heal fast, and if treated in time, we don't scar."

I duck my head, and my hair covers my eyes.

I lick my dry lips. "Perhaps, vanishing scars on your skin is dangerous. The damage is still there, underneath. If a pack can just hide all the bad and pretend it never happened, won't it simply repeat itself?"

The scars on my back phantom itch. I work hard not to scratch them. I startle, when Brey's hand lightly touches my elbow. When I raise my gaze, I meet her gentle one.

"Huh, that's a good point." Jack wanders to the table with the paste, placing it down carefully. "But I want you to keep out of politics as much as you can. I'm teaching you how to be a Healer, Ryan, so that you'll have a respected position in this community. I don't want to add to your scars. Your aunt was an even better Healer than me, and she'd be proud that you're learning the tradition."

When my gaze searches out a smiling photo of my aunt on the wall (she looks so young and desperately alive), Jack's mouth twists just for a moment. "I wish that she could be here now."

Jack's hands clench. "Look at it this way. Death is only your shadow passing to join the Great Shadow Wolf, remember?" He shivers despite the fire. "I don't fear death. It's this weather and the Deep. Those who are closest to nature can feel it the most. The animals have been unsettled for centuries longer than us, and the humans have barely picked up on what's coming..."

Brey's eyes narrow. "What's coming, Uncle?"

Jack ignores her, tapping the jar, instead. "The ingredients in the Lunar Salve and others are a closely guarded secret that's been handed down through the Healers in the Shadow Wolves for generations." He glances up at me and smiles. "And now I'm teaching you."

I straighten my shoulders. "I won't let you down."

Jack arches his brow. "I know that, buddy. But I'm mostly teaching you so that you can stay independent and not have to bow down...too much...to the Fearless or the Alpha. Because you're not the bowing type, am I right?"

I snort. "Aye, I'm more the *Rebel Without a Cause* type."

"Rebel without a clue," Brey snickers. "And I'm more

the lass with the ax, than the one who gets on her knees."

"That's not what your last boyfriend told everybody," I mutter.

Brey waves the Overcompensator in front of me. "I'm literally holding a knife right now."

"I'm literally not shaking in my boots."

All of a sudden, there's a loud banging on the front door.

"Healer, open up!" A panicked voice hollers.

Brey may be the one with the knife, but she's still my wee sis. I shove myself protectively in front of her.

Jack's expression becomes tight, as he bustles to the door and swings it open. Two Moon Wolves, who look nineteen or twenty years old like Brey and me, stagger through, carrying an unconscious third wolf.

Brey gasps.

The wolf who's being carried has been savaged: he's a mess of bruises and blood.

What in the name of shadows has happened to him?

"Put him on the table," Jack commands, instantly in control. He surveys the injured wolf, pausing only to check his pulse and then wipe the dark hair back from his bloodied forehead. Jack's voice is controlled but furious. "Who did this?"

The two wolves, who carried in their fellow pack member, look similar with close cropped blond hair. They exchange nervous glances. They're both dressed in muddy overalls like they've been working in the fields or as gardeners.

The taller Moon Wolf answers, "A gang of Sun

Wolves who in term time go to college with us. They just wanted to keep us in line."

Rage bubbles through me. Sun Wolves can transform in the day, but Moon Wolves can't. What kind of cowards would use their wolf against an untransformed pack member?

Wolf fights wolf.

That's always been our way. Here in Fable, however, the power that the Sun Wolves wield under their Alpha Queen makes them act like dicks.

I growl, stalking to the table, as Jack scoops his fingers into the paste. I scrunch up my nose at the powerful scent, as I rip away what little remains of the injured wolf's shirt.

I wince. Even with the Lunar Salve, those bite marks will take a couple of days to heal. At least his friends had the sense to bring him straight to Jack.

Jack's brow furrows in concentration, as he spreads on the paste. "Bring me some bandages from the drawer, Brey. We need to make sure that the herbs are held tightly onto the wound, and that he loses the least amount of blood possible."

Brey nods, ashen. She pulls out the bandages, hurrying to Jack's side to pass them to him. I don't miss the way that she pats the shorter blond on the shoulder.

She knows them…likes them.

At my raised eyebrow, her eyes flash. "They're in some of my classes." She nods at the injured wolf. "Dex here too. He's nice, you know, smart. Before you put on your growly big bro act, don't bother. I have friends, even if *you're* into the lone wolf thing. And Dex isn't the sort to start anything, although he's strong enough to finish it, if he's not ganged up on."

I focus on pressing a bandage over one of the worst wounds to hide my anger. If Dex is Brey's friend, then that makes him mine to protect as well. Okay, so I do have a wee problem with needing to own and control.

Sue me.

The pack with the power in a territory is meant to protect the others and not harm them, unless they're challenged. At least, that's what Da taught me. It's how it was with the overking and the packs beneath him in Ireland.

Except, I'm not in Ireland anymore, and here the Sun Wolves reign.

Jack shakes his head, sadly. "I gave my oath to heal every wolf, no matter what pack they come from. But this rivalry and fighting between packs has become crazy." He wags his finger at me. "You don't go getting any ideas. Stay out of it."

"I didn't say anything."

"You don't need to. I can hear you thinking it."

Sometimes, I wonder if he really can, or if my broody look is as bad as Brey claims.

When I study Dex's clawed chest and feel the sympathetic pull of the scars on my own back, I remember why it doesn't matter how enticing the Alpha's daughter smells, she's from this vicious Sun pack.

Won't she be just the same?

"You make sure that he looks after these wounds now," Jack says. "I'll give you more ointment to put on them, and he'll need the bandages changed."

The tall blond boy nods but then sighs. "I guess that means we all miss the initiation. I'd promised to support Hunter. He'll need it."

"Initiation?" I ask.

Something moves sickly in my gut at the way that Jack stiffens.

He wipes his hands together, avoiding my gaze. "Hell, I was going to tell you later." He lets out a chuckle, but it sounds strained. "Probably about an hour before we had to get dressed up all fancy for it. The Fearless have summoned a gathering, but this is precisely the sort of thing where you need to stay quiet and not get involved. I know you, Ryan, your wolf will be clawing at you to be noticed. You think everything's your battle. But not this time. Unless you want to end up with more scars, keep your head down and hide your wolf."

My eyes blaze, and I growl.

Here's the thing of it, no one's born to be an Alpha. But some wolves are born to battle to become one. In a world where the fear of the Deep is driving the packs to snarl and turn on each other, I can't hide from my inner wolf or my duty.

Even if I end up with more scars.

CHAPTER 4

WYNTER

For a moment, I stare at my reflection, convinced someone else is looking back at me. It can't possibly be me… the girl in the mirror is too beautiful and perfect. I'm just an ordinary girl with dark shadows under her eyes.

But now, I seem to be glowing.

Golden eyeshadow glints in the light, fake eyelashes bring out the violet in my hazel eyes, and my lips are as ruby as the petals on the blossom trees. My hair is combed off my face with a golden headband that has rays sticking outward around my head like an aura or more like the glory of the sun to represent our pack family. Dark hair falls half way down my back in small ringlets.

I don't recognize myself at all.

"You look incredible," Mom gasps, as if she can't believe her own eyes either. "You'll be the envy of everyone."

I look at her through the mirror's reflection, frowning. "I don't want to be the center of attention. Perhaps, I should wear my jeans instead of..."

I glance down at the black leather pants, which follow the curve of my legs and hips and the golden corset that's close to crushing me. It's decorated with golden coins to represent the sun, and has a heart-shaped design across my bust. On the bright side, this lung-crusher does give me the tiniest waist in the world.

Mom huffs like I just made a terrible joke. "You're the daughter of the Sun Wolves' Alpha, and anything less from you would be a stain on our name. You're expected to outshine everybody at the initiation."

I frown and look out the window where the snowfall has paused and the moonlight beams across the land with a silvery hue. I'd rather be out there in the fresh air, than going to a fancy event. I turn my attention to Mom, who's collecting a golden cape from the closet. She hooks the fabric over my shoulders and attaches the clasp around my neck to keep it in place, while the fabric drops to my ankles.

Perfect, now I look like a bad-ass superhero from a Marvel movie.

Mom, on the other hand, wears a gown that billows out from her waist like those Victorian dresses; it's white and woven with golden thread. Her long sleeves will keep her warm, while I fear I'll freeze.

But there's no gain without pain for the sake of beauty, right? I almost roll my eyes at my own thoughts, as I recite Mom's words.

"Beautiful," she says, stepping back to study me.

For so long, I've wished for her to look at me that way for just being myself, not because I was dolled up.

But *wishing* for things is dangerous.

"Faith," Mom yells abruptly. I wince. Moments later, the housekeeper appears at the doorway to the dressing room. "Help Wynter into her heels. We're already late."

"I'm not good with heels, Mom," I call after her, but she's already marching out of the bedroom.

"Miss, it just takes a little practise. You'll get the hang of it," Faith says.

I breathe easier around Faith. Well, as easy as the corset allows.

"It's a bit much, right?" I turn on the spot, trying to look at myself from behind.

"Not at all," Faith smiles. "You're the embodiment of the sun itself."

I almost burst out laughing but I hold it back to not hurt her feelings. I'm the farthest thing from representing the sun. Mom wanted me to be that, ever since I was a baby. But I disappointed her even then.

"You're a Moon Wolf. You don't have to lie like you actually admire us Sun Wolves." I study Faith. "Don't you wish that I could look like the moon?"

Faith's expression becomes more serious, and she clasps my hands. "I've never much believed in pack differences. We're all simply wolves, and we have our different strengths: Sun can transform in the day; Moon can transform in the night. It's like, we're simply the opposite sides of each other. And together, we're stronger."

I stare at her in shock. *She means it.*

"Like shadows?"

Faith's gaze meets mine. "Shadowmates."

My hand becomes sweaty in Faith's hold, and my heart speeds up.

Shadowmate?

Please, let it be true…

"Wynter, we need to leave now," Mom calls from downstairs.

Faith pulls away from me, hurrying to the back of the dressing room. She doesn't meet my eye like she's told me something that she shouldn't have. She drags open the door to a closet, which is filled with shelves of shoes, then she returns with a pair of black heels, dangling from her hand. They glint and thank the Goddess, they're wedged heels, rather than stilettos.

Looks like I may not break my ankle tonight.

Once Faith straps the shoes on my feet, I make my way down the stairs on wobbly legs and in one piece. Mom has the door open, and I step outside. Addison waits for us. He takes Mom's arm, and I totter alongside them, trembling from the icy breeze.

I don't even know where we're headed. If my home is a house of lies, then Fable is a town of secrets.

When I raise my head from concentrating on not falling over my own feet on the heels—because walking in slushy snow makes this even more of a lottery if I'll end up on my ass or my corset squeezed tits—I realize that we're heading into the woods behind the town.

Wow, that means we're going to Wolf Grove in the forest. I'm going to turn into a popsicle.

"It's freezing." I wrap the cape around myself, as I

slip and slide down the path alongside our home that takes us right into the woods.

Mom saunters gracefully by Addison, on the other hand, like the Alpha she is.

Like she owns this territory...which she does.

The night sky is bright and sharp with stars.

"So, are you going to tell me now where we're going and what this initiation means? I'm guessing it's something big for us to get dressed up like this. You're making a statement about the Sun Wolves' power, which is weird because don't the wolves already know who rules here? And it must have to do with you summoning the Fearless, right Addison?" I narrow my eyes.

Mom's lips twist into a wry frown. "Don't be so rude. You call him *Father* in public."

What?

It's been...thirty eight days...since my *real* Dad died. And now she wants me to play pretend with Addison...?

My expression shutters. "Not happening."

It's Addison who smiles at me, softly. "I'm not trying to take your dad's place. This is just about appearances, and only when other people are around. Pretend that we're acting. It's what I do."

And I can see it. Addison's blank expression; that far away stare he does. How often is he acting? *What's real?*

If he can do it, then so can I.

I nod.

Mom huffs. "Today is special, Wynter, so please do your best not to ruin it. Do you know how hard it's been for us to explain that I allowed you to leave Fable to live with humans and their doctors for the past four years?"

Allowed? I remember Dad snatching me away.

I bite my tongue, when I notice another family from down the street emerging from their home. It's an older couple, and the woman is in a gold and white flowing dress, the man in a white suit like Addison. They're definitely coming this way with their fancy clothes.

Lowering my voice, I say to Mom, "Maybe if you don't keep me in the dark about what's coming, then I can do my best not to embarrass you."

"You haven't told her yet?" Addison murmurs.

So much for *Father* being on the same page as Mom.

Mom pauses, her lips pinched, and she takes a side glance to the neighboring couple, who are walking in our direction, then looks me directly in the face. "This is a once in a lifetime event. An extravaganza that no one alive today has experienced. But I can't tell you anymore. I've been sworn to secrecy. The Fearless will be making a big announcement, and I cannot break their oath by revealing their proclamation."

"I'm your daughter," I hiss. "You're the Alpha of Fable."

She takes my wrist and pulls me into the woods. "Do not make a scene," she warns. "Addison and I have worked so hard to abide by the rules, to keep everyone safe, and you'll show the same respect."

If I bite my tongue any harder, it'll bleed.

We continue in silence and soon reach a set of stone steps that are built into the mountain, ascending up the steep hill. Arched branches, which are stripped of leaves, encase the stairway. Despite the burning torches that guide our path, shadows crowd around me. I shiver. This is too much like my dream.

Midnight Goddess, protect me.

An ominous feeling settles around me. Just like the dream, I feel like I'm walking into a trap.

Mom said we were late for an initiation earlier, and now I'm swallowing past the lump in my throat. Has the town introduced new rules for anyone who's been away for years from the pack like me?

Is it because I'm a hybrid?

The farther we travel up the stone steps, the more my stomach knots. I'm not a flashy person, or someone who loves the spotlight, which is the opposite of Mom.

Everyone says I take after my dad.

Once we reach the top of the stairs, the landscape stretches outward down a windy path, which is covered by more branches that are strung with tiny lights. Like the steps, the passage has been cleared of snow, so at least I don't risk slipping on my ass here.

I may be tottering toward a deadly initiation but I can still look for the silver lining, right?

Mom nudges me forward. Voices come from up ahead, and anxiety has me tensing.

I bet my arrival is the talk of the town, and like Ri said, I'm the *sick girl* who's returned, which means one thing: everyone will be staring at me.

I cringe, crossing my arms. Despite the cold, perspiration rolls down my back.

I follow Mom and Addison into Wolf Grove. I pause

at the edge, taking it all in, trying my hardest not to hyperventilate.

Gatherings attract top pack members and families, and today there are close to one-hundred people mingling in the vast grove that looks more like a fantasy wonderland. Enormous trees drape over the flat land from the edges, and from their branches dangle lanterns that cast golden light in the dark.

At first, my gaze sweeps over the spectacular dresses, the groups forming of chatting people, and the workers who are serving drinks — all Moon Wolves, of course.

I snort. *Wow, what fakery.*

They pretend to be friendly but almost everyone in the three packs, Sun, Moon, and Shadow, despise one another and would tear out each other's throats to gain the power in Fable. I saw them as a kid, petitioning Mom for positions, jobs, and influence.

The packs mingle here — the plain clothed Moon pack in cheap one-piece suits the color of silver with a deep V neckline for females. They have white crescent moons painted in the center of their foreheads. The dark Shadow pack wears all black: sleek dresses and suits, long gloves, and a black transparent fabric, which covers their heads and falls down to just below their eyes. Their official ritual clothing has always looked eerie to me. Then there's the Sun pack wreathed in bright silks — and the air's thick with social awkwardness.

It almost makes me forget my own social anxiety.

Addison claps loudly, and I flinch.

Silence falls on the crowd, drawing their attention our way. I feel every single gaze on me.

The sick girl.

The girl who's lived with humans.

The half-breed girl.

I squirm, *hating* this.

Mom places her hand on my lower back, pushing me forward. I stumble, before straightening. Heat rushes up my neck.

Mom's smile is relaxed, as her gaze glints with dominance. "It's a pleasure to see everyone together as one big family. It's been too long since we gathered, and it's unfortunate that it's under such circumstances."

I glance at her. What circumstances? My arrival?

Everyone bows their heads to her in response, placing a fist to their chests as a sign of respect to their Alpha.

Mom leads those living in Fable, then each faction has their own pack leader as well. She gets the final say on decisions. Just as much as they look up to her, they fear her.

"I bring happy news. My daughter, Wynter, has come back home for good." Mom's beaming, as everyone starts clapping like it's a huge achievement *for her*.

She glides toward the closest crowd, who are the Sun Wolves and eager to congratulate her. They hover around, lapping up their Alpha's attention. Addison is by her side, both of them masters at diplomacy.

Me — the actual daughter — is abandoned.

People stare at me, their gaze sliding up and down

my body, then they turn to the person next to them, gossiping about me.

I grimace. Who knew I was so interesting?

I steel myself. Well, I'd better get this over with. Nobody died from *mingling*. Except, tell that to my heart because it feels like it's about to burst from my chest.

When I step forward, however, the wolves back away, giving me space, and well, if there's anything to make a girl feel insecure, it's being treated like you have leprosy.

Or perhaps a freak in an overbearing sun headpiece, corset, and superhero cape...?

Was it Mom's idea the whole time to make me stand out like this?

Yeah, of course.

When another girl edges away from me, I groan.

The Sun Wolves are too scared of pissing off Mom by even looking at me wrong, let alone chatting to me. I can't help the way that my lips curl into a smile at how Ri spoke to me because at least he wasn't scared of either Mom or me.

Perhaps, he wasn't a stalker, he was simply crazy.

I glance around...just maybe...checking to see if he's here. But it's too hard to tell through the ritual clothing of the Shadow Wolves, which makes me shiver.

Unexpectedly, from across the grove, my gaze meets Paige's. She used to be my friend at school, and she looks just as I remember, with strawberry blonde hair and large blue eyes. I smile at her, lifting my hand to wave, but she turns abruptly away and pushes into the crowds.

Hurriedly, I lower my arm, feeling stupid. My cheeks flush with embarrassment. I hunch my shoulders and hug my arms around myself. It seems a lot has changed.

At least Mom's still having fun being flattered by her fangirls and didn't see me making a fool of myself. *You're my daughter and should never approach others first. They come to you, they grovel for your attention,* she'd command.

Well, that's just not me.

"Hey, Wynter. How's it going?" A soft voice asks.

Lost in my thoughts, I jump. "Sorry, do I know you?"

I peer at the Sun Wolf teenager who's standing awkwardly next to me. She looks a couple of years younger than me and is familiar, but I don't remember who she is.

Her curly chestnut hair is draped over her shoulders, shining beneath the lantern lights, as is her dark brown skin. She glances shyly at me from underneath her eyelashes. She's beautiful, her smile contagious, and I'm surprised she doesn't have half the teenage guys in the room following her around like puppies.

When I look into her hazel eyes, however, I recognize the familiar innocence that I know too well and it has me grinning.

"Iris," I snatch her hands between mine, "how could I forget my favorite neighbor?"

Iris lived in one of the neighboring manions to Sun House, but she'd only been a kid when I left.

She bites her lip. "You know Mom still calls me the Sun Mouse because I'm so quiet. I'm not sure if it's just because she never hears me entering a room or because everybody forgets me."

I nudge her with my shoulder. "You could become the ultimate assassin."

"Or ninja." She studies me. "Wow, Wynter, you look..." She's scanning me head to toe. "Let's just say, everyone's talking about how stunning you are tonight. They're jealous." She leans in close, whispering, "Let them drool. O.M.G, the look on their faces was priceless, when they saw you!"

She's always been a fast talker, but I can also just imagine the things the others are saying about the hybrid, who's trying to fit in with the wolves.

But having Iris smile at me softens my tension, and it cheers me up to have someone from my past talk to me like I'm normal.

I sway my hips. "It's the cape, isn't it? So sexy."

She smothers her laugh on my shoulder.

"So happy to see you." I hug her, a strange relief washing through me to find someone who isn't judging me.

She giggles. "You've been gone for too long. I'm sorry I couldn't call or see you, but you know there's no reception here and no one would let me leave town." When we pull apart, I notice people are watching us. "You don't know how boring this place has been, and I missed you, not to mention all our adventures exploring the woods."

When she winks, I laugh.

"Right, like the time we got chased by a boar and fell over, tearing our pants. Then we had to lie about it to not admit we ran from the animal, instead of hunting it."

"But it was too cute to hunt!" She protests.

She's giggling, and I've missed the sound so much. She may be two years my junior, but we used to hang out a lot outside of school, before I left Fable. Those moments with her I cherish and always will. I had a few friends in town, but I notice that none of them are coming to say hi now.

From the corner of my eye, I sense Mom watching me chat with Iris, and it's hard to tell if she's unhappy about it, but I don't want to find out either. I tilt up my chin and turn my back to her.

Iris is smiling widely. "Welcome back home," she teases. "It's quite the show they've put on for you."

"Oh, I don't think this is for me. Or at least, I hope it's not."

When I cut the crowd a side glance, my attention lands on one of the Fearless members, who's a greasy man with hair combed off his face, looking like he's oiled it. His teeth are so sharp, I bet he files them to a point.

"Oh, who gives a hell about them," Iris whispers, drawing me back to her. "Seriously, most of them are so afraid of not fitting in and of displeasing your mom, that they walk around like they have something huge up their *you know what*."

She's brave enough to sass about the Alpha but still can't get herself to say *ass*. I love that.

"Where were you yesterday when I arrived? I could

have used the cheering up," I say, my attention sweeping the crowd.

Suddenly, it's like I'm jolted with electricity because this time, I find him...*Ri.*

He's looking at me intensely from across the crowd.

Despite the black transparent fabric covering his eyes, his emerald eyes shine through. He's a Shadow Wolf, the pack who hides everything. Yet in the moment, it feels like he's revealing himself to me as well.

My breath hitches.

Next to him, stands Jack, the Shadow pack leader, and the gorgeous girl Ri had been battling in the field. Her black dress follows every curve, and I notice the guys near her studying her, when they think she isn't looking.

"Ahh, didn't take you long to spot *Ri,*" Iris draws out the name dreamily. She leans toward me, whispering over my shoulder. "You know, the girls in every pack are drooling over him. He's already gotten into a fight with Ballard in the woods. Of course, no one told the adults, but there's already talk of retribution against him from Ballard and his buddies. So, that should be a brutal fight. But between us, I could look at Ri for a long time, no matter how moody he is. It's clear he hates it here. Is it strange that makes me drool over him even more?"

"Ballard's always been a dickhead," I say, remembering the Sun Wolf from school, and how he'd trip and shove me when he got the chance. So, to hear that Ri stood up to him, earns him brownie points...or earns him some back for being such a jerk in the woods.

"Yeah, Ballard's cruel. He reminds me every chance he can get that I still haven't had my first shift." She sighs heavily.

I grab her hand in mine.

"He's a bully." My shoulder blades tense; it's where I hold my stress.

"I just stay out of his way." Iris glances away.

I hate how she's lost her enthusiasm, so I steer the topic away from Ballard to distract her.

"Why did Ri come to Fable, anyway?" I lower my gaze from him, though when I lift my head again, he's still watching me like nothing can tear him away.

"Something happened with his family back in Ireland. No one really knows what because he won't talk about it. That's what the fight was about: Ballard was stirring it about his family. Anyway, he and his sister, Brey, were sent to live with their uncle, Jack, here in Fable. I heard someone saying his uncle is teaching him how to heal, and Ri can heal me any day of the week."

I gape at her.

Thank the Midnight Goddess! That girl with the fiery hair and the insanely badass moves is his *sister* and not his partner.

"He's still staring at you," Iris singsongs.

"As is everyone else," I remind her.

"No, this is different. He hasn't paid anyone else this kind of attention, and trust me, I've seen other girls trying to chat him up. Maybe you should go over there and talk to him...?"

I almost choke on my tongue, while she's watching me with her sharp stare. "That's never going to happen. I've already had a run in with him, and he's a major douche. Plus, he hates me."

We're both looking at him now, and to my relief, he turns toward Jack, who's talking to him.

"Maybe he's just moody after being forced to move here," Iris suggests. "He's had it rough. The other packs haven't made it easy on him and his sister. It's kind of become a game: trying to find one of them alone. I mean, Fable's not exactly welcoming to newcomers."

"Don't I know it." I study Ri's broody outline.

A loud clap draws our attention to Mom and Addison, who stand before the crowd. Mom steps forward, her arms by her side. She glances out at everyone, before momentarily pausing on me.

I can't read her expression, but her smile is fierce.

"We summoned the gathering for an event to take place that we hoped would never need to come to pass in our lifetimes. But circumstances have changed, and our hand is forced. Please take your place for the Fearless to address you." Her voice raises; her eyes are filled with excitement.

Astonished, frightened whispers fill the crowd.

What's going on? *What are the Fearless about to tell us?*

"Oh," Iris says, her voice brittle, "this is it."

Her nerves are just as highly strung as I feel. My mind races with worst case scenarios of a ritual I'll have to do, new rules, or who knows what, until I'm breathless in the span of a few seconds. Locked in place, I can't move, but I stare at Mom, hanging on her every word. My fingers twist around my cape.

It isn't long before an eerie silence forms. Then in compliance with Mom's command, everyone begins moving about the grove, crowding around in a circle.

With people in every direction and my head spinning, I lose sight of Iris, and I stumble about, trying to work out where I should stand.

It's only when I slide between two women to get past them, that I run practically right into Hunter.

My breath catches in my chest, as I never expected to see him. Yet of course he'd be here.

Hunter's gaze darts in my direction, as if the shock of standing right in front of me startles him too.

Golden blond hair tumbles around his face; his sky-blue eyes are as piercing as I remember them. But the rest of him has changed. He's no longer the young boy I hung around with, who I secretly crushed on.

I swallow hard.

Now, my stomach tingles with butterflies because the guy standing in front of me is a man. Sure, he's only a couple of months older than me, but he's taller with shoulders broad enough to carry the world, and sweet Midnight Goddess, he's more beautiful than I remember. Such strong cheekbones and jawline. He's wearing the Moon Wolves' silver suit, and while it looks gorgeous on the girls, on Hunter, he's turning heads in every direction, and if my heart beats any faster, I may rupture a rib.

When did he get so buff?

"Hunter," my voice cracks, while my entire body softens under his heavy stare.

"I heard you were back but didn't believe it. I can't...I mean...You've been gone for four years." He's giving me a tight grin, and his deep voice brings back memories of our last time together.

The time I told him that I wouldn't leave Fable without him and I wouldn't forget him...

But then, I left the very next day.

Did he think I abandoned him? Left him behind?

Except, I did.

Yet what choice did I have, when Dad bundled me into the car and drove me to New York? I never got the chance to say goodbye to anyone. And with no phone reception in Fable or mail delivery, how was I meant to contact him? Maybe that's why so many others in town look at me with venom in their eyes.

They think I abandoned all of them for the human world.

I don't respond right away, as I have no idea what he's thinking and how upset he is with me.

"Yeah, things are never what you expect them to be," I finally say, shifting uncomfortably.

I can't explain now; there isn't time. Plus, I want to have that conversation in private, where I'm not being spied on.

"They aren't around you," Hunter replies, and his expression shutters. "Like you expect someone to be there forever, and then suddenly, they're gone."

"Listen, maybe we should talk," I say; my guts churn. "Later, okay?"

Hunter and I have been friends for a long time. In fact, we were best friends, despite being from different packs. We did a lot of things together as we grew up because his Mom brought him over to Sun House, when she had to work as housekeeper, after his dad died and she had no one to watch him.

Mom accepted Hunter because Faith had worked for our family all her life, but that of course was under the proviso that we remained friends and nothing else.

Mom had made it clear that I must remember that Hunter was *only the housekeeper's son*, and wouldn't be worth my time, as soon as we became older. She'd made that even clearer to Hunter by harsher methods.

Perhaps, I'd been foolish to feel anything between us could happen. Sun and Moon wolves can't be together. Mom would murder me...or murder Hunter.

Except, standing in front of Hunter again brings back too many emotions from our past. Nerves. Anger. Unrelenting attraction to something I can't have.

People are nudging past, pushing against me, but it's only when an iron-grip snatches my wrist, that I'm snapped out of my trance.

I look over to Mom, whose frown has me rearing back.

"Hurry up and get to the front of the circle," she commands, "so you don't miss this."

So *I* don't miss it?

I glance back to Hunter, but he's gone, and unease twists in my stomach at the meaning behind his words.

He isn't happy, but maybe it's better this way: safer, for both of us.

That earlier dread claws through me once more, and I start to slide forward, dodging around the crowd to emerge in the front of the large circle in the middle of the grove.

I can't shake away the sensation that whatever trap Mom has set is just about to tighten around my neck like a noose.

CHAPTER 5

HUNTER

*A*Moon Wolf's taught from the moment that they can howl to serve and *know their place*.

Except, what happens when you're the kind of asshole whose shadow howls to be Alpha?

You learn not to howl at all.

Plus, you learn to wear a mask like the blank expression, which hides the emotions that storm through me, when I'm standing in front of my Wyn again.

I clench my fists, until my nails bite into my palms.

My Wyn…curse the moon, what am I thinking? She's *Wynter* now with her glittering makeup and ruby lips and not *my Wyn*.

Does she even remember my nickname for her?

She stands in the shadows of Wolf Grove, surrounded by the gathering, which doesn't exist for me now that she's here and lit by the golden light of the lanterns and the tiny, sharp pinprick of the lights, which are strung in the arching branches of the trees.

I narrow my eyes. It's like she doesn't even know that to me, she's a ghost.

Like she doesn't know that I've grieved for her.

Like she didn't kill me by leaving me behind.

Does she think she can just turn up here, and everything can go back to how it was, like she never vanished? *Abandoned me?*

Can't she guess what I went through to find her?

My stomach twists in knots. My hands ball into even tighter fists.

I'm opening and closing my mouth like I'm talking. *Am I?*

Only the stars know what I'm saying. I could be reciting last week's soccer results for all I know.

Huh, it's no wonder Parker always jokes that I have less swag with women than Addison, but then, the poor guy *is* married to the scariest wolf in Fable. Parker doesn't know that I haven't seriously dated anyone because deep down, I always believed Wynter would come home...to me.

And now she has, and it hasn't changed anything because she was never mine in the first place.

Honestly, everything's in a daze and has been from the moment that Wynter glanced over at me earlier, through the crowds. She didn't see me then. Instead, she looked past me and focused on that new wolf.

The dick.

What's his name again?

Yeah, *Ri.*

As I said, the Shadow Dick.

I flared with jealousy and almost stormed over. Yet I

battled to hold myself back because there's still too much I don't understand.

Why did she leave me? Where's she been this whole time? And what's brought her back now?

The last time we spoke, Wynter promised that we'd be together forever.

In the Moon pack, words have power. If you swear on the moon, then it's binding. I'd sworn on the moon that I'd always be hers.

When she disappeared, I'd been frantic. I'd searched Fable, both the town and woods, for months. I'd barely slept or eaten because guilt had wormed under my skin. I'd been sick with it.

What if the Alpha had sent her away, punished, or murdered her?

And it would've been my fault.

Only the week before Wynter had disappeared, the Alpha had cornered and threatened to have me grounded to my room for the rest of the year like a pup, if I so much as *looked at her daughter inappropriately.*

And I'd looked at Wynter like she'd hung the moon...

Then she'd vanished.

At last, I'd become desperate enough to sneak into her bedroom in the Sun House on my mom's day off, searching it for clues. It was just my crappy luck that the Alpha caught me, as I was rifling through her daughter's pantie drawer.

Awkward.

Plus, the only time that I've felt like fleeing and hurling at the same time. Mom had warned me often enough about the Alpha's temper, but here I was, a Moon Wolf, acting like a criminal on her territory.

She had the right to hand out her own justice. *She could do anything to me.*

The Alpha crossed her arms. "So, you're a thief and a pervert. Just as I suspected."

My heart hammered, but I still lifted my chin.

For Wyn, for Wyn, for Wyn...

"I just want to know where Wyn is."

"Her name is *Wynter.*" The Alpha stalked across the bedroom, snatching me by the ear. "Since you're so keen to spend time in her bedroom, then so be it."

She yanked open the closet and thrust me inside into the darkness, then she banged shut the door. My breath caught, as I heard her turn the key, locking me in the black.

Moon God, save me.

I banged on the oak door, as my chest became tight.

Was she going to leave me here?

Silence.

I kicked the door for good measure. My own breath sounded too loud in the quiet black. The shadows were suffocating.

Had the asshole done this to Wyn? Was Wyn trapped somewhere as well?

I hollered, hammering on the wood, until my fists were sore.

Bang, bang, bang.

"Stop that noise instantly," the Alpha's furious whisper wound from the other side of the door, making me jump. She was still there, listening to me.

I fell quiet.

"That's better. Now, I shall only tell you this once. Wynter is gone. If you continue to make a fuss about her, then I shall fire your mother, and neither you nor your sister had better even think about working for the Sun pack, which will be a pity because Faith has been in my employ, since she was a girl."

What have I done?

I pressed my hands to the wood. *"Don't.* I'm sorry. On the stars, I won't be a bother anymore. Mom needs this job, and Tala shouldn't be punished because of me."

"Then think of them, before you act like a little monster," the Alpha snarled. "Pack should keep to pack. You owe your duty to me first as Alpha and then to your own pack. You've become confused, pup, and over my daughter who would laugh if she was here." My chest constricted. She wouldn't, right? "Did she even bother to say goodbye to you?"

Even though the Alpha couldn't see me, I shook my head dumbly.

I've been such an idiot.

"I allowed my daughter to play with you because you're no more than an interactive toy," she continued like she wasn't savaging me with each word. "You were just something amusing to keep her from distracting me, while I was working, and stop her from getting bored. But Moon Wolves are only good at being workers, weapons, or toys."

She rapped on the door to emphasize each word. I huddled back, sliding onto my ass and wrapping my arms around my knees.

I'd prove that she was wrong. I'd find a way to change how my pack was treated in Fable.

"Now," her voice was deceptively soft, "tell me what you are."

No. Way. In. Hell.

I bit my lip to stop myself from repeating the words she wanted to hear: that I *knew my place*. That I'd been nothing but Wynter's *toy*.

I didn't care if it was true.

I didn't care what the Alpha did to me.

I wouldn't say it.

The Alpha sighed. "Enjoy the dark, toy."

Mom found me huddled in the closet on her next shift a day later. She scolded me, pale with fear, then hugged me. She promised that the packs could be friends and mates because after all, weren't we all wolves under the same moon and sun? Didn't they shine on our skin the same?

Except, they don't shine on our *fur* the same...and hey, that's the point.

Packs aren't meant to be forced so close together, fighting over territory and power. But everything's been screwed-up for generations. The land shrinks, as less pups are born, and we can no longer feel our own shadows.

The Deep's coming.

Is it as screwed-up for all the supes in their different territories: the dragons, vampires, and fae?

Everything's changing...*everyone*...and not only Wynter.

I had a choice to make after the day and night that

the Alpha left me in the closet: servant, toy, or weapon.

If I couldn't protect Wyn, then I'd protect my pack. And I could only do that if I trained to become a *weapon*.

Wynter's gaze is intensely on mine. It's a struggle not to look away.

Wynter used to say that I had the bluest eyes in Fable, and that I should've been born in the Sun pack because *they look like the sky*. Does she still think that?

I clench my jaw. I'm not the same kid she knew. I'm grown up now: athletic, strong, and *why in the name of the night couldn't I have ironed my shirt properly?*

Oh yeah, because I was hanging out with my crew, playing basketball and forgot the time.

At any rate, I'm wearing my least crappy suit to this gathering. Okay, it's my *only* suit.

I may be poor but I can do my best not to look it. I have my pride; all Moon Wolves do.

My tongue darts out and wets my lips. Wynter's grown up too. She looks like the sun has fallen from the heavens, whereas I look like I've just tumbled out of bed.

My wolf feels like it'll always know her, but then, my wolf is being an asshole, which is kind of not a surprise. He's seriously dominant. And right now, he doesn't want me to stand here stiffly, hiding how I feel, he wants to bury his nose against Wynter's neck and breathe in her woodsy scent. He wants to claw the sun headband off her perfect locks and lure out the wild beast inside her to meet mine.

He wants to hold her tight and never let her go, so she can't leave again.

But of course, I'm not an asshole. And I don't do any of that.

On the moon, surely I can tell Wynter...warn her...*something*? I made an oath to protect her, after all.

But just as I open my mouth to warn her what's really going on in Fable, a steel grip settles on my bicep, hard enough to bruise, and I wince. I'm yanked away from Wynter and back toward the Moon pack and the circle that's forming around the Fearless.

"You'd let that brat Sun Wolf...the Alpha's daughter...distract you now, after everything she's done? How she wrecked you by leaving?" Flint, the Moon pack leader, whispers harshly, before swinging me around to face him.

He towers over me, hell, over every wolf, and his eyes, which are as dark as his long hair, blaze. The crescent moon that's been painted on his forehead gleams brighter than on any other wolf to mark out his status.

I struggle to meet his gaze and not twist back to look for Wynter.

Flint growls, shaking my arm. "Focus."

I give a tight nod.

I'd never disrespect Flint. He's like a dad to every fatherless pup in the pack.

Finally, Flint lets go of me. "You were the one who came to me and *begged* to be chosen and trained. You've become our only real chance to seize power. I trust you."

"I know."

Does he think that I've forgotten the strict warrior routine over the last four years: hours every morning before school and late into the evenings? Being woken up in the middle of the night and dragged out of bed to be hunted, which had almost made me piss myself the first time it'd happened with no warning, because only then would I be toughened up enough?

"You don't." Flint takes a sharp breath. My stomach cramps at the pain in his expression. "I trained you like *I* was trained. I was chosen as the strongest wolf in the pack, just like you've now become, and if you think that I've been a hardass to you, well, you never met the old pack leader. You have no idea what it's like to be driven relentlessly every day to become stronger, pressured to train and give up everything else in your life, punished if you don't beat your old scores, as your pack all idolize you like only *you* can save them."

Is he serious?

My mouth twists. "I may have some idea."

Flint's expression darkens, as he glares across the glade at the Alpha. "Don't backtalk me. You don't have a clue because I waited, and waited, and...*nothing*. I was never allowed to make a move against the other packs. So, I trained you." He gives a wicked grin that makes my insides squirm. "And tonight, at last, something's being announced that will make both our waiting worth it."

He shoves me to the front of the circle.

Bright lanterns, which are shaped like wolves, have been set up to create a circle in the center of the shadowy grove. The three packs cluster around them, separated once more: the brightly colored Sun Wolves, the Shadow Wolves in their mysterious ritual clothing, and our silver Moon pack.

I swallow, as I notice that all have pushed their most powerful wolves to the front.

For a moment, across the circle, my gaze is caught by Ri's. If I think *Shadow Dick* hard enough, will he hear it?

I smirk.

Then Ri's gaze slides to Wynter, who's standing in front of her mom, also in the circle.

He better not be getting any ideas about my Wyn. My lips curl back, and I bare my teeth at him. Except, Ri only glances lazily in my direction, before giving an amused smile.

Dick.

My hands curl at my sides.

All of a sudden, the three Fearless, one from each of the packs, prowl into the center of the circle. Their faces are covered with wooden masks; the Sun Moon's is topped with a sun disc and the Moon Wolf's a crescent moon. The Shadow Wolf's is faceless.

I shudder, looking away. That one freaks me out the most. I had nightmares about it as a kid.

I hate the Fearless. Perhaps, I'm broken because I should respect them. They're meant to link to the Great Shadow Wolf and the birth of our packs.

Bullshit.

I know about hiding behind masks, and they're just frightened men, using the power of our beliefs to manipulate us. But hey, it's working.

My heart thumps, and my wolf circles my mind, restless.

What did Flint mean, anyway? What's being

announced?

The Sun Fearless holds up his hand; everyone watches him. "For generations, there has been no new Alpha. For generations, it's been handed down through the Sun Wolves, without the ancient Wolf Trials and Wolf Games. But tonight, it's our will that from those gathered, nine will be chosen as initiates to take part with the chance to become the new Alpha of Fable."

Shocked murmurs and gasps break from the crowd.

What in the name of the moon…? Is this real? *The Wolf Games?*

This is my chance: for Mom, my sis, Parker, Dex and Jex, Flint, and for the entire Moon pack…

"Be silent," the Shadow Fearless bellows.

Now, there's nothing but the quiet night, and my pulse thrashing in my ears. I don't dare look at anything but the faceless mask of the Shadow Fearless.

This. Is. It.

"As there are three sides to the wolf – the Sun, Shadow, and Moon – so there will be three initiates from each pack. Only choose your best warriors because the trials to prepare them shall be dangerous and the games will be deadly," the Shadow Faceless coldly explains.

When I shiver, however, it's not out of fear but anticipation…by my stars, *excitement.*

Bring it on.

If you've been dragged out of your bed aged fifteen, had a bag thrown over your head, forced to march into the middle of a wood with thoughts you were about to be executed because hey, sometimes I was dramatic, and then been hunted by your entire pack in the name of *training*, no warnings about the *danger* could put me off becoming Alpha.

The deadly part sucked though.

The rest of the crowd must've thought so as well because there was a shuffling of feet and nervous glances.

The Moon Fearless twirled around, pointing at each pack in turn. "The Deep is coming: the cold devourer of the long, dark night. It's already stolen our shadow-mates. We must look to the old ways for balance and bring forward warriors to lead us to a new future. But for that, we need a sacrifice: our young. Select the initiates, who'll train in the Wolf Trials and then battle in the Wolf Games for the prize of becoming the Alpha."

I rock back and forth on my heels in excitement. This is my chance; I can taste it. My wolf howls. I chose to become the weapon, rather than the toy. If I succeed in this, then my pack will never have to make that choice again.

My neck prickles. I can sense Flint and everybody watching me. The air's charged with expectation, and it chokes me.

I won't hesitate; I won't let them down. I grit my teeth. I wish the Alpha had allowed Mom to have the evening off work, so she could've seen this.

But then, soon she won't be the Alpha.

If I win, I can let Mom rest as much as I want. The Sun Wolves can work for us.

I don't wait to be picked. Instead, I'm the first to step into the circle.

This is my choice.

When I raise my chin, my gaze meets Ri's again across the circle, and to my surprise, it's *Ri* who bares his fangs now like I've already stolen the title of Alpha from him.

I glance back over my shoulder, and Flint smiles at me, proudly. Warmth flushes through me. Then Flint lays his hand on Jex's shoulder. Jex is my friend, one of my crew along with his identical twin Dex; they're both wiry and dark-haired, but the smartest wolves in our pack.

My stomach twists at the thought of Dex, who was attacked by a gang of Sun Wolves earlier. It'd hurt to see how he hadn't even been able to walk, when he'd been brought back from the Healers, and now, he's missed out on seeing his twin selected as an initiate. Since birth, they've never been apart.

How on the cursed moon, are they going to cope with being parted now?

Jex sucks in a breath to steady himself but stands squarely at my shoulder.

Flint walks along the line, before tapping Parker on the shoulder.

I can't stop the goofy grin, as Parker swaggers forward, shooting me a wink.

Okay, Parker will bring the fun to the dangerous.

He combs his hand through his thick, black hair, pushing it back from his face. His caramel skin is flushed, like he's posing for photographs. Hey, I don't blame him for enjoying the spotlight. He didn't train like me, however, so why was he chosen?

Jack, Healer and leader of the Shadow Wolves, steps forward but he's scowling. "How does this help us to face the coming storm with unity? Pitting the packs against each other will tear us apart. This...spectacle... of the games is pure entertainment. You're distracting us from the truth because you don't have a real solution. Why would you risk the precious lives of our next generation? This is smoke and mirrors."

"Cease to question our decisions, or you'll be thrown out of the gathering," the Shadow Fearless snarls. "Do you wish us to pick your initiates for you?"

"Don't you dare." Jack's eyes flash. Then his expression gentles, and he turns back to face the Shadow Wolves. I study him in surprise. Has Flint ever looked at me like that? Huh, it must be nice to have a pack leader who stands up for you or even studies you with that type of concern: weird but kind of nice. "I'm not going to put any of you forward. This is more dangerous than they're letting on. I'm a Healer, and I took an oath not to cause harm. All of those who are of age, you can make your own decision. Shadow Wolves don't need to be Alphas; we survive as we are. So, you step forward or don't. We won't snap at another's heels for power."

A tall wolf with ebony skin steps silently into the circle with a fluid grace; I don't know him, but he's powerful.

Jack nods. "Okay, Teo."

My eyes widen, as Ri stalks forward.

Shit. I knew it.

Shadow Dick wants to steal the wolf I love and now my chance at becoming Alpha.

I'm going to kick his ass.

Then Brey, his sister, snatches him by the arm, and her voice vibrates with fury and fear, "I'm the warrior, and you're the Healer. We agreed."

Ri tries to pull himself free but fails; I smirk. "Away with you, that was before I had a chance to fight for Alpha."

"*You* had the chance...? What about the chance to die? I can't lose you as well."

He nudges her shoulder. "You know why I have to do this, right?"

Brey sighs, before letting go of him and holding his hand, instead. "Then we do this together."

She walks forward next to her brother.

I stare at them, sizing up my competition.

Jack's expression is tight. "You know what I'm going to say, and I also know that you're going to do this anyway. But remember what I warned you about scars?"

Ri cocks his head. "Aye, and remember what I said about not hiding them?"

"Three moons, three shadows, and now we only need three suns," the Sun Fearless intones.

My gaze shoots to Wynter. She stiffens. She's pale and panicked.

The Alpha inclines her head, before with a swish of her long, white dress, sweeping behind Ballard.

Stars above, not that asshole...

When the Alpha curls her hand onto Ballard's shoulder, Ballard gives one of his patented haughty smiles. He's from one of the poshest, richest families after the Alpha and he makes sure that nobody forgets it with his stupidly perfect golden hair, chocolate brown eyes, and immaculate clothes.

He's also a vicious bully, who gets off on the power he holds over the other packs. I shudder at the thought of what life will be like in Fable, if he becomes Alpha.

Ballard's gang has beaten me up more times than anyone else: they keep score. They play a game with tallies: Moon or Shadow. They've got a bet going on which pack they'll manage more beat downs on.

You see, I'm a *secret* weapon. Flint's been training me because he promised that one day, I could have a shot at wrestling back the power, and he hinted that it could be legal or even a coup.

This right now is my shot.

But if you're a *secret* weapon, then you have to take the beatings or you reveal yourself too soon.

But not anymore. At least, not the moment that the trials begin. Then Ballard will be in for a shock.

The Alpha pushes Paige into the circle with a shove, and I can't hold back the snort. Ballard's eyes light up, and he wraps his arm around her possessively. She *eeps*.

Paige isn't a warrior. Is she more like Ballard's bonus?

I glance at Wynter. Why isn't she stepping into the circle? Doesn't she want the chance?

Can I help the way that my wolf's desperate that she shares this experience with me?

When the Alpha hesitates on the final selection, the Sun Fearless marches toward her.

"As the Alpha's daughter," the Sun Fearless

commands, "the rules state that she must take part and fight."

The Alpha shakes her head. "She's too weak. Sick. You all must remember that."

I don't miss the flash of pain across Wynter's face.

Weak, weak, weak.

The Alpha's sick daughter.

How many times had pack members whispered that when they didn't know Wynter and I could hear? They'd also been the Alpha's favorite words to spit at Wynter in that special disappointed tone she saved just for her daughter.

But Wynter wasn't weak.

It took strength to keep going, despite rejection. To remain kind and funny in the Sun House. To be in pain every day but never complain about it.

It took a quiet strength to live in a pack that valued one type of power, when you held another.

I wish I'd told her that.

Hell, I wouldn't let her be shamed like this because then the packs would never let her forget it – ever.

"By the moon, let her fight," my voice rings through the grove, and everyone turns to stare at me. My pulse thrashes in my ears; my face is hot. "She's back with us now...one of us. Or is it the Alpha who's weak?"

I wince at the shocked gasps, which are followed by a deathly silence.

Whoops. Too far?

What in the wild wolves have I done?

Flint grabs me by the ear and twists; I grit my teeth. "Have you lost your mind?"

I'm dead.

"I just wanted…"

"Remember your true allegiance," Flint hisses. "As soon as we're home in the Moon Quadrant, I'll be sure to remind you."

Awesome, something to look forward to.

Flint let's me go with a shove, and Jex catches me before I can stumble.

Jex pats me on the back, pulling a sympathetic face. He knows what *reminding* means.

But it's worth it. Wynter always is.

I glance across the circle at her with a grin, but it fades, because she isn't smiling back. She's staring at me in shock and then she frowns.

"I don't want to fight in some freaky games for the pack's amusement," Wynter says, and each word stabs through me. "I don't have anything to prove to anyone."

It looks like I really don't know her anymore.

The Alpha's white with rage. Does Wynter know what she's done?

There are hundreds of wolves here tonight: the top families and every pack, and they're all intently watching each other. After all, soon the dynamics may change entirely. Soon, there could be a new pack on top.

The Alpha grabs Wynter's elbow and propels her into the center of the circle. "You'll fight and you'll win."

Wynter shakes her mom's hand off. "Not happening."

"Then who should take your place?" The Alpha glances around the circle, before she settles on a young wolf (far too young for the trials). "I pick Iris."

Iris' eyes widen.

"You can't," Wynter pleads. "She hasn't even shifted yet." When the Alpha merely arches her brow, Wynter hangs her head, clenching her fists. "Okay, I'll fight."

Wynter's shaking. I'm desperate to dive across the circle and wrap her in my arms, as I would on cold winter days down by the bridge over the frozen river. I want to tell her that I'll protect her. My wolf needs to.

But I can't. She's a rival.

I'm being torn in two.

My Wyn would've grinned at me. She'd have wanted to go on this adventure with me as equals like when we quested into the woods as kids, even if this time it's deadly.

But this is Wynter…and she's spent too long in the human world.

Now, I've condemned her to take part in the Wolf Games, when she didn't want to.

Does she hate me?

The Shadow Fearless nods, satisfied. "Nine initiates are selected and—"

"Wait," the Alpha holds up her hand, imperiously. "I've yet to tell the initiates what the trophy is. When they win the Wolf Games and become Alpha, they also get to mate with my daughter."

Blood rushes in my ears; my heart thuds in my chest. Someone's growling…

Wait, it's me…and Ri.

Wynter isn't property: a trophy or a prize.

I can't let anyone else win, if it means that they mate

with Wynter. My wolf says she's mine. My wolf would die if she became someone else's.

Wynter is staring at her mom, horrified. "Don't do this. *You can't.* I won't be forced to mate with the winner."

The Alpha's expression hardens. "Then it appears that you have enough incentive to win. Then you get to choose who you mate with from the initiates."

Wynter's mouth gapes, and she scans along the initiates in the circle. I straighten like somehow that can tempt her to pick me.

The Alpha is ruthless. No wonder she doesn't look terrified at the fact that she's going to lose her Alpha status. Either the Sun Wolves win and they retain the power, or they don't, and she still does, through the mating.

The packs have never been joined in mating like this before. It wasn't allowed. That's the exact reason the Alpha punished me as a kid. So, is this a desperate attempt to draw us all closer together or stop us breaking apart?

All I know is that if I win, I'll save my pack and mate with the woman I'm desperate to have a second chance with.

But what's the point, if she hates me?

I glance around the circle at my rivals. Except, am I looking at a circle of ghosts? The trials and games are deadly, the stakes are the highest in the wolf world, and the prize is everything.

Yet my guts churn at the thought that in these Wolf Trials, we're really nothing but sacrifices.

CHAPTER 6

WYNTER

Growing up, Mom used to say that I'd be lost without the Sun pack.

But it's a lie.

I lived four years away from Fable and I was fine. In fact, I was awesome. I had non-furry friends, school, and Doritos.

Now, I suspect that it's actually *Mom* who'd be lost without *me* to continue her legacy.

The Deep's approaching, panic is setting in, and it's been a long time since the last Wolf Games were held. I get why the Fearless have decided that now is the time to determine the best Alpha to lead Fable through the upcoming dangers. But it terrifies Mom to lose her position.

Did she urgently call me home for no other reason than the Wolf Games? Didn't she care at all about Dad's death? Instead, she knew that the initiation for the games was being called any day and she needed her pawn.

That's me!

But do I want to be caught in the middle of her web and be used by her?

Hell no!

I rush down the main street of Fable in the early hours of the morning, making my escape from Mom, as the sun is only just peeking over the horizon, with Hades on my heels. My backpack's flung over my shoulders, and I pull the hood of my snow jacket over my head to keep the icy cold away.

There's an early morning bus that goes past the main road, where the crash happened at seven a.m., and I intend to be on it.

After the initiation gathering yesterday, I didn't sleep a wink. I tossed and turned with Mom's cruel words whirling through my mind.

When they win the Wolf Games and become Alpha, they also get to mate with my daughter.

I inhale sharply, as anger burns through me, despite the cold wrapping itself around my body.

How can I remain in Fable? I felt like I might die, when Mom threatened to put Iris in my place if I didn't obey her, and sold me as a mate in front of everyone, just like Addison was sold to her.

Tears of rage tremble at the corners of my eyes.

Mom doesn't care if I win the games or not because either way *she* wins. To her, it's not about what's best for the wolves of Fable, but what's best for her.

And I refuse to be part of her games. I can't stay around in town to watch her do this.

Hell, I miss Dad.

He'd have put his arm around my shoulders and promised: *it's gonna be all right.*

Like he did when I fell over and skinned my knee.

Like he did on the day that I first overheard the word *half-breed.*

Like he did every single damn medical test that I went into hospital for.

Some days my grief feels like a broken rib: no one else can see the agony I'm suffering, but I can feel it with every breath I take.

It's why I'm leaving and taking Hades with me. I want to be around things that remind me of Dad again. I have a few friends in New York, who'd let me crash at their place, and I'll do a bit of couch surfing, until I get a job.

I'm not *weak.* I'm strong enough to do this.

The world suddenly spins around me, and I pause for a moment, resting against the window of a store front. Hades nudges against my legs as if to steady me.

"I'm okay, buddy." I ruffle the fur on his head.

I took my meds this morning, before sneaking out of the house, but anxiety makes my illness worse.

If I'm being honest with myself, I expected to hate Fable more, but after catching up with Iris last night, then seeing Hunter again, so many old memories resurfaced. There are things I miss from my upbringing, and they all revolve around my friends.

Everytime I think of Hunter, my stomach knots. I begged Dad, as he drove me away from Fable to *take me back.* It'd killed me to leave Hunter without saying goodbye or letting him know what was happening.

I thought about him every day for months.

It doesn't help when my thoughts sweep to Ri as well. I almost melt on the inside at the thought of his intent emerald eyes against his pale skin, yet why does he have to be such a jerk?

I sigh, scuffing my feet along the slushy road.

Gorgeous as they are, no guy is a good enough reason to remain in town, when I'll end up being Mom's puppet. The way I see it, once I'm gone, Mom won't put Iris into the Wolf Games. She won't risk losing the games.

Besides, I'm not a fighter, so how am I supposed to win? It's just for show. She really means to marry me off.

I reach the edge of town and make my way across the field, sticking to the shadows. Snow crunches under my feet, and I dart into the woods as far from the main track as possible to avoid any detection by guards.

Please let the cold keep everyone out of the woods...

The trees and even the rising skyline bleed into darkness.

Trekking through the night or early hours into the woods may be forbidden to the younger wolves and carries severe penalties, but there were many from school who risked it. The bold would venture out as far from town as possible for their own parties.

I attended one, mainly because Hunter took me with him, though I stayed on the fringes, since I was only thirteen years old. Still, any excuse to pretend that

Hunter and I were allowed to hang out like regular friends.

I watched the older students drink and go off into the shadows to kiss. I always wondered if I'd do the same when I reached their age. There was a beautiful brunette, who gained the eye of three guys that one night, and they ended up asking her to choose between them or they'd fight and the winner got her. But I could see the tears in her eyes, the impossible answer she couldn't give. I never did find out what she decided that night as we left early, but I remembered thinking how nice it would be to have such attention.

Yeah, I was a moron.

Now with my return and feeling like I have the attention of the whole town, I wish that nobody would ever fight to win me.

Yesterday, Hunter and Ri had glared at each other like enemies and not simply rivals. The tension between them had been explosive.

Seriously, I don't need that kind of anxiety in my life. It's clear I don't belong in Fable.

I move quickly through the forest, and Hades stays close. The ascending land is slippery under my feet with the thin layer of snow.

Quiet. It's so very quiet this early in the morning. The wind is blowing upwind, and I sniff cautiously.

Where do I know that scent from?

I pause, placing my hand on Hades' back to hold him still, then I lift my head and take a deep sniff this time.

Woodsy with a hint of masculine perspiration.

A wolf.

My expression hardens.

Ri.

Is he stalking me again? Is that seriously his whole thing: stalker-vibe with some assholery brooding?

Except, he's in front of me. At least with the way that the wind's blowing, he won't have detected me yet.

Perhaps, I should've christened him Mr Lurker rather than Emerald Eyes because just like the first time that we met in the wood, he's lurking in the forest by himself.

Is that his hobby?

Okay, now I feel bad for him.

Perhaps, he's trying to fulfil the human stereotype of the big, bad wolf in the woods?

Hades has his nose in the air, sniffing. There's no growling, but his ears are stiff and swiveling like radar discs.

I exchange a look with Hades and crouch down, looping an arm around the back of his neck. "Can you smell him too?"

He makes a groaning sound and pushes his head against my hand.

"You big cry baby." I scratch him behind the ear and get to my feet, before I stick my hands in my pockets and start walking again.

But it doesn't take long before I'm brought to a stop by a vicious growl.

I freeze.

Shit.

Perhaps, coming out alone into the woods without telling anyone where I was going, wasn't my best idea.

The thing about Shadow Wolves is that while they can only transform during a full moon, which isn't happening right now, they can call on the power of their wolves while still in their human form.

At any time.

I've always believed they're the scariest of all us wolves, the most dangerous, so that makes me wonder what Ri is really up to. And why is he growling like he wants to savage something?

Midnight Goddess, don't let it be *me*...

Dad once told me: *never mess with a wolf who isn't afraid of being alone.* When I asked him why, his response surprised me.

Because those wolves will win every time, Dad explained. *The most dangerous are those who don't need anyone, even pack.*

Ri may be a Shadow Wolf, but at the gathering yesterday, he stood out like he didn't belong there, not even among his own kind.

What secret is he hiding?

The deep growl rumbles again.

I peer through the trees, before I spot movement through an obscure opening amid a dense section of oaks.

Someone's standing there with their back to me, seeming to swing something through the air. Only when the glint of dawn sun shines against the silver end, do I realize that it's an ax.

Yeah, that's Ri.

He's practicing that strange fight again, and even from my distance, I'm captivated by how swiftly he moves. He's dressed in all black, and his eyes gleam in the dark.

A strange tingling starts in the base of my belly.

Next thing I know, he's darting deeper into the woods away from me, and I'm stepping forward after him almost instinctively, as if it's a given I'll follow him.

I'm drawn after him, and it's like by his leaving, a part of me has been ripped away.

I stop myself and glance down at Hades. He's staring at me with a judging look.

"Hey, it's not what you think," I whisper. "What if he's up to something bad? What if he's a serial killer? I'd never live with myself if I did nothing. Just because I don't want to fight in some crazy games, doesn't mean I don't care about this town." My voice is barely audible, and I cringe hard on the inside at my terrible excuse to follow Ri.

It's not like I care about a certain Shadow Wolf.

Not at all.

I have time before my bus arrives. If I leave now, I'll always wonder what he's hiding, and I definitely don't want to carry that kind of burden around with me. I have enough on my mind already.

"Let's go, but keep quiet," I tell Hades in a hushed voice.

Then I dart in the same direction as Ri.

I glance at the trees around me, which are like shadows in the darkness, watching me.

My mind screams that this is a bad idea.

What if Ri catches me following him like a stalker...again?

I blush. At least then, I could be his Mrs Lurker.

Those gorgeous lips of his would probably smirk, before he narrowed his emerald eyes and blurted some arrogant assholery.

Weirdly, that thought no longer makes me only furious but also flushed with warmth.

I shake away the thought.

I keep moving, focusing on keeping up with Ri, focusing on making as little noise as possible. I make quick work of ducking low branches and rushing over dead logs.

I blink through the darkness, scanning the land. Where did he go?

Excitement builds up within me at the chase.

Hades takes a step to my right, farther down the slope. The woods have become sparser the farther we travel, and when I see movement ahead of us, I duck behind a pine tree. Hades remains concealed by a cluster of shrubs.

My heart beats hard.

Will Ri see me?

He's going to be so smug to have caught me.

When the crunch of snow reaches me, I peer out from behind the tree.

Ri prowls across the wide, frozen river. His steps are fast and sure over its icy surface, then he jumps across to the opposite side before making a break for the woods.

Determined to not lose him, I square my shoulders and follow. Stepping out of the woods sends a shiver jolting up my spine. I'm exposed here. The river is at least fifteen feet wide with no bridges out here in the forest. I glance around, seeing nothing but trees in every direction. Only one way to fix that. I sprint across the river.

I glance over my shoulder. "Hades," I hiss as loudly as I dare, "get your furry ass over here."

But Hades waits on the riverbank; his tail hangs between his legs.

I stand still, unsure whether I need to drag him after me.

It looks that way.

I sigh, marching back toward the riverbank. It appears I'll lose this hunt.

All of a sudden, my foot slips right out from under me across the ice. I gasp, and my arms flail.

Then there's a terrifying cracking sound beneath me.

I grit my teeth in terror, and adrenaline rushes through me.

It all happens too fast.

I fall onto my ass, the ice shatters beneath me, and I drop right into the unbearably cold river. Fear bangs in my chest because I've left my heart somewhere back in the woods, while the freezing water steals all my warmth in seconds.

Shit!

I throw my arms and legs about, dread pricking at the edges of my mind that I'm going to die out here in this hole in the ice. But I keep fighting, trying to grab hold of the edges of broken ice, which only crumble under my touch.

A biting cold grips me, digging claws into me, as I sink.

My screams are stolen, and the last thing I hear is Hades' desperate bark, before I slide down beneath the surface.

CHAPTER 7

HUNTER

I shove my hands deep into the pockets of my long, silver coat against the cold of the dawn. I'm only wearing a thin t-shirt underneath because my wolf snarled at me to get my ass to the Sun House, and when he snarls, you don't hang around for things like dragging on a sweater. Instead, I just snatched my coat and rushed out into the freezing shadows.

So, I blame that asshole for the shivers wracking me. I wrap my arms around myself. It's nothing to do with the dread that's settled in my stomach.

Nothing.

Blaming your inner wolf works a lot of the time, but never with Mom, especially when used as an excuse for stealing cookies.

Sorry, my dominant wolf got hungry. Should I eat Tala, instead?

That makes my sis squeal every time.

I grit my teeth, as slush soaks through my shoes on each step, and stomp down main street.

It's quiet.

Why can't I be back in the room that I share with Parker? He'd be up for some pre-training basketball. I need to drive the thought of my Wyn and her transformation into *Wynter* from my mind: her ruby lips and violet eyes. She looked like the sun itself in the golden glow of the lanterns. After all, Parker's an initiate now as well, and I must make sure he becomes a weapon like me. He won't be able to battle with his smart mouth alone.

He'll try. And he'll get his ass kicked.

Jex's weapon is his brain. He's just smart, period.

My shadow whispers that they're both mine to protect because they're as close as family. I'll do anything to keep them, Mom, and Tala safe. But by the cursed moon, is there something broken inside me that makes me so fierce?

Because no Moon Wolf should feel like that.

They should *know their place*.

Accept the will of the Great Shadow Wolf.

And be prepared to sacrifice anyone.

Bullshit.

We're taught that the Moon pack howl with one voice in joy, triumph, or sorrow. No one wolf is above the other, and no one death is to be mourned more. If a sacrifice is needed for the good of all, then it's to be celebrated.

Moon Wolves don't protect their own. And I definitely shouldn't be thinking about my rival, Wynter.

But as I said…*bullshit.*

After all, Parker's parents died protecting him.

I was only a tiny cub, but I still remember the screams on main street, and how Mom dropped her shopping and pulled me onto her hip, pushing my head away with a hushed *don't look*, before dragging something squirming and sobbing onto her other hip.

I sneaked a glance.

Parker.

I gasped. Parker's terrified silver eyes were surrounded by a sea of red. His face and clothes were coated in it but it wasn't his.

It stank: coppery and tangy. The pavement was covered in crimson puddles.

"Mom," Parker sobbed, "Dad."

He clung to Mom, and she clung to him. I'd never seen her look so determined. It was the only time that she fought with Flint, insisting that she foster Parker.

No one ever discovered who murdered Parker's parents. But then, who looked hard for the killers of two Moon Wolf servants?

In training, I once slashed a punching bag to pieces. "It's so screwed-up. The Alpha only cares about what happens to her Sun pack. The Sun Wolves get away literally with murder. On the blessed moon, how can they claim there's any justice in Fable?"

"There isn't and never has been equal justice for all the packs. Accept it," Flint snapped. "There's justice for Sun Wolves, revenge for Shadow Wolves, and a silent grave for Moon Wolves."

I clench my fists. *But not anymore.* A weapon doesn't

go silently to its grave. It fights and sends others to theirs.

And it was Flint who honed me.

Last night, when Parker and I returned from the gathering, we were still psyched from being chosen as initiates. We hadn't stopped grinning all the way home. It was like something inside me was ready to spring free.

Things had a chance of finally changing in Fable.

After we'd been able to persuade Tala to go to bed and tucked her in (against her loud protests that she wasn't a cub and was old enough to stay up), Parker and I had stood looking at each other in the lounge.

"How about we break open two packets of chips, before Mom gets back?" I offered.

We might be poor but we knew how to party.

What would Mom think when she heard both Parker and I had been chosen? Would she be excited? Worried? Angry?

My stomach turned with nerves.

"Why not? Let's go crazy." Parker laughed.

I caught the glint in his eye the moment before he pounced. I ducked to the side but allowed him to tumble me to the floor. I still reversed our positions, pinning him beneath me. We both laughed, as I pushed my arm against his throat.

"Okay, okay, *uncle*," he spluttered. Unexpectedly, his expression became serious, and I just *knew* that he was thinking of that day on main street with the crimson puddles and his desperate cries for his Mom and Dad, who'd never be coming back because they'd joined the Great Shadow Wolf. "This is it, bro."

I nodded; my throat was dry. "This is it."

Then the door pushed open, and Mom stumbled in. She looked exhausted like she did after every shift, but her eyes were red-rimmed, as if she'd been crying.

I exchanged a glance with Parker, before we both pushed ourselves up.

"Are you okay, Mom?" I asked.

She blinked, dazed. "The Alpha has a temper on her. I warned you, remember? She stormed in and she was furious. She started throwing books and vases and…" I growled, stepping closer to her. She hung up her coat, mechanically. "Addison tried to calm her down like he always does, but she snatched my arm…"

My eyes widened, and I gently traced over the purple hand print on Mom's arm.

I was going to tear out the Alpha's throat. Okay, she'd tear out mine first but…

Mom patted my cheek. "Don't even think about it."

"What?" I said, innocently.

"We both know what."

I glanced over my shoulder at Parker, whose expression was as tight as my own. "Ice."

"On it." He dived out of the room and into the kitchen.

Mom clasped my hand. "The Alpha said you'd both been chosen. That I'd let you *forget your place*. My own sons. She said that my family is getting above itself, and she tried to teach you a lesson, but it clearly wasn't effective. So, she's demanding I bring Tala to work as a maid, so she can do better with her than she did with you."

"*No*," I snarled, snatching my hand away from Mom.

My wolf circled inside me, snapping and biting.

I couldn't let this happen. *I wouldn't.*

My fangs descended. I was barely holding in my wolf. When I looked at Parker, who was standing in the doorway, he was doing no better than me. His claws were piercing the ice that he was crushing in his hands.

"She's fourteen," Parker said, coldly.

But hey, why would the Alpha care that she was ruining a Moon Wolf's childhood and education?

I struggled to breathe.

Dark. Dark. Dark.

I was back in the closet, banging on the door to be let out. Alone and trapped and…*that could be Tala.*

If I left for the Wolf Trials, who'd be here to protect my family?

Parker's gaze met mine.

Yet could I throw away all the years of dedicated training, the agonizing tests that Flint had put me through, and the pressure as the hope of the Moon pack? Flint would say I couldn't give that up for the sake of two wolves.

A sacrifice should be welcomed.

Screw that.

"I'll win the Wolf Games for you," Parker whispered. "I'll do it."

Mom slammed her hand on the wall, and I jumped. "You'll both get a chance to win." My eyes widened, and her mouth curled into a smile. "Why do you always think you can hide things? Moms are all-knowing. Like the times that you used to sneak out past curfew, and I turned a blind eye, well, the same for your secret training with Flint."

"Busted," Parker muttered.

Mom crossed her arms. "And do you think that you hid your love for Wynter? That I couldn't see your friendship becoming something more?"

I flushed. "Mom…"

"It was beautiful. But she broke that. Stole it. I had to watch, as you suffered. So, you enter the trials and you fight for all of us. But most importantly, you fight for yourself, you hear me? I believe in you."

Now, I squint up at the sun, which is just peeking over the horizon and lighting up main street. I shift my shoulders. Dawn, just like twilight, is a weird time for us wolves. It's the transition between sun and moon, when neither holds the power. Instead, there's an uneasy balance.

I can't transform fully, but my wolf is at its strongest with the greatest hold over me, and right now, it wants out.

All night, I had laid awake, worried for Tala. Then my wolf had enough and threw me out of bed and stalking down the street toward Sun House.

My wolf is all about action.

I may not be able to save Tala, while I'm away in the Wolf Games. Until they start, however, I can at least try to protect her. I've just turned eighteen; I'm not a cub anymore like Tala. The Alpha is angry with me, so I'll let her use *me* as the punching bag, even if I end up slashed to pieces.

If I offer myself up, then she may leave Tala out of it.

A strong wolf isn't ashamed of another's dickish actions. My dominant wolf is an asshole but he knows that whatever the Alpha does to hurt or humiliate me shames her…and not me.

Wait, who's that walking towards me?

I push my floppy hair out of my face, narrowing my eyes. I sniff, catching a faint pine scent. My wolf howls.

My Wyn.

I pull back to make sure she won't catch sight or scent of me.

Does she hate me for getting her chosen for the Wolf Games?

By the moon, don't hate me, Wyn.

It'd wreck me.

She's so lost in her own thoughts, however, that even if I stood in front of her in a clown costume and honked her nose, she wouldn't see me.

She's no longer wearing the glittery make up or luxurious jewellery but plain jeans. She looks cute in a huge snow jacket and jeans. I smile because I'm looking at the real Wynter beneath the mask and she's beautiful.

She's more beautiful than she was last night.

She's real.

Even if she doesn't know it, she's mine. My wolf longs to hold her close, warm against the cold, and never let go…to bite kisses down her neck and claim her. But then, I tilt my head in confusion. Her hood is pulled up, and she's carrying a backpack.

Why in the name of the wild wolves would she be out dressed like that at this time of the morning, unless...?

She's running away.

She's leaving Fable again.

She's leaving me.

The desperation and desolation of those first few months after she disappeared wash over me.

She wasn't even going to say goodbye this time either.

The Alpha was right. I was only ever a toy to her.

Wynter doesn't care for me like I do her with such an ache in my shadow that I don't know whether I want to hold her forever or tear her apart just to be free of her. She would've left me behind like I'm just another Moon Wolf who's worthless. But I'm not and I'll show her.

She promised me that we'd talk, and we will.

I bare my fangs, as I prowl after Wynter. When she reaches the edge of town, she crosses the field and then darts into the woods.

Is she making for the human world? I sigh, as I follow her. What did she find in it that tempts her so much? Is it because she's a hybrid?

I've heard it whispered about her throughout Fable *that no hybrid will ever find a home with wolves because they'll be called away to the siren song of humanity.*

Is that what draws her away from me? How can I get her to understand that she does belong in Fable?

The wind blows through the tree's branches, and I

carefully climb the steep wood. The snow is slippery. I'm not losing Wynter.

She has no clue that I'm behind her.

Okay, that came off as stalkery. But I'm a wolf. Deal with it.

Then I freeze.

There's another wolf in this wood. One who's as dominant as me. I take a deep sniff, scenting out the trail. Then I jerk in shock.

Ri: The Shadow Dick.

Perfect. On my way to offer myself to the Alpha for punishment, I find my first and only love skipping town, then I come across the most dickish of rival wolves.

Although, Ballard gives Ri some competition. Perhaps, we can get them both to fight each other in the trials.

To my surprise, Wynter hesitates and then sniffs like she can smell Ri too. Why can she smell him and not me? I know that I'm awesome at concealing myself, but it's like she's connected to Ri.

I ball my fist, stiffening.

Yeah, that idea doesn't make me want to smash in his smug face at all.

Except, it seriously does.

I fall further back from Wynter, watching from the shadows. When Ri begins to growl, I roll my eyes.

Shadow Wolves are posers. *Look at me, I'm such a scary wolf, hear me growl.*

When I spot Ri in a glade of oaks, swinging around

an ax, I have to slap my palm over my mouth to smother my snicker.

I reckon Ri likes to sneak into the woods and pretend that he's an Alpha with his shiny ax. It's stress relief for him after last night…like jerking-off.

When Ri darts further into the woods in that *I'm so mysterious and broody* way of his that makes all the girls in the packs swoon and all the guys want to kick his ass, I grin. Now he's gone, I can finally have that talk with Wynter. I'd better not wait any longer or who knows who'll step out next…knowing my luck, the Alpha and her Sun goons.

But then, Wynter whispers to Hades (I've always loved that dog and I miss him), and follows Ri like he's compelling her.

My mouth falls open.

WTF?

I only bite back my own growl by nipping the inside of my cheek. I stand, rooted to the spot.

I trusted Wynter. Her above anyone else. We were best friends, and we told each other everything. But I don't know her anymore. We're no longer cubs, and we both have secrets.

How can I trust her?

Would she choose Ri over me?

Finally, I straighten and prowl after her. As soon as I catch up, I'll make her *see* me as much as she does the Shadow Wolf.

He's the outcast. Newcomer. Psycho.

Wynter thinks that she knows me but she only knew who I was. She has no idea who I am now or how dangerous I am. There are different types of strength and not all are as obvious as those wrapped in black leather.

I leap over fallen logs, and duck under branches that paint scratches across my cheeks. I pant, as my adrenaline spikes.

All of a sudden there's a sharp *crack*, followed by Hades' desperate barking.

Something's seriously wrong.

My pulse thrashes in my ears, as I sprint out of the wood and slide down the slope to a wide, frozen river.

I stare around, wildly.

Where's Wynter?

Hades stands on the riverbank with his tail tucked between his legs. He barks, high and frightened.

My breath catches. My heart *thump, thump, thumps*.

My gaze fixes on the jagged hole in the ice.

No, no, no.

I don't even hesitate, as the wolf takes over. I edge to the riverbank.

"Wyn," I holler, "please, Wyn."

Nothing.

I desperately glance around, before rushing to a tree on the edge of the wood and snapping off a low branch. Then I throw myself to my knees and crawl to the edge of the ice.

The branch will reach the hole, but only if Wynter's able to pull herself out and reach it. With ice thin enough for her to fall through, it's too dangerous for me to get closer. If I drag myself out there to help her, then I'll simply fall through and drown us both.

I howl with a desperation that I never have before, so that Wynter can hear me and follow my voice back to the surface.

I howl for Wynter's shadow.

I howl for her to live.

Wynter bursts out of the water, gasping and icy-blue in shock.

Tears are caught in the corners of my eyes, as I smile in relief. "Call to your wolf."

Her eyes are closed, and she shakes her head as she scrambles desperately at the ice.

"I believe in you," I say in a rush. Mom's words reverberate through me, warming me against the cold. "The Wyn I know wouldn't let herself be beaten. She's strong."

Wyn's eyes flutter open, and her gaze fixes on me.

Thank the moon, she finally sees me.

Then her claws extend, as she partially transforms, with the sun shining over the trees behind her, blinding on the frozen river. Her claws stick into the ice. My knuckles are white around the branch, as she uses her claws like picks to anchor herself to the edge of the hole.

"You can do this," I call.

I shoot her a reassuring smile, and her eyes narrow with determination.

She snarls, as she drags herself free by her claws, before rolling onto the river on her side. She curls in on herself, gasping for breath and trembling.

"Don't try to move. The ice is still weak." I lay down

on my belly and reach as far to her as I can with the branch. "Grab onto this."

When she snatches the branch, I shudder. Our gazes meet. It's electric.

For this moment, in the quiet, wintry dawn that could've ended in death, we're connected in life through the touch of this branch.

I'll never forget the way that she's looking at me now.

That I saved a Sun Wolf.

So much for Moon Wolves not protecting their own and that includes Wynter.

Slowly, I drag Wynter across the thin ice to safety. As soon as she's on the bank, Hades jumps around her.

Gently, I push Hades back. "Give her room to breathe, buddy."

And she needs it.

Wynter shakes, hyperventilating with shock. Her eyes are wide, her eyebrows already white with ice.

Let her be okay.

She isn't okay.

I push myself up and haul her into my arms. She's frozen. I drag off her soaked snow jacket, before slipping my own coat off. I wrap my dry coat around her shoulders, and she huddles into it, pulling it closer. Her teeth are chattering, her whole body convulsing with tremors.

I shiver, as the breeze cuts through my thin t-shirt.

Inner wolf, you asshole, this is why you pause to put on a sweater.

I pull Wynter onto my hard chest, giving her my

warmth like I wanted to earlier. For years, I never thought I'd see or hold her again.

But I could've done without it being like this.

Life as a wolf in Fable sucks.

I hush Wynter, as she tries to talk, rubbing her shoulders. "Concentrate on taking slow breaths. Like this."

I force myself to slow my own breathing. I can feel Wynter copying me, and at last, she's able to breathe. We're in sync, connected.

There's no one but us, breathing for each other.

The tremors subside. Wynter's gaze is intent, as she studies me.

I push a wet strand of her hair off her forehead. "Look, you're in shock. We need to get you warmed up quickly. I don't know where you were going but..." I bite my lip. "You belong with the wolves, whether you can see it yet or not. Maybe we're only strangers now. A lot has changed since you left. But you're surviving, Wyn, even if I have to carry you every step of the way."

Her eyes widen, as I slip my hands underneath her, then I stumble to my feet, carrying her in my arms.

It's a long way back through the freezing wood, fields, and town to the Sun House, but I'm not the weak cub that Wynter once knew. I'm a warrior. And I'd carry her forever if I had to.

Wynter loops her arms around my neck, resting her head on my chest. "T-t-thanks..."

Her teeth still chatter.

"Hey, don't try to talk now." I start my way up the

slope away from the river, clicking for Hades to follow me. "Just concentrate on breathing."

Will I be breathing, however, if I turn up in Sun pack territory, clutching the bedraggled and half-dead Alpha's daughter?

The Alpha is the type to tear out throats and ask questions later.

Especially when it's me.

One summer when we were cubs, Wynter and I had been on one of our adventures in the woods. She rushed ahead of me, and didn't slow up when I called. Instead, she only ran faster, before she tumbled into a small ravine. She twisted her ankle, and I helped her limp back to Sun House.

When she saw the leaves in Wynter's hair, her ripped dress, and her swollen ankle, the Alpha reddened with fury but she didn't explode at Wynter. Instead, she backed me against the wall.

I whined, expecting to be savaged.

Yet I'd ended up wishing that the Alpha *had* savaged me, after the hour-long scolding. She grounded me to the Sun House or my own home for the rest of the Summer, but at least that meant I could keep Wynter company, as her ankle healed.

Wynter was still free to sit outside in the warm garden, however, and I wasn't. I only watched her through the window, crowned by sunlight, as I was trapped inside in the dark.

Is Wynter now my rival, childhood friend, or the wolf who remembers that she promised to be with me forever?

It doesn't matter.

She's the woman who makes me forget every time I'm with her that the three packs are enemies. Yet, it makes my guts churn with unease just how much I'll risk for this Sun Wolf.

Once, I allowed myself to really fall for Wynter with everything that I was, until I drowned in her. And she left me to die in the icy water.

If I let myself fall for her like that again, it could be my entire pack who freezes to death.

"How dare you harm my daughter!" Mom snarls from the doorway at Hunter.

Her grip on my elbow is like iron. She's shaking her head, and her face is red with fury at being woken up too early, when Hunter banged on the door for help.

She looks like she's barely holding herself back from diving for Hunter's throat.

I tried to tell Hunter just to leave me and go, but finding my voice was hard between chattering teeth and shaking so unbearably hard that I was in pain.

"S-stop it," I say, tugging on Mom's arm. At least I manage to draw her death glare from Hunter to me. "He s-saved me."

Mom huffs. "Don't mock me, girl. I can see the truth in his eyes."

She swings back to Hunter, who stands tall despite her anger and the driving snow, which hits him in the back. Yet he never lowers his head or shows submission.

Back in the woods, he told me so much had changed in town over the past four years, and that includes him.

I see that now.

There's a confidence, where once there'd been uncertainty, muscles instead of a wiry frame, and a piercing determination, with what I swear is dominance rather than the meek Moon Wolf who I once considered my friend.

But I'm drawn to him now in a different way. Okay, I admit it. Could he become *more* than a friend?

Yet life in Fable has grown complicated with the upcoming Wolf Games. Hunter will be participating, and that's driven Mom to truly detest him or perhaps, she *fears* him for the first time.

And that'll make her vicious.

"*You*," Mom growls. "A Moon Wolf has no right to touch a Sun Wolf. But maybe it's my fault for being lenient, when you were both younger. That won't happen again."

I meet Hunter's gaze, and he doesn't bat an eye like he's become so used to Mom's ranting that it's washing over him.

Footsteps close in behind me, and I turn to find Addison entering the hallway, dressed in a long, white robe, sleep still in his eyes. He runs a hand through his hair. "Do you know what time it is? You'll wake the whole neighborhood, and the gossip will be running wild before we even have breakfast."

"Go back to bed, Addison," Mom hisses between clenched teeth.

When he winces, I tighten my jaw.

I hate how she talks to her mate. A matching shouldn't be like that, right?

"Just go easy on the poor wolf," Addison urges.

When I look at him, I can't tell if he's referring to Hunter or me. Either way, it won't make a difference. Mom's fuming and won't back down.

While I appreciate that Addison tried to stop her, a sharp ache of disappointment strikes, when he shrugs and strolls into the kitchen with his hands deep in the pockets of his robe.

He's giving up already...?

I guess he's learned that the only way to deal with my mom is to let her win. She's the Alpha, after all. Isn't that what the whole of Fable does? Who has the courage to stand up to her?

Except, Addison has to live with her. The guy's been worn down. If I'd stayed here, would I be like him now?

"Upstairs and get into dry clothes," Mom barks.

But I'm not going anywhere. I won't leave Hunter again.

As much as I want to scream at her to leave Hunter alone, I know as well as Addison that it won't work.

So, instead, I reach over and touch her arm. "I asked Hunter to bring me home, after I fell into the river. It was my fault. If it wasn't for him, you'd have lost a daughter today."

Mom studies me for a long moment and then her scowl deepens. "You can't keep your toys in perfect condition forever. There comes a time, when they'll break or be thrown away."

Hunter's hands ball into fists.

Mom doesn't believe me.

I shouldn't be surprised and yet I am. Mom thinks lies and manipulations are part of being a successful Alpha. I bet she's secretly proud of me.

I shake at the fact that Hunter's witnessing how shattered my relationship is with my mom. When I was young, I always envied how close he was to Faith. They made loving each other look so easy.

"Don't take it out on him." My grip on her arm tightens. My gaze meets Hunter's: we both know that *it* could mean so many things in Fable...and between us, since we grew up together in this house.

Mom shakes me off. "Take a bath and warm up. I'll call the Healer to check that you're okay. Tonight is the Blossom Ball to welcome you back and celebrate the Wolf Games. All the initiates will be the stars, and you'll shine brightest."

I bristle. My attempt to escape ended in an icy near-death failure. But I'm not Addison. She hasn't broken me yet.

"I won't shine. I'm not an initiate, if I won't fight."

Gaping like a landed fish is a good look on Mom.

I almost snicker, but then Hunter shoots me a confused glance.

Why does he look so disappointed? I guess he was the one who spoke up for me joining the Wolf Games in the first place. Does he think that this is just another great adventure like when we tracked bears as kids?

Can't he see that if Mom wants this, it's going to be a terrifying nightmare that we can't escape?

Mom's expression darkens. But instead of attacking

me, she shifts like a chameleon from being vicious to a dangerously calculating woman. "Fine, then you leave me no choice but to force Iris to take your place."

Awesome, the guilt game again.

But this time, I can't back down. I just...*can't.*

If I do, it'll be the beginning of the nightmare.

I hold her stare.

Frustrated, Mom turns and faces Hunter. "And for your disobedience and forgetting your place in Fable, I'll teach you what your pack have clearly failed to. I revoke your invitation to the Blossom Ball tonight. Instead, you'll learn where you belong and help run the party."

When Hunter's eyes widen, I see the pain gleaming in them: the hurt that he'll be publicly reminded of how much lower the Moon Wolves are than the other packs.

That he has no place at the Ball but as a servant like his mom.

"You can't do that," I protest. "He has every right to attend. He's earned it."

Mom marches into the hallway. "And he will attend by serving the drinks."

She slams the front door in Hunter's face, shutting him out.

I'm trembling with rage. "H-how could you?" My body is still shuddering from the cold, but now a newfound fire ignites within me, and it burns through my veins. "How could you treat him like that? He's my friend. His mom has worked here for decades. He's practically family."

The way that Mom turns on me reminds me of a

viper rearing back before it strikes. Ice cold eyes pierce my soul, and she grabs my arm. Her fingernails dig into the sleeve of my coat so deeply that I gasp.

"Has your time in the city blurred your judgement? Have you forgotten the structure of the packs in Fable? Hunter is not our family," Mom spits out the words like it pains her to even consider such a thing. "He was something for you to play with, when you were growing up here, so that you weren't alone. And that's it. The Sun Wolves would've used their own kids to jostle for position in the pack. The son of our house-keeper was far simpler and safer. But now it's time to leave behind your childhood and take your place along-side me. Time to prepare for becoming an Alpha."

I rip my arm from her grasp. "I haven't forgotten one bit how you treat others in this pack. And I'll never be anything like you."

I shake with anger.

"You've become soft, Wynter. Hunter stares at you with those pretty eyes of his, and his golden hair, and muscles that half the idiotic wolves in his own pack swoon over, and you act like you wish to join them. But here are some hard truths. He'll never be good enough for you. The Moon Wolves' participation in the games has done nothing but show us disrespect. What they need is a reminder of our rules."

One of her manicured eyebrows arches.

"You're wrong," I whisper.

"We'll see, won't we?" She pulls her robe tighter around her chest and sweeps into the kitchen.

She's talking to herself, making a racket in there.

I march upstairs, fury flaring through me. I wipe at my burning eyes.

This is why I dreaded returning, and each passing day grows darker with problems.

Once in my room, I slam shut the door, dragging at my clothes. I realize that I'm still wrapped in Hunter's coat. I sniff at the sleeve, and it smells reassuringly of him.

Does he own another coat? He'll be cold on the walk back to Moon pack territory now. I hug the coat tighter around me because at least then, it's like having my best friend back with me.

Right now, I don't have control over much but I'll do the only thing I can and that's resist Mom. Wouldn't Dad want me to? After all, he ran away with me from the wolves.

I can stand up to her.

I want to make Dad proud, but it's so hard to figure out what would do that. The rules are different here than the human world I've grown used to. Mom's right about that at least.

It seems that many in town have given up resisting Mom, even Addison.

Yet Hunter hasn't, and I respect the hell out of him for that.

I curl in on myself, burrowing my nose in the sleeves of Hunter's coat, and close my eyes, wanting to vanish from this dangerous world.

I wake in a daze, pushing myself up onto my elbows. The sudden movement makes me dizzy.

Most mornings, it takes me long moments to find myself, still not settled to the idea that I've left behind New York. Except, when I look at the time on the bedside table, it's past midday.

I reach over and open the drawer, collecting my plastic tube of meds. I pop two into my hand and throw them into my mouth, then chase them down with the water that I keep near my bed. They'll help calm me, just as they aid in the exhaustion that's been wearing me down.

Some days, I can barely get out of bed.

The thump of footsteps hitting the floorboards outside my room, jolts me upright in bed.

I quickly wipe my eyes, although my tears have long dried.

When there's a quick knock on the door, I don't respond, but the door opens regardless.

Mom walks in, wearing her best fake smile and a flowing dress, which is the color of ripe mandarins. Her hair is perfectly styled off her face with bobby pins, and she's even wearing heels in the house.

Mind you, it's freezing outside, but she's the Alpha, right?

"Someone's here to see you." Her smile is tight, and I tilt my head to look past her to the town Healer, who steps into my room. "Jack's here to look you over.

I can't have anyone think I don't care for my daughter."

She laughs, though it's forced.

I may have just vomited in my mouth at how transparent she is.

"Hello, Wynter," Jack's voice is soft, and there's kindness behind his words.

He's in his early fifties, rugged and strong. I notice many of the Shadow Wolf males are built like that. Snow peppers his dark hair that sits messily like he ran over to our house on command from Mom.

Yeah, I bet he did.

There's something reassuring and powerful about Jack. I like him. I always did. He's the leader of the Shadow Wolves, and from what I've learned so far, uncle to Ri and his sister.

What would Fable be like if he was the Alpha?

"The Alpha tells me you fell into the river," he says with more care in his voice than my mom could muster up all morning.

"Alright, Jack, I'll leave you to tend to her," Mom says his name like a taunt.

Everyone calls him the Healer, except Mom, who must think that using his first name degrades the Shadow Wolf beneath her rank.

She turns on her heel and *clicks clacks* out of the room.

Jack's silvery eyes study me, and he smiles gently. "Did you swallow a lot of the icy water?"

I shake my head.

"Good." He places a hand to my brow, then sets a

thermometer under my tongue. "The Alpha also told me you're still taking tablets. Can I see them?"

I nod and point to the top drawer by the bed, which I drag open. Sitting inside are two of the pills in small, orange containers. As I sit back, he studies them, reading the label.

He settles down on the bed beside me and places two fingers on my inner wrist to feel my pulse, looking at me with a caring expression. So much about him reminds me of my dad: the way he used to read me stories on the days I felt the sickest, or would order in Chinese that we'd eat in my room, so I didn't have to move.

Sometimes, it's the small things that make the biggest difference.

We sit in silence for close to ten minutes, his hand on mine as his eyes close. The warmth coming from him radiates in waves. He has a magical ability to heal, although it costs him.

When Jack finally opens his eyes and takes out the thermometer from my mouth, he says, "Wynter, you know as a wolf, you don't really need to take these human medications."

I blink at him. "I'm a hybrid, you know that. The doctors don't have a clue what's wrong with me, but the exhaustion that comes over me is crippling."

"Maybe your ailment is something human medication can't fix." He places a flat palm on his chest. "All of us wolves have a shadow inside us. We're connected to the Great Shadow Wolf. It's from where we gain our strength and our healing. The repair I do on wolves is for quick fixes, but in the end, each one of us has immense strength within us."

I shift in the bed, thinking hard about what's told me, before I say, "But what if my shadow is broken?"

He doesn't respond right away.

A cold ball forms in my stomach. I didn't want to be right.

Who wants to be broken inside?

I haven't transformed into my wolf for four years and barely sense her. And no wolves experience illnesses like me.

"You don't really believe that, do you?" His brow creases in concern. "Your mind will always believe what you tell it."

Except, no matter how much he may not be on the same page on this as me, I'm the one who's lived with the lethargy and mystery illness for years, where I suddenly can't get out of bed and sleep for days in a row.

The meds help; I know they do.

Just like I know that something is wrong with my wolf.

I stare hard at my lap. "Maybe I'm not made for the wolf world. I should never have come back."

He takes his hand away from my wrist, seeming to not have any issues with my pulse.

"I want you to know that you can trust me. Come and talk to me anytime; I promise, anything you say will be in the strictest confidence." He studies the thermometer. "My dad once gave me some advice. He said that in order for us to become what we're meant to be, we have to transform into something new. We can't do it by staying the same."

He stands up, picking up the black satchel bag that he brought in with him. "You're perfectly okay, Wynter. There are no side effects from your fall into the river. I'll let the Alpha know there's no need to worry."

"Thanks for being so nice," I say. Jack turns to me, taken aback. "It's just that you talk to me like I'm a person...I mean a wolf...*crap*, I just mean not someone to be ordered around. Like we're equals."

Jack looks shocked, before he leans closer. "For all our sakes then Wynter, if anyone from the Sun pack is going to win the Wolf Games, let it be you. We're long overdue for change in Fable and a new type of Alpha who sees us all as *equals*." His words are soft, meant only for my ears.

He lowers his head, before hurrying out of the bedroom and shutting the door behind him.

I flop back onto my bed. His words spin around my mind.

But what if the *wrong* Alpha wins?

Will the packs and leaders like Jack simply accept them or will there be war?

I don't know how long I've been in my room, when the faint chatter of female voices reach me from downstairs. Curiosity gets the better of me, and I'm on my feet, opening the door.

I startle at the sound of Mom's laughter. "Oh, you look incredible."

The heavy dose of sugar in her voice makes me frown

and step out into the hallway. I edge my way down the stairs. I blink, when I'm confronted by Iris, who's standing on a small stool in the middle of the living room, dressed in a pink gown that looks like she's swimming in it. The seamstress is pinning the dress in along Iris' side, while Mom watches, resting her chin on her hand.

"We need it tighter across her bust," Mom orders.

Then she lifts her head in my direction and grins. There are no words exchanged between us. Instead, she goes back to giving the Moon Wolf seamstress instructions on how to make the dress fit Iris.

"It has to be perfect," Mom says.

"*Hmm*, I'm not too sure if this is going to work," Iris murmurs; her voice is timid.

"Hush. Of course, it will. At least you have a strong will and know what you must do for your pack."

Iris lifts her gaze toward me.

My breath catches. *She's terrified.* Her eyes gleam with tears that she's struggling to hold back.

Iris looks at me, imploringly. My insides twist with guilt. I should've known that Mom didn't bluff. She'll force a girl who hasn't even had her first shift right into battle.

It sucks to have a conscience.

I duck my head, strolling toward Iris with my hands in the pockets of my jeans. Then I flop down on the couch to watch them.

"Doesn't she look magnificent," Mom crows.

Iris scrunches up her nose, shaking her head for me to say the opposite. Her curly chestnut hair sweeps over her shoulders, and her hazel eyes are large and frightened.

I don't want to give in to Mom but I want to betray Iris even less. I'm not a monster.

Plus, maybe I've been looking at the Wolf Games all wrong. What was it the Healer said about needing to *transform*? Remaining the same is never going to change my situation, right?

Shit, it hasn't exactly worked for me so far.

Would running to live alone in New York really be any safer for me? At the end of the day, I'm a hybrid. I don't fit in either world, and I don't have Dad any longer to help me. Plus, if I leave the Wolf Games up to Mom, she'll marry me off to anyone who wins, so she retains her hold on power over Fable.

But what if *I*... by some miracle....win the Wolf Games?

I'll end up as the Alpha of Fable.

I get to choose who I mate with, and if I'm the one in charge, who's to say I must follow Mom's rules anymore? Sure, it'll be dangerous as hell, and will mean I'll need to play politics to change the way things are run but if I can change the systematic prejudices that divide the packs, then won't it be worth it?

Won't it be worth risking my life...*risking everything*?

"I'll do it," I call out, and all three women turn their heads in my direction. "Yep, you can stop putting on a show, Mom. I accept entering the Wolf Games, but swear on the Midnight Goddess that you'll never drag Iris into any of your schemes again."

I sit deadly still. It's hard to tell how Mom will react. She is as unpredictable as a grumbling volcano.

Mom stares at me as if she hasn't heard me properly. Iris is already stepping off the stool, however, and throwing herself into my arms.

"Thank you, thank you, *thank you*. I could kiss you." And Iris does, on my cheek. "Crap, I almost thought I had to enter the games. I mean, I would've died. I'm putting it out there, but death was on the cards for me."

Mom clears her throat. "That's quite enough, Iris. That's not the kind of talk I want to hear from any Sun Wolf."

Iris nods, grabs her clothes from the table, and then rushes into the bathroom.

"I've never seen her move so fast," I joke.

Mom watches me like the wolf she is. "You have my word on the Midnight Goddess about Iris. But in turn, you must stop behaving like...*a human*. There's no more running away in the middle of the night and no more associating with Moon Wolves. Understand? You have one focus, my dear." She prowls closer, pushing loose strands of hair off my face. "You've brought enough shame to our pack with your weakness. Now it's time to make us proud and to increase our power. Show me you have worth."

Her words are like whip strokes, lashing me for a nature and sickness that I can't control.

Yet something darker shifts beneath her tone.

What happens if I don't make her proud? If I'm not judged to have *worth*?

Will she destroy me like she has so many other wolves?

I force myself to smile. "Don't worry. I'll show you."

Except, I'll show her what I'm *really* worth. And it's becoming an initiate, training in the trials, and then fighting in the Wolf Games not to increase the power of the Sun Wolves but instead, to secretly increase my own power and topple hers.

CHAPTER 9

WYNTER

I scrunch up my toes in my high heels. The cavernous room in the upstairs of the Town Hall is all gleaming marble and columns. But it's hard and cold.

"Tonight you're the Blossom Princess at the ball. For our town to survive, we must follow the old traditions, Wynter," Mom says.

She stands at my side, straightening the blossom flower in my hair, which has been styled with long curls falling down my back, held in place with ruby pins. She straightens the red moon earrings that drip from my ears.

My fake eyelashes feel awkward, and I blink.

Mom pulls back and starts fussing over the fabric across my middle. "Tuck in your stomach. There, perfect."

I stiffen at the sound of the guests in the Grand Ballroom downstairs. My nerves are frayed and fragile like they could snap.

Mom strokes over the blossom in my hair. "After tonight, everyone will forget your disobedience at the initiation gathering."

"Except you," I reply.

Mom freezes for a moment, before she gives the blossom a final caress and steps back.

The flowers are sacred to her. They are to me as well. Yet how much has she spent preserving them, while the other packs suffer?

I clench my jaw. I know why I'm going through with this charade of a ball now. I have a purpose and that means letting Mom believe it's her rules I'm following. The consequences of not succeeding crush my chest with anxiety.

Addison appears at the door. He looks quite hand-some in a crisp suit, which is as black as the night with a red shirt and tie underneath, to match all the Sun Wolves, who are dressed in cherry red.

The whole pack is the epitome of the blossom flowers that Mom loves.

My gown follows the curve of my body from my shoulders where the neckline takes a wide sweep across my shoulders and glides all the way down to the tips of my blood-red shoes. The fabric glistens like stars have been sewn into my dress, and when I glance in the mirror at myself, I have second thoughts about going downstairs into the crowded ballroom.

The starry dress is extravagant, only matched by the glow of the ruby gems that are draped around my neck.

Midnight Goddess, this isn't me.

Give me jeans, a movie marathon, and a family sized packet of Doritos, and I'm happy.

I'm a cheap date.

What I'm not, is a Blossom Princess.

I bite the inside of my cheek.

Remember the long game: pretending to obey in order to take the power.

Still, it sucks.

"Are you ready? Everyone's waiting." Addison runs his hand through his hair.

He looks as nervous as I feel.

"You're so lucky, my dear, that you didn't catch a cold or worse from falling in the river. It must be a sign from the Midnight Goddess that this will be a most auspicious night for the Sun Wolves." Mom straightens her red gown that has long, lace sleeves; her skirt is full and billows with each move she makes.

My stomach clenches.

Time to make our entrance and begin my performance.

I force myself to plaster on a smile, tilting up my chin.

This is how a proud Sun Wolf acts, right?

Mom will use this party to show me off to prospective mates, should they win the Wolf Games.

Let her.

I'll use it to weigh up my rivals.

Like I've said before, I live in a town made of lies. And tonight, I choose to become one of those pretty little things, who weaves my own web.

"Quickly." Mom nudges me forward. "Now, remember, dance with those participating in the Wolf Games.

But only Sun Wolves or Shadow Wolves, you understand?" Her fingernails dig into my skin, where the fabric of my dress dips half way down my back.

Because it'd never do for the daughter of the Alpha to dance with a Moon Wolf...

Gritting my teeth, I nod. Then I slowly walk through the wide hall to the top of the sweeping, marble staircase.

A band plays a soft ballad. Sparkling chandeliers give the ballroom a glittering effect, and fabric the color of blossom flowers is swept across the white walls. Statues of snarling wolves are posed in every corner, and servants weave between guests in black pants and shirts, making sure everything runs smoothly.

Mom and Addison stand behind me, their breaths on my back, and I look down at the crowds. It doesn't take long for the wave of whispers to spread across the large ballroom.

My breaths become ragged. *They're staring up at me.*

My gaze sweeps the guests, while my pulse thrashes in my ears.

I swallow past my dry throat, wishing to be anywhere but here. But instead, I take my first step down the elaborate, curving staircase. It looks like it was made for royalty. I can't help but shake that I may miss a step and fall on my ass in front of everyone.

Yeah, that'd make them all forget about my *disobedience.*

I take a deep breath. *I can do this.*

I lift my gaze and glide down the stairs. Coming around the curve, I realize that most people have paused to watch me. I stumble. My heart is beating too fast, my cheeks are on fire, while my mind is drowning in panic at the judgement on their faces and how intently I'm being studied…

Then I see him: *Hunter.*

And my breathing slows; my panic subsides. I regain my footing, steadying myself.

I'm not here alone, I truly can do this.

Hunter stands at the front of the crowd at the bottom of the stairs. He's dressed in black like the rest of the Moon Wolf servers. His hair is brushed back, and it still surprises me how much he's grown and how handsome he's become.

He's not the friend I remember growing up with, although if I look hard enough, I can see the ghost of the boy I loved. The guy standing there is the opposite of who Hunter used to be, and it scares me.

What happened to change him?

Anxiety mingles with anticipation. They both flutter their wings in my stomach at seeing him stare at me like he's desperate to come up to me and sweep me into his arms.

Either that, or I've been watching too many human rom-coms.

Hunter's holding a silver platter with drinks, but his eyes are only on me. *All* for me like he's completely forgotten where he is. And there's something else that I don't expect.

Desire.

It leaves me breathless, and I'm half smiling. My pulse races

I want to talk to him, to thank him for saving me, to apologize for Mom's rudeness. I just want to be near him and chat with him like I used to. We'd laugh about this dress together. He's the only wolf who'd understand how much this evening sucks, I'm sure of it.

He's also the only wolf who I truly want to dance with.

But he's a Moon Wolf, and I'm not allowed to dance with him, even if he wasn't a servant.

When Hunter smiles at me encouragingly, for the first time this night, my smile becomes genuine.

But then, I remember Mom's warning that Hunter is nothing but a *toy*, and my smile fades.

Hunter looks confused, and his eyes gleam with hurt, before he straightens his shoulders, defiantly.

All of a sudden, I spot Ri. He pushes through the crowd behind Hunter. Then he pauses, and his gaze locks with mine.

My stomach somersaults.

Ri's wearing a midnight black suit with a matching button up shirt that's open at his throat. The sight of him has me gasping for air. With his broad shoulders, his clothes sit on him like a second skin, revealing his powerful stature.

Okay, so he's from an opposing pack, but he's every bit what I expect from an Alpha. The power radiating from him is magnetic.

Like everyone else, he's watching me. Shadows dance under his gaze, and I can't work out if he loves or hates what he sees.

Why should I care?

Why *do* I care?

My attention sweeps from Hunter to Ri, and I flush.

Perhaps, Hunter isn't the *only* wolf I want to dance with.

Hunter and Ri eye each other warily.

Why does it feel like they're waiting for me to go to them... *to choose?*

That's crazy, right?

But the thought lingers, and I can't chase it away.

I'm sweating under their gazes in a room that's too perfect, grand, and indulgent.

Ri moves back into the crowd and is swallowed by it. A guest yanks on Hunter's arm, demanding his attention, and he's distracted by serving drinks to a surrounding group of Sun Wolves.

To my relief, Iris greets me at the base of the stairs.

Her lips are painted scarlet, and she looks spectacular in a red dress that pulls in tight at her waist with a ribbon and tumbles to her knees. Her chestnut hair is pulled back into a braid, and blossom flower earrings match the one hanging from her gold necklace.

"Girl, every guy in the hall is going to ask you for a dance, so be ready." Iris nudges me.

"I'm not interested," I whisper back, then force a smile to my Mom and Addison, who join us.

Mom and Addison encourage me to mingle. I remain close to Mom's side, just as she instructs. Iris has fallen behind, talking to her friends, while I'm scanning the room for Hunter, eager to slip away and sneakily chat to him.

I hate the way things were left, after he saved me. He

should be enjoying himself tonight and his new status as initiate, instead of being forced to work.

When I notice Mom has been caught up with her followers on the other side, I grin.

My chance to have some fun.

Yet I've only taken a few steps of freedom, before I'm staring into familiar eyes from across the room.

Ri stands amid a crowd of Shadow Wolves but he looks bored.

He truly does have the dark and broody thing going on.

Yet he's throwing lingering glances in my direction. He pushes the curls out of his face and doesn't look away, when I boldly meet his gaze.

Wow, his confidence is intimidating.

There's a quirk at the corner of his mouth, as though seeing me is mildly amusing, and it bothers me. I curl my hands by my side, as he turns his back on me.

Jerk.

Doesn't he want to be seen with me in public?

Unexpectedly, someone steps right into my view. It's an older man, who I recognize from one of the Shadow Wolf families. There are so many members in the three packs. When I left at fourteen, I never got the chance to know everyone.

The man has white threading his hair.

He offers me his bent arm to take. "You look lost. How does a dance sound to help?"

Except, he isn't who I want to dance with. I want to find Hunter.

I bite my lip. *Where is he?*

When I glance around me, however, I notice the wolves watching to see what I'll do. They're like starved predators, waiting for their turn, and I hate how it makes me want to run out of the Town Hall.

Instead, I narrow my eyes and shake my head. "Thanks, but I'm okay."

I step back from the Shadow Wolf and bump into someone else. Startling, I turn.

Goddess save me, it's Mom.

Mom's smile is faker than mine. She snatches my arm and her nails dig into my skin. "Don't embarrass me by rejecting a dance offer. He has connections in the Shadow Wolves, and right now, I need you to be more like honey than vinegar."

I stare at her. "When have *you* ever been like honey? And I'm not dancing with a man who's older than Addison."

"I told you to call him *Father*."

Mom's lips thin, but in seconds, her expression morphs back to her fake smile, and she scans the room. "There," she says.

With a tug of my arm, she turns me on my heels to face the corner of the room, directly where Ri stands. He's not even looking my way, but my veins turn to ice.

"Go and ask him to dance." Her hard push at my lower back has me stumbling forward a few steps.

This is not happening…

Except, it is.

After all, I'm the Blossom Princess, right? It's not like Ri can reject me.

Squaring my shoulders, I stroll across the room. The

other guests move out of my way, as I carve a path directly for Ri. Those around him pause as well. His buddy shoves a playful hand to his shoulder, teasing him, as I approach.

On the inside, I'm dying.

But on the outside, to hell with it.

Tonight I'm the Blossom Princess, a Sun Wolf, and the Alpha's daughter.

Why can't I be the one to take charge? It'll do the asshole Shadow Wolf some good.

Upon my approach, Ri's friends vanish like shadows.

Ri stands before me. He's taller than me. His piercing emerald eyes smolder, as his gaze glides over me. He tilts his head to the side.

Then he puts his bent arm out for me. "Dance?" The surprise on my face must've shown because he gives a small laugh. "Away with you, it's not a trick question. With the fierce determination on your face to reach me, I guessed that was your intention. I just wanted to be the one to ask first."

See, jerk.

I stare at him intently. "Sometimes, what's expected of us isn't our true intention."

I raise an eyebrow at him, while draping my arm over his.

He radiates warmth. It shouldn't excite me as much as it does that we're so close, but his cologne is captivating and makes my knees weak.

"You know what they say about expectations, right?" He turns us toward the dance floor, and if I thought everyone had been watching me before, now it feels like the entire hall is staring. And that definitely includes Mom, but I don't expect anything less from her. This is what she wanted, after all.

"You mean, assumptions," I correct.

I let Ri swing me onto the dance floor, joining other couples, both young and old.

"Nay, I really don't." Ri loops his strong arm around my lower back and draws me toward him so forcefully that our bodies clash. I struggle to slow down my thunderous heartbeat. "Expectations are just resentments that'll eventually sneak up on you."

"D-did you just make that up?" My words come out breathless.

I'm unable to focus on anything but the close proximity of our bodies and how he towers over me.

My wolf howls inside me.

"Get on with you, I read it in a book," he says, nonchalantly.

Then he releases me from his grasp, creating a small gap between our bodies to mirror the other dancers.

One of his hands takes mine, while the other is still low on my back. I curl my fingers on his strong shoulder.

Compared to the first time I ran into him in the woods, everything about Ri now is suave in his fancy suit, and I can't deny that this look is made for him.

An awkward silence falls between us, and my gaze drops to his broad chest. He has the body of a god, and the smile of a sinner.

I can tell that he's used to getting his own way.

But why?

He's only the nephew of the Healer, right? How does he know how to dance like this and command a room like he's the Blossom Prince?

"The flower in your hair looks beautiful. But does the Great Shadow Wolf allow it to be taken from the sacred trees?" Ri stares into my eyes, as he speaks like he's looking for something.

The faintest trace of heat shivers over my skin like a feathery caress.

Except, his smooth words carry an accusation. Blessed Sun, who's he to judge?

"We only use the flowers that have already fallen. No Blossom Tree should ever be touched." My gaze hardens. "Though you seem to have no problem tempting fate by using axes so close to them that you could easily lose control and cause damage."

He cocks his head to the side. "Lay off, I never lose control. I know how to handle my weapon." He winks, and I flush. "But if you must know, I've received permission to fight in the sacred fields."

"From my mom?" I gasp.

Ri's long lashes hood his eyes.

Then he nods once. "Aye, from the Alpha. I carry healing magic, as does my family. So, my duties include protecting the Blossom trees from the ongoing Deep."

I pause.

So, he isn't a total douche then because he cares about protecting the trees like me. Plus, nature wouldn't respond to his magic if he was.

On the other hand, maybe it just means that his

goals are closer to Mom's than I'd thought. After all, she's practically giftwrapped me for him tonight.

And that means being with Ri can't be a good thing.

I tighten my hand around his. "So, your axe fighting does that?"

"My presence does." He bares his canines in a smile that's all predator, and I shiver.

What's his problem?

Ri leans closer. "Why don't you forfeit your position in the upcoming games? It's like this, see, you're clearly not serious about it. Then you can offer your spot to one of the other packs...who are."

A flare of shock climbs through me, followed by a jolt of fury.

Has this been his plan all along? Is he ruthless enough to try and take away a spot from the Sun Wolves?

My guts churn. Has he been seducing me and getting close to Mom, just to take me out of the Wolf Games?

Or is he trying to protect me? Midnight Goddess, why am I desperate that it's his totally asshole attempt to keep me safe?

Yet there's no way in the world that I'll let him make my choices for me. I won't allow him to push me out or win for that matter. Not now.

His presence may protect the blossoms but he has no right to take control of my life.

"Maybe I only want you to think I'm not serious," I hiss. "I know I'm weak but I can still try."

When Ri laughs, my gaze becomes steely. "Aye, right."

"I don't even know why I came to you for a dance," I say, trying to pull my hand free from his iron grip.

"You *think* you danced with me because your ma told you to, but the truth is, you've wanted to dance with me from the moment you entered the ballroom."

Wow, egomaniac alert.

I'm going to ignore the fact that he's right.

Yep, ignoring.

I look around, and Mom is still watching us. Her expression is stern like she's waiting for me to fail even at the simple act of dancing.

To be fair, it's likely.

The couples dancing near us are shadows that melt together in the background. Every nerve in my body is taut, and I tear my hand from Ri's.

"Are you sure you want to do that?" He cuts a quick glance to the room surrounding us. "Gossip can be cruel."

"They need more excitement in their lives, if they waste their time on me."

Ri collects my fallen hand back into his and leads me into a dance once more. "I'm sorry. We're in this together, and you're going to need help to survive. Look, as initiates, we'll be all anyone talks about, until the end of the Wolf Games."

Reluctantly, I keep dancing with him for the length of the song.

The silence is uncomfortable. His gaze is concerned, as it sweeps across me.

I duck my head, avoiding his gaze.

Where's Hunter?

Hunter held me in his arms after my fall into the icy river, and it'd been like truly coming home. He'd flooded me with warmth and security.

Yet now, everything about this Shadow Wolf screams danger and that I should run as far from him as possible.

How is he already so powerful?

Ri's my adversary in the upcoming games. Both Hunter and him are in truth, and I've let myself get blinded by emotions that I shouldn't be feeling.

But if there's one thing I've learned tonight, it's that Ri and I aren't that different after all. We're both playing a long game. We're both wearing a mask. And we're both lying.

Plus, for some reason, he wants to win the Wolf Games with a desperation that I can feel howling through his wolf.

Joke's on him then.

Especially since I have every intention of making him believe that I don't want the crown for myself. That way, he won't see me sitting on the throne, until it's too late.

Let him pretend that he's my destined prince.

For now.

CHAPTER 10

"No, Cinders, you may not go to the ball," I mutter sarcastically, scuffing my shoe against the marble floor of the ballroom.

Huh, who knew it'd mark? It's kind of satisfying.

I don't get to attend the Blossom Ball (unless serving drinks counts), and do the Prince Charming routine that I'd planned but I can still mess something up for the Sun Wolves. It's my speciality, seeing as they've perfected the art of ruining Moon Wolves' lives at every chance they get.

Lowering expectations is important if you're a Moon Wolf. Mom taught me that when I was a kid and would walk past the bakery in the center of Fable with the delicious muffins and cupcakes in the window.

Moon Wolves don't buy from here, she told me firmly, *we bake our own cookies.*

Once I win the Wolf Games, Moon Wolves will buy from any shop they want, and I'll bring home a whole tray of cupcakes for Mom and Tala.

I glance around at the wolves in their beautiful suits and ball dresses that drip with jewels and back up a step. I wrinkle my nose against the intoxicating scent of perfumes and champagne. The room is suffocating with music and laughter; the walls are blood-red.

Nobody will notice a small black mark in an expanse of gleaming white, right?

I balance my tray with gleaming flutes of champagne and red and white wine on one hand. If I try, really...*really*...hard, it's not that different to balancing a basketball.

Can I get away with spinning it?

I narrow my eyes and raise the tray. The glasses *clink* ominously, and a passing Sun Wolf snarls at me.

I bare my teeth back.

Then I adjust the thin, rough black shirt that was shoved into my hands by the harried Moon Wolf in charge of the event, when I arrived.

I was shivering because I left my coat with Wynter earlier, and the walk to the Town Hall was freezing. At least my snarling inner wolf hadn't been enough of a dick to stop me from pausing to put on a sweater.

But then, he wanted to come to this ball, even less than me.

Tonight should've been my moment of triumph. To the Sun Wolves, I was only known as *the housekeeper's son*. Yet I was invited into the elite because at last I'd shown my hand.

I was an initiate and potential Alpha. I should dance, drink, and act as an equal to every other wolf.

How was that for a finger up to the Alpha, Sun pack, and Great Shadow Wolf himself?

Moon knows, I could've survived in that moment – memory – for the rest of my life.

Instead, I'm standing here, watching the other eight initiates dance and drink, and battling to stop my wolf from bursting out and showing me up as the beast, rather than the prince. Too much is at risk and I wouldn't put it past the Alpha to find a way to kick me out of the Wolf Games. So, I swallow my damn pride and think of the larger picture.

Still, my fangs itch to descend. A growl rumbles in my throat.

Only catching sight of Jex and Parker's dark hair, as they dance with Shadow Wolves in the corner, steadies me.

I bet my claws they'll be boasting about the pretty wolves they hook up with tomorrow.

I smile, softly, remembering the moment that I saw Wynter descending the grand staircase. Jack had told me that he'd checked her over, and she was okay.

But I had to see it for myself.

Wynter looked stunning in a sweeping red gown and shoes with a blossom in her hair. My breath caught at the vision of the Blossom Princess. Then she stumbled, and I stiffened, convinced that she was about to fall.

And there was: *my Wyn*. Only she could fall on her ass on her dramatic entrance. I was torn between chuckling and throwing myself through the crowd to catch her. But then, she steadied herself without me.

The stars know, I was proud. She was strong. She didn't need a guy to save her.

As our gazes met, I wasn't able to hide my smile. She swept down like *she* was the Alpha, even though I knew that underneath, she was thrumming with anxiety.

I bet she wishes that she could shed that glittering dress and dive into a pair of jeans.

How awesome is it that no matter how much has changed, the girl who I adored is still in there?

Still, my wolf howls that I'd die to protect her, and that's a complication I don't need in the games.

I frown. Am I making a bigass mistake by letting myself feel so taken by her?

Moon Wolves are taught to shield our eyes from the sun because that way, we won't be blinded.

Bullshit.

I'm ready to look directly into the sun.

I push through the throng to the edge of the dance floor. This is what I've been avoiding: *watching Wynter dance.*

A fire kindles deep in my stomach, when I see her.

Once, I took her to a forbidden party in the woods. It was the only way that we were able to hang out and pretend we were friends. I think it was too much for her. I wanted to dance with her like the other couples, but it would've been too dangerous if anyone saw us.

I'm an idiot.

Why did I hope that tonight, she'd dance with me for the first time?

Of course, that wouldn't happen, not with her hawk-eyed Mom watching every move she makes.

Yet if we had our special moment together, I'd hold her close, make her laugh, and feel her body against mine. And I'd listen to her talk about New York and what it was like living outside Fable.

In that moment, there'd be nothing but us in this messed up world that's creeping closer to the edge of the Deep.

Yet dancing with a Moon Wolf publicly would be dangerous. To dance with a Moon Wolf servant would be a scandal.

So, yeah, I was an idiot to hope.

All of a sudden, I catch sight of Wynter twirling across the dance floor like a blossom caught on the breeze. Except, my heart clenches.

Ri's arms are clasped around my Wyn like she's *his*.

A deep guttural growl rumbles in my chest. My wolf knows what's ours and to see her in someone else's arms (especially his), has me fuming.

He's stealing my moment. My girl. My time.

I shudder. The glasses on the shaking tray *clink*.

The asshole outsider intends to steal what I've waited years for: the role of Alpha, Fable, and Wynter.

I'm going to kick his ass.

My inner wolf circles furiously, wanting to be let free.

It's night. I can transform.

But there are rules, and no wolf would break them without serious consequences from the Alpha. At civic events, there are to be no transformations.

I can't break the peace or risk punishment.

What would the Alpha do to me, if she gets the chance to brand me a criminal on her territory?

Chill out, I whisper to my wolf, *my Wyn isn't tricked by the Shadow Wolf's stupidly handsome face, all those muscles, his suave suit and...*

Okay, not helping.

When Ri yanks Wynter commandingly towards him, my lips pinch.

I can't hear what they're saying, although it looks kind of heated. "Why, I'm just a big, mysterious, psycho wolf," I add my own commentary in a mocking Irish accent because hey, it's the kind of thing Ri would be saying, right? *Why is he holding her so close?* "Nay, don't be shy. Why don't you have a feel of my manly biceps...I mean, dick? I am the Shadow Dick, after all."

I snort. Wynter wouldn't be looking at Ri in that starry eyed way, if she knew about his secret past.

None of the female wolves who swoon over him would.

My guts roil. I'm not a gossip. Sun Wolves are the ones who play those games. But Dex, Jex's twin, dated a Shadow Wolf, who heard something troubling from Ireland.

Should I warn Wynter?

When a Sun Wolf with a sweep of ginger hair and cold eyes snatches a drink off my tray, almost overbalancing it, I stiffen.

He ignores me like I'm a statue.

Jerk.

"Here to serve," I say, brightly. "And you're so welcome." I tilt my head. "Wait, you didn't thank me."

Whoops, my dominant wolf is showing.

The Sun Wolf turns slowly to look me up and down like I've just gone from invisible to prey. Then he nudges his friend's shoulder and the wolf turns around.

I freeze.

Shit.

Ballard raises a haughty eyebrow, although his smile is predatory. His golden hair is gelled back like a halo, and his silk shirt is a slash of blood-red in his black immaculate suit.

He clicks his fingers, and in a moment, I'm surrounded by his entire gang.

Awesome. Now my night is complete.

I'm about to receive another beating from my favorite bully and his goons.

Ballard crowds closer to me, and his chocolate brown eyes are fixed on mine like he expects me to drop my gaze.

Not. Going. To. Happen.

His lip curls into a sneer. "Give me wine."

Right away, asshole...

I snatch a white wine off the tray and hold it out to him.

He stares at it like I've just offered him my dick to suck. "I didn't say white wine, Moon cur."

The urge to pour the wine over his head pulses in my veins.

I grit my teeth and slam the wine glass back onto the silver tray, picking up a red wine, instead. I may be holding the glass too tightly because as I pass it to

Ballard, I spill the wine, which slides down like blood to coat his fingers.

Ballard hisses. "Clumsy, bitch."

I flush.

He says *bitch* with such venom that the word carries. I feel that it must be able to be heard over the music. I resist looking over to Wynter. I can sense the gazes of too many in the hall already.

Heat climbs up my back; my wolf snarls in my chest. Ballard is all Alpha, and I want so much to whack the drink tray over his head and ram him into the wall.

My eyes flash, as I hold myself rigid. "I'll see you at the trials. Then we'll find out who's the real *bitch*."

Ballard becomes pale with rage; his cheek twitches. Then, just for a moment, he smiles.

WTF?

Unexpectedly, he slices his hand through the air and knocks the tray out of my hold.

My eyes widen. I flail, trying to snatch the tumbling glasses, and I'm covered in mingling red and white. The cold wine splashes over me, and I gasp.

It feels like it happens in slow motion, but I still can't stop it.

The glasses smash to the ground and shatter.

I wince, and the other Moon servants hunch their shoulders.

I'm dead.

Ballard takes a neat step back like the mess that he's left behind has nothing to do with him, as he adjusts his cuffs. "See? Clumsy."

I stare at the shattered glass on the floor. If not

everyone was looking at me before, they definitely are now.

"You'd better clear it up, before the Alpha sees." Ballard smirks. "Or before I tell her because how much do you think those cost?"

I clench my fists. Probably, more than Mom earns in a month. How will I pay for this? No one will care that I didn't drop it. "How about you clear it up, and I'll pay the damages."

There has to be a trick. There always is with Ballard.

"Okay, sure," I hiss between clenched teeth.

He leans closer. "And you're so welcome. Wait, you didn't thank me."

"Funny," I grit out.

"Get on with it then."

"But I don't have anything to…"

"You have your hands, don't you? On your knees."

His cronies snicker.

Don't let Wynter be watching.

I can't let Tala go without the schoolbooks she needs, or Mom the new boiler for the house. We can't lose our savings over this.

I drop to my knees, carefully edging the glass shards together onto the tray. I force myself not to react, as they nick my fingers. Dark droplets of blood mix with the sea of wine. My face is burning up, and I loath Ballard.

He watches me coldly.

I bite my lip at the sharp pain of glass slicing my skin, again, and again, and again. It hurts so much, but I bite down on my tongue and refuse to show them or anyone that I'm in pain.

I won't let Ballard hear me yelp or gasp.

I won't let him win.

I won't be his bitch.

"That's quite enough," Addison's voice rings out, as he pushes through the Sun Wolves to Ballard's side.

I peer up at him, holding my cut hands to my chest; they mark my shirt but it's black so good at hiding the stains.

I bet that's why the wolves choose it, just like the mafia.

I like Addison. The guy has always been fair to me and kind to Mom and Tala. But he feels more caged and repressed than me. Of course, he is married to the fiercest wolf in Fable.

He's lucky he still remembers that he has fangs.

Ballard points at me. "This cur is only—"

"Bleeding," Addison snaps. Then his expression softens. "*I'll* pay for any damages. Go to the kitchens and sort out your wounds."

I nod, breathing hard, as I push myself up.

Instantly, my gaze meets Wynter's horrified one across the room. She's seen the whole thing.

And I thought this night couldn't suck any worse.

I storm out of the ballroom.

I know everyone's watching me: the initiate with hands sliced to ribbons. Did Jex and Parker see?

Thank the moon for fast wolfen healing. I can already feel the thin cuts knitting together. I find myself pacing, instead of following Addison's orders to go to the kitchen, however, and all I can think about is how much I want to march back in and challenge Ballard to a real fight.

Yet I can't, and it's tearing me apart.

Perhaps, I can at least find something to bandage my hands, so I don't bleed on anything else, while the cuts heal. But I can't handle seeing the other servants.

They're my pack. I know they've all experienced Ballard's cruelty. But I don't want their understanding. I'm their champion and I owe them one thing: to win the Wolf Games and save them from Ballard.

He's shown tonight what Fable will be like if he becomes Alpha.

I shudder, as I stalk through a narrow corridor of the Town Hall and then shoulder through a back door and out into a small courtyard, whose walls are overgrown with ivy. It isn't snowing tonight, and the ground has been cleared but it still glitters with frost like it's been embedded with diamonds. The music drifts out from the ballroom; it's ghostly.

I can still feel the hardness of the ballroom floor in the ache of my knees, and the glass slicing my skin.

I suck viciously on my bleeding fingers; the blood is tangy and sweet. Then I rest my head on the cool brick of the wall.

Wynter's horrified expression fills my mind. Was she horrified to see me bleeding or horrified that I'd been brought so low?

Did she finally think that her mom had been right about me all along?

But how can I blame her, when I'm hiding who I've

become? The secret inside me, which right now is desperate to escape.

I sniff at the freezing air, shivering. The moon is high and swollen. The fur itches beneath my skin; my gums ache.

I can't hide anymore. I need this escape...*this freedom.*

The door bangs open behind me.

I swing around but not fast enough. Instantly, I'm slammed against the wall. The breath is knocked out of me with an *oomph*, and the back of my head connects with the wall.

For a moment, the night sky is lit up by falling stars, as my head spins.

Huh, pretty.

Then Ballard's hand is around my neck, choking me. His fist flies to my face so fast, I can't block it. It clips me on the side of the head. Sharp pain zigzags across my skull. But I don't cry out, don't move.

I growl and meet Ballard's cold gaze.

Okay, that's one way to sober up fast, even from a head injury. I groan; it feels like glass is being shoved right through my brain.

"Did you think that weak Alpha's bitch could save you?" Ballard almost sounds bored, as he tightens his hand at my throat, and raises his other one to my cheek; a shard of glass glistens in it, which sparkles in the moonlight. It's edged crimson already with my blood. The wolf inside me...*snaps.* "We're not finished."

"Yeah, we are," I snarl.

My heartbeat pounds in my ears, while fury builds in my chest.

Moonlight explodes from me in shimmering rays. I feel like I'm being turned inside out, as my wolf takes over, and I transform.

All of a sudden, the night is alive with intense sensation. The moonlight is brighter, I can feel the slight breeze moving every strand of fur and smell the sharp night air and the call to the pine forest.

Like this, I'm free.

Like this, I'm dangerous.

My fur is the color of moonlight, and my eyes are intense silver. I'm bigger than any other wolf in the Moon pack, apart from Flint.

Ballard stumbles back in shock, as I snarl and sink my claws into his immaculate suit, slashing it to shreds. My bleeding paws stain his shirt in matching red. But with it comes the sharp pain from my glass cuts across my paws.

Everything hurts, hurts, *hurts*.

My head and paws are in pain, and this *enemy* wolf attacked me from behind like a weasel.

My eyes narrow, and I knock Ballard to the ground with my heavy weight. The broken bottle tumbles from his grasp. My ears press to my head, and I pin the shaking enemy beneath me with my huge paws, baring my fangs and letting out a low, rumbling growl in his face.

Ballard throws punches to my head and chest, but I don't feel them. Adrenaline soars through me. My wolf demands that I finish him, as he's a threat to the pack.

I take a deep sniff. My snarl's loud and dominating.

Ballard flinches under me, feeling the power I carry. I can smell fear on him.

I'm the leader. I should tear out his throat.

"He submits, don't you think?" a soft voice says behind me.

I turn to see Wynter.

When did she come into the courtyard?

I raise my head to howl my greeting to my Wyn, while I work my hind claws swifty down to Ballard's crotch. He yelps. I keep him locked in place, until I'm ready to release him.

Wyn rushes forward and with no fear at all, lays her hand across my mouth with a laugh.

When I lick against her palm, she pulls a face. "*Eww*, you win. But you need to keep quiet, before someone else hears you. We don't want anyone to find out about this episode. It's a shame because you're cute. I didn't know you'd look…so powerful and striking."

When she takes away her hand, her words play on my mind.

She called me *cute*. Did I hear right or is she teasing me?

Wynter smirks, then glares down at Ballard. "Not so tough now. Are you, Ballard?"

Ballard stubbornly keeps quiet, staring up at the sky like he hasn't heard her.

"I'm the Blossom Princess. This is *my* night," Wynter hisses. "Imagine if I told Mom that a certain Sun Wolf ruined it for me."

That makes Ballard notice Wynter, and his attention snaps to her.

His eyes grow wide and panicked. "You wouldn't."

"Try me."

Ballard's jaw works for a minute, before he reluctantly forces out, "Fine. You've both made your point. Now get off me." He darts a glance at me, before baring his neck in submission.

It clearly costs him.

Awesome.

I growl at him.

Ballard shudders and mutters, "Get the hell off."

My Wyn strokes over my ears, and I push eagerly into her touch. "Wow, your fur's soft. But can you change back now, before someone discovers you?"

It's hard to give this up: the freedom and connection to nature. It always is. Yet for my Wyn, I'll do anything.

Moonlight shimmers around me, and I transform back into my human form. My clothes are still tainted with blood and wine because our transformation comes from a place of magic, which means that our clothes don't need to be shed and are in just the same state as we left them before the change.

In my case, a terrible state.

I get in a strategic knee to Ballard's balls, as I push myself to my feet (because hey, satisfying).

Ballard moans and doubles over, before scrambling up as well, groping himself from pain. "There's grave punishment for transforming without permission at a civic event, cur."

He shakes, attempting to adjust his damaged suit.

I cross my arms playfully. "I think you mean *big, bad wolf?*"

Wynter laughs.

Warmth unfurls through me at the sound. I've missed hearing her laughter.

Ballard is ashen. "You'll be bound in a pillory on Main Street. You'll be—"

"He *won't*." Wynter sweeps to Ballard, and he watches her in shock, as she fusses with the lapels of his suit. "Here's what's gonna happen now. You'll make an excuse about your torn clothes and go home. Invent something embarrassing like you have such explosive diarrhea that you ripped your own clothes with your claws in your rush to...you know..."

I smirk, and Ballard reddens.

Ballard begins to choke out a protest, but Wynter hushes him, brushing at the shoulders of his suit.

I've never seen him so confused.

When did Wynter become ruthless? I eye her, warily. Does she know the power that she could hold?

"And you'll tell no one about Hunter's transformation." She takes Ballard's hand as gently as if she's about to lead him in a dance. Instead, she pushes him to the door, holding it open for him. "If you do, then I'll tell Mom that you started a brawl on my special night. And called Addison a *bitch*."

Finally, Ballard pulls away from her, diving through the doorway, but then he hesitates. "You heard that?"

"Uh-huh."

"Then why didn't you stop the fight?"

Wynter's lips curl into a smile. "Because I wanted to see Hunter kick your ass."

I grin.

The look that Ballard shoots me over his shoulder promises retribution.

Wynter slams shut the door. Then she turns to me, and unexpectedly, appears shy. Her cheeks pink, before she hurries toward me. Instantly, I inhale her beautiful floral scent, mixed with pines.

I stiffen. It's weird being this close to her after so long.

Watching her sweep down the grand staircase in her fine dress and jewels or across the dance floor was one thing, but crossing the small courtyard and now, so close that I could touch her, is another.

She steals my breath.

And then, she's touching me, running fingers down my arms playfully… not like the Wynter who's returned to town after so long.

She reaches for my cut hands, pulling them to her lips. "Can I kiss them better?"

I stare at her, making sure I heard correctly. When we were kids, and I turned up to play with a bruised cheek or arm and teary eyes, she'd ask: *can I kiss it better?*

I never told her where I got the bruises. I reckon she guessed.

The question pulls at me and makes tremors run through me.

But I nod.

She lifts each of my hands to her mouth in turn and kisses over each cut. It makes them feel like war wounds.

And as if she may destroy me one day.

You see, I'd be her warrior if she asked. I'd bleed for her. *Kill for her.*

I can't tear my gaze from her soft red lips on my hand.

She never breaks her touch, as the moonlight covers us in its silvery web and the sweet melody bleeds out to us from the ballroom.

Then her expression becomes determined. "Dance with me?"

My breath hitches.

Did I think that this night sucked?

Best. Night. Of. My. Life.

Wynter, Sun Wolf and Alpha's daughter, asks me, Moon Wolf and servant to dance...!

I totally forget about the ache in my head or smarting hands. I forget everything.

I'm so lost in happiness that I kind of forget to answer.

"So, that's a nope, then...?" Wynter says, disappointed, her eyebrows pulling together.

She drops my hands.

I wrap my arms around her waist, drawing her to me, and sway to the music. She laughs, curling her arms around my neck.

She's warm against the cold. I can feel the thud of her heart in her chest. *And it's perfect.*

"I've just waited for this moment a long time," I reply. "I wanted to enjoy it. You don't mind breaking the rules, right?"

"I'm a rule breaker," she sighs. "Well, I am for you."

I tighten my arms around her and let myself have

this: Wynter in my arms, our special moment, and the dance that I never thought I'd truly have.

We don't need a fancy ball. This courtroom garden to ourselves at the back with the stolen music and the moonlight is better than marble, suits, and fakery.

I wish that we could dance in our wolf forms in the woods.

Then Wynter pulls back but only to reach up to the blossom in her hair. I blink at her, as she unfastens it and then reaches out to fix it in *my* hair.

"Tonight, I choose you as my Blossom Prince." Her eyes crinkle, as she smiles.

I'm the ball's Blossom Prince? Is she serious?

No Moon Wolf has ever been chosen as the prince for the princess. It breaks all tradition.

My eyes widen. "You can't choose me."

She tilts up her chin. "Haven't we already agreed that I break the rules?"

"But I'm a Moon Wolf," I whisper.

She strokes over the flower in my hair. "You're not a Moon Wolf. You're my Hunter."

My Hunter.

Am I hers, as she's mine?

Does she mean it?

My heart's racing.

Let this be real.

Does she understand what it means to choose a wolf as her Blossom Prince? It's a promise of a mating. *Sacred.*

Yet she danced like this with Ri; she was also in his arms tonight.

I look down. "Wouldn't you rather give the blossom to a Shadow Wolf?"

She stiffens and bites her lip. "You saw that, huh?"

"I had a ringside seat."

"I only danced with Ri because Mom insisted." She leans closer and each word gusts across my lips, "He saved the flowers' lives, but you saved mine."

My chest tightens.

"You've no idea how much I want to kiss you right now," I murmur.

"Probably about as much as I want *you* to kiss *me*."

Her words surprise me, but I don't hesitate and press my lips to hers, tangling my hand in her hair. She moans and sucks on my lower lip, before our tongues entwine in a dance of their own. I kiss her, passionately...desperately. I've waited for my first kiss with her for so long.

How many nights have I dreamed of her?

Of this?

My hands fall to her waist, and any self control I have is gone with the way that she pushes closer to me, asking for more. A growl rolls through my throat, as I taste her sweetness. Kissing her is nothing like I imagined. She's in my arms...real...and she chose *me* to be *hers* tonight.

Her kiss is mind-blowing and heart-stopping. And with her soft moans, the way her body melts against me, my dick thickens and hardens. My heart thumps louder, as I walk her backward, until her back kisses the wall, pinning her beneath me. There's nothing else I want but her. Here. Against me.

And this moment – memory – is the one that I could survive in for the rest of my life.

Even if she chooses to never kiss me again.

When she draws back, her pupils are dilated, and her cheeks are blushing pink.

Then she smiles and softens further into my arms like she's never left them. It makes my shadow howl.

Except, a twinge of guilt shoots through me.

If her mom pushed Wynter into Ri's arms, then it looks like she's seeking an alliance with the Shadow Wolves.

How can I let Wynter rest in my arms like she's safe, when I know she isn't?

She deserves to hear the rumors and make up her own mind.

I don't want to break the moment but I have to warn her.

I can't hide the truth, even if it scares Wynter. It's always better to know the danger that lurks in the shadows.

When my expression becomes serious, Wynter's brow furrows.

She traces her finger over my lips. "Hey, didn't you enjoy that? I mean, I did. But was I too...?"

By the moon, how could she think that kiss wasn't *everything?*

I pull her closer, stroking her lower back. "It was the single most greatest moment of my life." She relaxes. "But I need to tell you something I heard about that Irish Shadow Wolf."

Her gaze hardens. "I'm kind of wondering if you're

crushing on me or *him* because you're acting kind of obsessed."

I gape at her. "I'll pretend I didn't hear that."

"You do you," she teases.

I nip her lip in retaliation. "There's this rumor…"

"I don't listen to gossip."

"You should listen to this. Ri and his sister, Brey, they're like this deadly duo. Assassins or something. They wiped out their own pack to take their power. At least, they're the only ones left, so how did they survive? It's suspicious, right? Then they were chased out of Ireland for their crimes. They're outcasts in Fable. It's why they're given a hard time. It's only your mom who's attracted to Ri's ruthless power, which isn't a surprise. If you get close to that brother and sister, you're gonna get hurt."

CHAPTER 11

WYNTER

The morning after the Blossom Ball, I'm wearing my unicorn onesie pajamas, staring at myself in the mirror. I'm exhausted, and even my favorite pajamas can't lift the heaviness of my illness, which drags through me.

The urge to climb back into bed and sleep for days calls to me.

Midnight Goddess, at least if I'm asleep, my joints and muscles won't ache. Yet I remain standing in front of the mirror, trying to steady my ragged breathing.

Yesterday morning, I tried to run away. Last night, I attended the ball as the Blossom Princess, danced with Ri, and kissed Hunter.

Wow, I've been busy.

But even though I now have a plan to take on Mom, I still know that regrets will bite me in the ass later.

I hate that I'm drawn to Ri and hate that I let myself kiss Hunter.

Is it because they're both so pushy and hot that it

makes my stomach flip each time that I see them, as if they're using an Alpha's unique gifts over the opposite sex to conquer and control?

Or is it because they both make my shadow spark with life?

Yet it's too dangerous to fall for any wolf right now.

If I want to save myself, Fable, and make my own choice of mate at the end of this, then it can't be more than a game to me.

Why is that so hard?

I bite my lip, as I remember Hunter's gossip about Ri and his sister.

Being talked about by an entire town hurts; I know that. So, this rumor about Ri and his pack could just be another cruel lie, right? But I trust Hunter. Was he warning me because I'm truly in danger?

Then again, it's obvious that Ri and Hunter don't get along. I also know my mom well enough to understand she wouldn't accept anyone into Fable without doing her own research on their background. There's no way on the blessed sun that she'd let in an *assassin*.

I mean, the guy's a jerk. That doesn't make him a killer.

I freeze. If Mom's angling for someone powerful to fight in the games and marry me, then a killer who'd been ruthless enough to wipe out his own pack for power was *exactly* who she'd invite in.

I need to talk to Mom and keep my distance from Ri. My heart clenches at the thought.

I stare at my reflection, running a hand through my

birdnest hair to smooth it down. My attempt at a smile comes out lopsided.

I glance at Hades' in the mirror. He sprawls across my bed, snoring.

"What are you doing?" I murmur to myself. "You let Hunter believe you want to be with him. Sure, he has incredible power unlike any Moon Wolf I've seen and kisses like the devil, but damn girl. He's going to be in the Wolf Games."

I sigh. I can't roll over for Hunter. Even if we're the last two standing, I'll battle to be the victor. And I have the feeling, so will he.

Then there's Ri. I don't trust the guy, but my chest tightens every time I think of him.

A laugh spills past my lips at how messed up things are already. And we haven't even started the trials.

I swallow, imagining Hunter's kiss. My body tingles at the way he walked me backward and pinned me to the wall. Something about him surprised me.

I loved playing Blossom Princess for the night. It gave me an unexpected sense of power, a bravado. Seeing Hunter in his wolf form affected me, making my blood pump faster. His energy was spellbinding.

I sigh. But it could only be for one night.

I missed Hunter so much, while I lived in New York. So, last night I let myself go there with him. I can't allow it to happen again. At least, not until I win and am declared Alpha.

Shit, Hunter's been my friend forever… and this is why they say don't get involved with your friends.

Now it's going to feel awkward between us, isn't it?

I close my eyes and breathe out heavily.

"New rules," I say to myself, firmly. "No more kissing Hunter. No going near Ri. And win the Wolf Games. Easy."

I cringe. *Then why does it feel so hard?*

Without giving myself another second to change my mind, I head to my bedside table and pop two of my meds into my mouth, chasing them down with the water from the glass. Then I head out of my bedroom and hurry downstairs.

I hunch my shoulders, as I trudge into the dining room. I wrinkle my nose at the delicious scents of bacon, coffee, and piles of sweet muffins from my favorite bakery on main street.

Awesome, I'm the first here. I flop into my seat.

I yawn, reaching immediately for the coffee and pouring myself a mug.

I take a long slug of the rich ambrosia, and it warms me. "So good."

"You're up early," Mom says from behind me. "Why are you still in your pajamas?"

"It's only seven in the morning. Anyone who doesn't want to be in their pajamas all day long is a monster."

Mom cuts me a sharp look, as she takes her seat at the head of the table. She's dressed perfectly in one of her fancy 1920s dresses, of course. This one is covered in tiny red cherries. She always looks immaculate.

My comment still stands, though.

"You're in a chirpy mood." Mom eyes me, placing her napkin over her lap. "Maybe the Blossom Ball last night was good for you. Who'd have thought?"

Does she need a side order of *she told me* so with her smugness?

I grab a crispy bacon strip from the pile in the middle of the table and take a bite of it, watching my mom delicately use a fork and knife to cut a fried egg.

"I can feel you staring. Is there something you want to ask me?" Mom arches her brow.

"What's the deal with Ri and his sister coming to Fable? Were they kicked out of their pack?" I half laugh as if to imply it's a joke, but I watch her carefully as I stuff the rest of the bacon into my mouth.

Her eyes lift to meet mine. "You like him?"

I rear back in my seat. "What? No! I'm just curious. I heard some people talking about them last night."

"You hate gossip." Her eyes narrow.

"I know, but they're new in town and call me curious."

"Curious."

"Hilarious," I mutter.

"See, wasn't I right to send you to dance with him last night?" The smallest of grins plays on her lips. "Like you said, he's new and it gave you a chance to get to know him for yourself and see what sort of person he is."

Yeah, a jerk!

I bite my tongue not to tell her what I truly think.

It's interesting that she hasn't answered my question about his past.

When I determinedly stare at her in silence, she huffs, putting down her cutlery.

"They were in trouble in their hometown in Ireland," she explains, "so, I took them under our protection."

"Out of the kindness of your heart?"

She flashes her canines. "That and because of their power over nature. Ri can make our sacred blossoms survive, despite the Deep. I thought you'd be the last wolf to listen to rumors. You know first hand how easily people in Fable turn to fabricated truths to justify their hatred toward others. It's why we have so much tension between our packs."

I keep my expression carefully blank.

Right, as if the tension between the three packs has nothing to do with the way Mom rules with an iron fist, the cruel hierarchy between pack members, or the blatant display of wealth by the Sun Wolves, when the other packs can barely put food on the table for their families.

I sink back into my seat, no longer hungry despite the mountain of food. Does Hunter ever get to eat a breakfast like this? I want to pack it all up and share it with the Moon pack who need it far more than us.

It's not like I don't know what it's like to go hungry.

When I hear the clink of cutlery striking a porcelain plate, I glance over at Mom, who's resumed cutting up her egg. "Do you think someone as respectable as Jack would accept Ryan and Brey into his pack, if they were anything but simply wolves in trouble?"

It takes me a moment to realize she means Ri. "So, it has nothing to do with their pack being the second most powerful in town or the fact that Ri stands a good chance of winning the Wolf Games?"

Mom's glare is instant, and my thoughts fly to her declaration at the initiation in front of everyone.

When they win the Wolf Games and become Alpha, they also get to mate with my daughter.

"You have a very sharp tongue, Wynter. Your dad had one too. Be careful of the words you free for they could strike back when you least expect it." She studies me, intently.

Yeah, that touched a soft spot.

I reach for my cup of coffee and sip on the nutty flavor.

Something's off about the whole Shadow pack.

The entire time I've known the Healer, he's been nothing but genuine with me. Has he simply been hoodwinked by Ri, or as Mom says, an over-exaggerated piece of gossip that's got out of hand and made Ri and Brey outcasts in town?

Yet I want to believe Hunter so badly...

Mainly to prove Mom wrong and make her eat her words. I'd love for her to admit she's put others' lives in jeopardy for her own gain. Another, more broken part of me, just can't stop challenging her because she was never there for me and doesn't care that I lost Dad.

Thinking of him brings back that jagged ache in my chest.

I stumble to my feet.

"You've barely eaten. Sit back down," Mom barks.

"I'm done."

"Why must you always defy me? We'll need to get our working relationship a little more functional, before you take a leading role in Fable."

I pause and look into her pale violet eyes; my spine stiffens. Her lips only quirk into a smirk, as they always do when she orders me around.

Unease tightens my stomach. The sun is barely up, and I'm ready to scream with frustration.

"What if you're wrong about the Shadow Wolves?" I counter, wanting to see her reaction.

She scoffs like that's a ridiculous concept. "I'm never wrong."

I step closer. "But what if Ri and his sister are more dangerous than you or any of us realize?" Her knuckles whiten around her fork. "What if they're playing you to get what they want?"

All of a sudden, Mom's on her feet; her fork clatters to the table. I flinch.

"I don't make mistakes," she hisses.

Mom hates being challenged. Anyone who so much as dares question anything she says or does has her fighting back with claws and fangs.

I'm no longer a kid; I'm not blind. It comes down to one thing.

Insecurity.

She's terrified of it being found out that she's not as great as she pretends. It's easier to lash out at others. And that only makes her more dangerous.

"Where's this coming from?" Mom demands. "Who's filled your head with lies?"

My own wolf is circling. I'm bristling inside, desperate to challenge Mom but knowing that I mustn't.

"It doesn't take a genius to see there's something odd

about them," I reply. "So, why would you want to align our pack with them?"

She's breathing heavily now. "How dare you! I'm doing everything in my power to ensure your future is secured, to make sure that a Sun Wolf continues as Alpha, to help everyone in this pack, and you question me?"

She's close to transforming. I can sense it.

Her hard exhale rushes past her lips, but I don't back away. Instead, I lift my chin.

"Hey, it's a simple question. I'm only worried about what they want." My heart's thumping in my chest.

Midnight Goddess, protect me...

Where's Addison or Faith or… anyone?

"What I do is none of your concern." Mom shoves past a chair and comes at me, standing in my personal space. "You have two days until the Wolf Trials begin." She grabs hold of my chin, pinching. I grit my teeth. It hurts, but I don't cower. It's what she wants. The flicker of arrogance in her eyes is now consumed by fiery rage, and a nerve twitches just below her eye. "You have two options, which you seem to have forgotten. You win or you partner up with the winner."

A bolt of anger shoots through me, and I shove her hand off me. I stumble back, hating that I had to do that. "Stop bullying me. I know what I need to do for *MY* future in Fable."

"Is that what you think? Ungrateful brat!" Her expression darkens.

My skin goosebumps, and I freeze.

Instantly, Mom sweeps her arm across the table with

a growl, knocking over the plates, drinks, and mountains of food. It all goes crashing to the floor. The porcelain and glass crack and smash; the sound slices through the silent house.

I gasp, jumping back in shock from the shards and growing puddle of hot coffee.

Blessed sun, all that waste...

Servants rush into the room but freeze in the doorway, when they see Mom with her teeth bared and her eyes blazing.

They retreat just as quickly out of here. *Smart move.*

Would they mind if I tagged along with them?

"You push and push me." Mom points a finger at me. "When all I've ever wanted is to give you a future, where you hold power like I do. Yet you look at me like I'm the worst person in the world. You question my decisions. You accuse me of holding secrets."

Yeah, yeah, and yeah.

My jaw muscles are clenched so hard that they hurt, and my eyes prick with furious tears.

But I won't cry in front of her. I won't give her the satisfaction.

"You've no idea how I feel." I snap back. "And I'm getting sick of being told what my future will be like, who I can dance with, or who I can't be friends with."

The wolf rises in her, mirrored in her eyes, which morph into pale violet wolf eyes. She's so close to losing control and transforming. But she doesn't back down. A dark fury swirls in her gaze, and dread curls up my spine.

"You've spent too much time among humans,

listening to their idiotic dreams about freedom and being independent. Those are a fool's words." She lifts a chair up off the floor like that makes a difference to the mess she's created. "The survival of your own pack is all that matters; the pack's needs come before your own."

I'm trembling with rage, stuck between staying in this home with her, and going to Fable Academy to train with Ri and all the other hungry wolves wanting to become Alphas, who long to take me down just as desperately.

Both scenarios are nightmares.

"Get upstairs and clean yourself up," she growls. "Put something pretty on and try to understand how everything I'm doing is for the survival of the Sun Wolves."

This has always been about her remaining in power.

An ache deepens in my chest. The room tilts around me; I'm woozy.

I can't do this right now.

The hatred.

The perfect little lies.

The gossip.

I storm out of the room, while Mom yells at the servants to clean up the dining room.

I shake, and my hands clench compulsively.

I hate her. I hate the expectations. I hate the whole cursed Wolf Games.

With my head lowered, I run toward the stairs.

"Wynter," Addison's soft voice calls, then his hand is on my elbow.

I tilt my head up to meet his gaze. He's still in his

pajamas too, although he's wearing a silk robe over them.

"We need to talk." He hurriedly cards his fingers through his hair, which is as messy as mine.

That startles me because he's usually careful to be wellgroomed.

His gaze flicks in the direction I came from.

I blink at him. "I'm not in the mood to hear that I shouldn't let her get to me or whatever *fatherly* pep talk you've got prepared."

His brow wrinkles like the thought of speaking about Mom is the farthest thing from his mind, and I wonder how much he actually cares for her.

With his hand curling around my arm, Addison guides me toward the front door, so we're as far from the dining room as possible. He takes a quick look back to make sure Mom isn't coming, then he faces me, his expression pensive.

"I heard you and your mom talking just then. And last night, I couldn't help but notice you were rather taken by Ri."

I rear back, giving Addison my best deadpan face. "If that means crushing on him, that'd be a *nope*. What's this about?"

He studies me. "Wynter, do you know how you can tell when you find that someone special just for you?"

I shrug.

"When you know that you can't live without them, when you can't get them out of your head, when you stare at them the way you were at Ri last night. That's why I needed to talk to you before it's too late."

"I have no clue what this is about." I can't help the blush that's creeping up my neck.

Goddess, was I really that obvious last night, when I danced with Ri?

Addison holds my stare and a pause of silence floats between us; his hand still rests on my arm. He looks toward the dining room and back.

Suddenly nervous, I'm curious to hear what he has to say.

"Your mother has made a dangerous decision in taking Ri and Brey into our town," he whispers.

My pulse races, and I force myself not to react.

I'm thrown back to the familiar words, which I heard from Hunter. Unease flares through me.

"How can you be sure? Or are you believing the rumors now too?"

"Every rumor stems from a thread of truth." He leans in closer. "And it seems you've already heard about them. Your mother doesn't allow me into most of the important meetings." He ducks his head, flushing, and he doesn't need to say it, but we both know he's the trophy husband. "I'm married to the Alpha and so, people tell me things." His gaze hardens. "The Irish Shadow Wolves are all dead...except for Ri and his sister. Whatever happened in their pack is shrouded in secrets and lies. No one knows the truth. And yet those two survived."

My heart is beating so hard that I'm certain he must hear it.

"Mom must know the truth. Why else would she welcome them into Fable, right?" I whisper.

"I don't know. She doesn't tell me about her business dealings. But you need to be aware of the devil in our town and that your mom intends to make an alliance with his family. Be careful, Wynter."

Suddenly, footsteps thump the floorboards coming towards us.

Mom.

Addison draws in a quick breath. *Is he scared of his own mate?*

Addison and I both snap our heads up, and Addison runs his hand through his hair, smoothing it, before straightening his shoulders like a soldier and twisting away from me. He leaves my side and marches toward Mom.

I don't want to face Mom again, so I turn and rush upstairs.

When I shut my door to my bedroom, my legs and arms feel as though they weigh a ton. I flop into bed, stirring awake Hades. He grumbles and curls back up, so I shuffle under the blankets, groaning at how hard just moving feels.

Is my sickness getting worse?

I've been so good since arriving in Fable. So good... until now.

Stress always makes it worse.

Two days until the trials, Mom said. *Am I really up to this?*

It's not like I have a choice, which means one thing.

Go forward with my plan.

I close my eyes and lean my throbbing head on my

pillow. Everything hurts, and I can feel a fever beginning to blaze.

This is dangerous. I shouldn't be up here alone.

Yet I am now...alone.

Then why is it, that before I'm dragged into unconsciousness, the last thing that I see in my delirium are Ri's piercing emerald eyes?

CHAPTER 12

RI

*D*a once told me, *when a wolf's forced into unfamiliar territory, he either shows his belly or his fangs*. As I prowl down the icy driveway along with the other eight initiates toward Fable Academy and the start of the trials, I've already bared *my* fangs.

I snarl; a low growl rumbles in my throat.

Who knows what nightmares lie ahead?

Fair play to the Fearless, at least they warned us that they'd likely be *deadly*.

Brey nudges me with her elbow. Her expression is studiedly blank, and in her all-black jacket, which is tucked into loose pants by a belt, along with her fiery hair, she looks as deadly as a blade.

I call it her *ninja outfit* but not to her face, unless I feel like making a run for it straight after. But then, we wonder why the Shadow Wolves have a reputation for being stealthy and mysterious.

We hide behind our wall of independence with our

veils and secret vendettas. But just because we're dangerous, doesn't make us safe in Fable.

I clench my hands and bite back a growl.

Honestly, my inner wolf is a growly idiot but he knows when there's danger, and here, it scents the air like blood.

Fable Academy's shadow swallows us. The building, which is gray stone and part castle, part fortress, rises out of the forest, which has grown up around it, taking it over. Ivy encases the front, winding in and out of the latticed, crimson windows. The highest turret has collapsed, and the arching entranceway is crumbling. On one side, there's a high, barred gate.

Our bags have already been dropped off at the academy by our packs. If they've damaged my guitar or Crown Breaker, my axe, I won't be held responsible for losing control over my wolf.

It's coming up to the full moon, right?

Never mess with a Shadow Wolf close to the full moon.

And aye, I've heard every variation on *it's that time of the month* gag.

I grimace, scrunching my nose against the stink of mold and decay. They've got the whole gothic vibe working for them.

Darkest shadows, I'd give anything to keep my wee sis safe, after all I've lost, but we've both *chosen* to join the Wolf Games. At least Jack allowed us to volunteer, instead of drafting in the initiates like the other packs.

It's a chance to take back our legacy and exorcise the ghosts that haunt us.

Perhaps, it's also justice.

Revenge.

We're owed that.

My gaze cuts to the Sun Girl who's also chosen this path, even though I've tried to warn her off at the ball.

Don't think about how she felt in my arms…with her warm hand curling onto my shoulder…the sacred blossom in her hair, which was saved by my magic…and her scent that drove me wild.

She had no idea that she was dancing with a monster. And she's got even less idea how monstrous she could become herself.

Our darkness could weave legends together.

Now though, she's pale. She's dressed in jeans and a warm snow jacket. Her eyes are too glassy, however, like she's feverish or has been recently.

My brow furrows. What's wrong with her?

Wolves shouldn't get ill. But then, she's a hybrid, right? I growl in frustration that I haven't learned much yet from Jack about healing them.

Brey notices the direction of my gaze, and her brow furrows even deeper than mine.

"Bad idea, pup," she mutters. "Try thinking with your head for once and not your dick."

Wee sis, you didn't just call me pup *in front of the other initiates…?*

I narrow my eyes. "I'm thinking with my wolf, *ninja.*"

As Brey splutters in outrage, I work my way through the snow to Wynter. She's walking by herself. She shivers. Should she even be out on this long trek to the academy?

"You can't mean to go through with this," I blurt.

Okay, not quite what I'd meant to open with, but it's too late now. "You look like you'll blow over in a gust of wind."

"I'm stronger than I look," Wynter's voice is cold and hard.

It's like a slap in the face.

I've been a jerk to her... I've been told I have this broody bastard thing going on... but she's never looked at me with that sort of icy calculation in her violet eyes before.

I hate it.

I straighten my shoulders, holding out my hand to her. "Want to walk with Brey and me?"

She recoils like I meant to hit her. "Why would I? Mom's not here to make me."

I lower my hand and take a step back.

Is that how she really feels?

She looks conflicted like she wants to say something else but is holding herself back. Yet there was a hint of something else in her tone, even though she tried to hide it: *fear*.

Her gaze is darting around like she's looking for an escape route, and I let her take it. She rushes to Hunter's side, and the three Moon initiates circle around her like they're protecting her from *me* in a wave of pale silver.

Hunter shoots me a glare, and I force myself to smirk back like I'm not torn up inside.

But I am.

My only moment of smug satisfaction is when Hunter tries to put his arm around her shoulders, and Wynter shrugs him off.

The same hurt flashes across Hunter's expression as flashed on mine at Wynter's coldness, before he hurriedly shutters it.

It's almost enough to feel a twinge of *kicked in the balls* man solidarity.

Almost.

I jump, when Brey rests her hand on my shoulder. She pushes me to walk on, down the long driveway, like nothing's happened.

You mustn't show your belly to other wolves.

Brey's grin is sharp. "This is the part where you sing *Brey is always right, and I'm always daft as a wolf's arse.*"

"Lay off, I haven't sung that since you invented the rhyme aged five."

"Aye, but you've never crashed and burned with a woman like that either." Brey pats my shoulder, before she drops her hand to her side. "What if Wynter's just not that into you?"

Except, I don't believe it. I've felt the way our wolves called…nay, *connected*…to each other.

So, what's happened between our dance at the Blossom Ball and now? What's the mystery between her and Hunter? I guess a lot can happen in three days.

I duck my head, and my hair tumbles over my eyes. "I haven't forgotten who she is. She's a Sun brat. *The Alpha's pawn.*"

Brey's expression hardens. "We're all pawns."

"Sun Wolves are monsters and killers. I shouldn't care if the Alpha's daughter rejects me. So, why do I crave to protect her?"

"At a guess: your inner wolf's feeling the effects of

the full moon." Brey rolls her shoulders, tipping back her head. "I am too, mind. But by the shadows, we need to cool him down, or you'll get yourself flayed."

I swallow, arching my back as well. Phantom pains from the web of scars prickle across my skin.

Brey is always right, and I'm always daft as a wolf's arse.

I can sing it in my head, right? When my lips quirk, however, Brey smirks like she's heard it anyway.

I stare up at the arched gateway entrance into the grounds of the Fable Academy.

Adrenaline spikes through me.

Almost there.

Teo, the remaining Shadow Wolf initiate, walks silently in front of Brey and me with a cool stealth. He's dressed in a black suit and coat that billows as he walks. He's a year older than me, and we're not friends. Teo doesn't have friends, only allies.

Jack's spent the last three days doing his best to prepare Brey and me for these trials, and that's included a run down on the other initiates.

Teo's ruthless, single-minded, and vicious.

Thank the Great Shadow Wolf he's in my pack.

But then, Ballard's also here, and he's a violent dick.

A violent *entitled* dick in a royal orange designer suit, and they're the worst. The bright sunlight shines off his golden hair, and his arm is looped around Paige, who smells less like an Alpha and more like prey.

Right, Ballard's prey.

Wynter is the outsider in her pack. Why's Ballard shooting Hunter and her venomous glances?

Shadow knows, he's only doing it when he's sure

that they're not going to catch him at it like a whipped wolf.

It's a good look on him.

Wynter appears to have been adopted by the Moon Wolves, who circle her protectively: Parker, a swaggering wolf who's been voted The Wolf with the Sexiest Ass for two years. *They really do vote on this stuff.* And Jex is the Moon pack's smartest wolf.

Then, of course, there's Hunter. Why did he put himself forward for this? Jack said he's not aggressive like Ballard and Teo. Surely, he hasn't been wearing a mask to hide his true wolf just like me?

And if he has, then is he as dangerous as me?

Parker's also his foster brother, and that means we have the same weakness: a sibling in the games.

If you know who someone loves, you know how to hurt them. And Hunter's the type of wolf who's been hurt and taken it all his life. You can see it in the hunch of his shoulders.

Yet now he dares to glance across the driveway at me and meet my gaze like he's my equal…like his wolf's dominant enough to be challenging mine.

Idiot.

I'd tear him to shreds.

I clench my fists, letting my nails cut my palms. I boot a snowdrift as I pass, and my feet numb in the cold.

I offered Wynter a place by my side with the Shadow Wolves.

With me.

Instead, she chooses the Moon Wolves and the *housekeeper's son.*

Back in Ireland, I could've chosen any mate. But here, I have to beg for scraps of attention or affection.

Here, I'm nobody.

Outsider.

Outcast.

Brey glances warily at the looming academy. "You could've had a life as a Healer with Jack. This should've been my fight. Regretting your choice?"

My grin is sharp. "Not a chance."

My wolf howls. Once I win, I'll be Alpha.

King of Fable.

The broken crown will be restored, and all this pain will forge me into something stronger.

Brey catches my hand in hers, and her grin is as sharp as mine. We stalk faster toward the stone building together.

I steer Brey toward the Moon Wolves because maybe I'm only scarring myself, but I need to overhear what Wynter's talking about.

Fine, eavesdrop.

"You okay, Wyn?" Hunter asks.

"Better, now that I'm free of the Sun House and Mom. I've been in bed for the last two days," Wynter replies, and her voice is filled with a warmth that's the opposite of the closed off coldness that she showed me. I bristle, and my chest tightens. "You know, stress and drama, it's tough on my illness. But I'm rested now. I can do this."

Hunter smiles and his sky-blue eyes light up like this

is one big adventure, even though he's shivering in a too thin silver coat.

See, idiot.

In fact, all the Moon Wolves are wearing threadbare, shabby clothes and suffering from the cold already. I tilt my head. That gives me an advantage.

"We're in this together." Hunter nods at the academy building, which is strangled by ivy. "So, are we betting gourmet dinners and silk sheets or bread and water and chains?"

"Kinky." Parker smirks.

"What is this place?" Wynter gestures at the tumble-down turret like she can't bear to look at it. "I thought it was a myth."

"It hasn't been used in a hundred years, since the last games," Jex replies in a calm, clipped voice. "It's been hurriedly renovated. Nature had claimed it, and the Alpha has taken it back."

"It's wrong," I growl.

Because I feel the truth of it...deep in my magic.

Hunter's eyes narrow, but he doesn't look round. "Nobody asked you."

I drag my leather jacket closer around myself and run my hand through my curls. I struggle to control my wolf and not slam Hunter's face into the snow.

"It's a lot freakier than I was expecting." Parker waggles his eyebrows. "If anybody wants to cling onto me in terror, then I offer myself up."

"Good try." Wynter laughs.

"Once, it was nicknamed Nightmare Academy," Ballard drawls like my interruption has broken down the barrier between the packs. "Because nobody escaped without suffering their worst nightmare, or transforming into it."

He flashes a sharp smile like he's excited by that idea, which is all predator.

"Don't," Paige breathes, clinging to him tighter.

"Ladies and gentlemen, our new Captain of Morale." Parker points dramatically at Ballard.

Jex attempts to smother his laugh on his sleeve.

Wynter rolls her eyes. "*We're* the nightmares. *That's* just an empty building with nothing in it but ghosts."

I stare around at my other initiates: the most dominant wolves of their packs and potential Alphas.

The nightmares.

The huge, crimson front door of the academy looms in front of us.

We're here.

Teo doesn't even look around; his voice is deep and biting, "I'm not scared of ghosts or nightmares. They should be scared of me."

All of a sudden, the back of my neck tingles. The hairs stand up on my arms.

Danger.

I crouch down at the same time as Brey does.

Nobody else even moves.

Unexpectedly, a group of masked men burst out of the academy's front door. They're wolves, but it's impossible to tell if they're from the Fable packs.

I holler out a warning.

Too late. *We're ambushed.*

Who are they? Instructors? *Assassins?*

The masked men are covered head-to-toe in scarlet: tailored shirts and pants with woolen coats that drag across the snow. Their heads are covered in hideous wolf masks. My inner wolf rages at the sight.

The strangers encircle us, raising short batons that are embedded with sharp wolf claws. They tip back their heads and howl.

It's so loud that I cringe.

It's a disorientation tactic.

A trick.

I draw in a sharp breath, and my pulse races.

Brey draws closer to me, and we drop into our practised defensive stance.

The Moon pack have been driven further toward the iron gate; they're circling Wynter to protect her. My heart clenches that I can't be the one to help her. The Moon Wolves are howling themselves, as the claw batons slash through their thin coats; their blood is bright against the white snow.

I raise my arm and block a baton attack; I grit my teeth at its bite, but the claws can't break through my leather coat. I glare into the masked face of my attacker and snarl.

Meet my wolf, bastard, and he's just under my skin, ready to rip out your throat.

Out of the corner of my eye, I watch as Teo high round kicks one attacker, smashes another in the face, and then spins around another to dive down the side of the academy.

By the shadows, he's going to be one tough rival.

I narrow my eyes, and when my attacker leans

closer, I headbutt him. Taken by surprise, he staggers and falls back.

I hiss out a breath, as sparks fly through my aching forehead. But still, worth it.

Brey gives me a quick nod, before punching another one of the masked dicks in the face.

Ballard runs in front of me; he's holding Paige's hand, shielding her.

Well, that's surprising. Perhaps, even Ballard isn't a total bastard.

When one of our assailants launches himself at Ballard, he dodges but too late. Ballard howls, as the baton slashes across his forearm, which he's holding up to protect his face. He looks more furious that his jacket has been ripped than by his injured arm. He's trembling viciously like he's struggling not to transform.

We've been warned not to transform without permission.

Yet Ballard looks like he has less control over the beast inside than I do.

Ballard's eyes are wild, as he throws himself on the man who slashed his arm, knocking him to the floor and smashing his fists into the mask like he's desperate to break it. I take the opportunity, snatching Brey's hand and jumping over Ballard.

"Run!" I yell.

Brey and I sprint around the academy, dodging attacks and sliding on the icy floor.

We skid into the barred gate, which blocks us.

Curse the shadows, why didn't we follow Teo's route? Now we're trapped.

Frustrated, I slam my hand against the gate with a clank.

Then I watch in shock, as Wynter slips away from the Moon Wolves and clambers onto the low ledge that runs around the front of the academy.

She's going to fall...

My breaths are ragged. My fingers claw around the bars. My fur bristles close under my skin.

Wynter swings herself closer to the gate. She shoots me a cocky smile, before shimmying through the bars and to safety.

Fair play to her, it's a smart trick, which I can't copy. I'm twice her size (and even Brey is too big), but Wynter's turned a weakness into a strength.

Despite everything, I grin.

She didn't need me to protect her after all.

I duck my head, waiting for her to leave me behind. If this is a test, she's beaten me.

On the other side of the gate, she hesitates. We stare at each other through the bars. Then she turns to the lock on the gate, which is on her side, and drags off the chains that bind it with a rattle. Then she pulls open the gate.

She stands in the open gate like a savior...queen...or Alpha.

She's the type of woman I could bare my neck to...if I wasn't going to win and be named Alpha.

This is becoming interesting.

Brey smiles at Wynter. "Thanks."

Wynter doesn't return the smile but turns and runs down the slope, which has been cleared of snow.

Brey lifts her brow at me.

Was Wynter saving Brey and me or only the Moon Wolves behind us?

Suddenly, there's a hand on my bicep, yanking me back. I'm turned by a tall wolf; his crimson coat is stained with his own blood, and his eyes blaze with fury through the slits in his mask. I struggle, but I can't twist free.

When he swings his baton at me, I can only dodge to the side, but it still catches my face. I yelp, as one of the claws on his baton slashes my cheek.

The sharp pain shocks me back into my memories.

Claws raking my skin...

Blood tears down my cheek.

Just like that other time, when I lost everything.

Dark. Alone. Dark.

The smell of Irish linen.

Screams and pain.

I'm frozen, breathing too fast, trapped in the flashback.

Brey snarls, sucker punching the masked man in the stomach, and then as he drops to the floor with an *oomph*, stamping on his back.

Brey grabs my arm; her gaze is assessing.

"Come on, bro," she whispers, dragging me through the gate and after Wynter down the slope that leads to the back of the academy. "You're here, now, with me, and we're getting our arses kicked in Fable. We're not in Ireland anymore. We're having a fine fight in the trials, instead."

I blink, shaking myself.

Right, battling for my life in Fable Academy, rather than Ireland.

Brilliant.

If this is the welcoming committee, then I understand why it's nicknamed Nightmare Academy.

But what's behind the academy? Is it something even deadlier?

CHAPTER 13

RI

*B*rey and I follow the side of the building, until we reach the back of the academy. I'm on the alert, as adrenaline races through me.

The sloping track opens into a vast parade ground, which has been cleared out of the dark forest that surrounds it. Stone pillars stand at either end, and nine large crimson boxes have been laid out in a line.

Right, looks like the fun and games are about to begin.

A giant of a man with bulging biceps and silver hair that sweeps to his waist stands with military bearing next to the boxes. His eyes are pale silver. He has a claw baton that rests next to him on the ground like a threat. I guess he's the main instructor then.

Brey and I exchange a glance.

Teo and Wynter already stand at parade rest in a line in front of him. It looks like we're being ranked on this already.

So, this was a test...? They launched an attack,

before we even had time for our wolves to settle into the territory.

Bastards.

When I prowl toward the line, the instructor doesn't even acknowledge me. His head tilts though, and I realize that he's listening to someone through an earpiece. Of course, he's being told how we all performed by the main attackers. In Fable, you're monitored secretly all the time.

I've become too comfortable with the freedom and privacy I had at Jack's.

Still, no one can control me.

I wipe the blood from my cheek; the cut is healing already. Then I lick the blood off my finger, as I meet the instructor's eye. I drop to the floor, sprawling on my back and pillowing my head on my arms.

Brey laughs, as she crosses her arms, defiantly.

The instructor doesn't even blink.

The Moon Wolves limp to join us; they've stayed together as a pack.

Interesting.

Like good little servants, the Moon Wolves stand in line next to Brey.

Finally, Ballard stalks to join us…last…and Paige trails after him. The Alpha would savage him for showing up the Sun Wolves like that. Scarlet spatters his orange suit like a freaky work of art, and I'm surprised by the crease of concern on Wynter's face.

I take a deep sniff; *it's not Ballard's blood.*

I push my curls out of my eyes, ignoring the cold of the floor beneath me, as I study Ballard. He's beaten me up enough times with his goons to know he's a bastard. But now I know that he's also a *psycho*, I'll keep an eye on him.

The instructor appears to be as well. He meets Ballard's fierce glare.

Then he scans over all of us, and his lip curls in contempt. "You're the special initiates…?" His sneer is harsh enough to flay. "*Pathetic*. Shadows, you act like you're humans and not wolves, thinking only of your-selves." Teo's hands ball into fists but he doesn't move out of position. "Moons, you're conditioned to be nothing *but* pack. You're not slaves here. Stop acting like it." The Moon Wolves shift and glance down. Hunter flushes. "And Suns…" His gaze slides over Ballard. "…Have no control."

"And are *you* the *special* instructors of Fable Acad-emy?" Ballard mocks. "*Pathetic*. You bleed, as easily as any wolf."

He draws his hand down the blood on his suit.

Aye, definite psycho.

The instructor steps forward in a quick, fluid move that takes me by surprise and backhands Ballard, knocking him to the floor.

Paige screams.

Ballard wipes the blood off his lips; his gaze meets mine.

Just for a moment, I think that he's going to go for the instructor's throat.

Stay down, idiot.

Then Ballard turns away his head, pushing himself slowly to his feet.

"And you bleed too," the instructor says, coldly. "I'm Thiago. You listen to me now. I'm training you in these trials to prepare you to survive the games, and we have a lot of work to do. The only one who passes today is the Alpha's daughter."

Wynter's eyes widen. "Me?"

"Yet even you can't hide that you're half human, although you're desperately trying to." Thiago strolls in front of her.

Why's he humiliating her like this? I growl, at the same time as Hunter.

Thiago ignores us. "Don't hide who you are; it's your strength. But then, every one of you initiates are hiding." He prowls down the line with his hands clasped behind him. "Only one of you can become Alpha. So, play as pack, hero, or monster. It doesn't matter to me. You're all lying." His piercing gaze meets mine; it's like he can see inside to my shadow. Like he knows my secrets... *the truth*. I shudder. "But don't lie to yourself. This isn't Fable, it's Fable Academy. If you don't let out the real wolf inside, you'll lose...or die." He shrugs. "With the Deep coming, isn't it the same thing?" Then he gives a bright smile and claps his hands. "Let's see what we have to work with. First fight. Stand in a wide circle around the boxes."

Grudgingly, I push myself up and join the others around the boxes, which I eye warily.

Away with you, when's anything good come out of a box in this kind of situation?

Brey stands on one side of me and Teo on the other.

Wynter's on the opposite side of the circle, and holds her head high like she's steeling herself.

The wind whips across the parade ground, cutting across my cheeks, and bringing with it the pine scent of the dark forest.

"You," Thiago points at me.

Of course he does.

When I strut into the circle like a gladiator entering an arena, Hunter rolls his eyes.

Come on, choose the housekeeper's son. I'm in the mood for kicking Moon Wolf arse.

Instead, Thiago points at Wynter. "You."

Of course he does.

Just the wolf I don't want to ever fight. Kiss, see if she tastes as delicious as she smells, and drive her so wild with pleasure that the only name on her lips will be mine forever...but not fight. I mean, rough foreplay if negotiated, can be exciting, but it doesn't include kicking each other's arses in front of an audience.

At least, that's not my kink.

My guts churn at the panic and fear that flashes across Wynter's expression, before she nods and strides toward me. She meets my gaze and doesn't look away.

It's questioning, unsure.

I prowl closer to her. "What's wrong?" I whisper, fiercely.

How can we fight with this tension hanging between us? It smarts me, every time she avoids my gaze.

"Just fight me," she hisses.

I step away. Fury surges through me, when I catch Hunter's smug smile.

If she wants a fight, then I'll give it to her.

"Go to the boxes," Thiago instructs.

My heart beats rapidly, as I step toward the crimson boxes that are laid on the ground with Wynter at my side.

What's inside?

Thiago crosses his arms. "Pick one each and open it."

An eerie silence falls across the parade ground. I can sense the wolfen magic, which hums through the boxes from whatever's inside. Each of the boxes is identical, but somehow, they have a different energy, burning hot, cool, or wreathed in shadows.

Wynter nudges me. "Age before beauty."

"Nay, you won the test," I reply. "You go first."

Wynter walks around the boxes, before her head tilts. "It's calling to me."

She drops to her knees next to one of the boxes, opening it with shaky hands. I peer over her shoulder, as she reaches inside and pulls out an iron dagger. The dagger's beautiful: sleek and dark. It's long with a heavy hilt, which is decorated with the rays of the sun. Its blade shimmers darker than the rest.

The dagger's deadly, and my skin prickles a warning. I know that sensation...*remember it.*

I take a desperate breath. I must be wrong.

Wynter smiles, as she lifts out a leather sheath from the box as well and slings it around her waist; it hangs down across her arse.

Can I be blamed for looking?

"Pretty, pretty knife," Brey murmurs. "That should

be mine."

"Would you take it easy?" I shoot Brey a quailing look. "She'll let you stroke it later."

Wynter stands up, slicing the dagger experimentally through the air. "Do I get to keep it?"

"You'll all get one of the weapons from inside these boxes," Thiago says. "The one that whispers to your shadow."

"All weapons should have a name," Brey says. "What's yours?"

I admire her restraint in not dragging the dagger away from Wynter.

Wynter's brow furrows for a moment. "Midnight."

When she reaches out to touch the edge of the blade, Jex takes an urgent step forward.

"Don't touch it," Jex warns. "My guess would be that it's been dipped in wolfsbane. I've studied about it; ancient weapons often were."

Wolfsbane.

I should've trusted my instincts and the prickling of my skin. You never forget the burn of that poison.

Wynter gapes at Thiago. "I'm not gonna fight with something that'll kill another wolf."

Thiago waves his hand dismissively. "It only burns and makes a wound heal more slowly. What it does in this fight, is balance the odds. You're facing off against a Shadow Wolf. He has the power of a wolf all the time… and what weapon will he get? Now at least, he has to be wary of getting too close."

Wynter stares at me in alarm.

I *knew* she'd forgotten why she shouldn't be bossing

me around.

I try to ignore the way that my skin crawls every time I catch sight of the blade in Wynter's hand and circle the boxes.

Right, let out my inner wolf. Don't hide or lie. Just feel...

Unexpectedly, I gasp, as from inside the box directly in front of me, a howling starts up.

It's primal.

Free.

And only I can hear the song of the wild.

This weapon is mine.

I fall to my knees, ignoring the crack as my kneecaps hit the hard floor, and throw open the box's lid.

Crown Breaker.

My ancient ax – Da's ax – rests on the scarlet silk lining like she's been waiting for me since the beginning of time. When I lift her out into the light, my grip tightens on the twisted handle, which is like black shadows. The steel head gleams.

I grin and leap up, thrumming with power and thrilling in the moment.

Until Ballard's drawl breaks it, "We were taught in Fable School that wolves fight with fangs and claws and *not* with weapons."

I slash the ax through the air with a fierce war cry. "I'm a wolf and I fight with an ax."

Ballard's eyes flash with contempt. "You're an Irish cur. Who cares what you do?"

"Actually, American wolves fight with weapons too, if they're skilled enough." Thiago's pale gaze pins Ballard in place like he's dissecting him. "You pups in college weren't at the advanced level. It looks like Irish wolves have their training wheels taken off at a younger age."

I chuckle. "We're early developers in the Emerald Isles."

"Early developers? Is that what you're calling it?" Hunter's voice is strangely flat.

I catch a glance that he's exchanging with Wynter.

What in the name of the shadows has Hunter done? What has he told her about me?

An ice-cold fear shoots through my veins, even as I raise Crown Breaker, and Wynter and I back away from the boxes. I ignore our audience now, focusing only on Wynter and the way that she's clutching the dagger, making quick, practising stabbing movements.

I wince: with the wolfsbane, that'll hurt if it cuts me.

Yet not more than the beatings and taunts of *outcast* and *killer* have since I arrived in Fable. Until I was the victim of malicious gossip, I never understood how it could flay you to the bone.

Words are as cruel as blows.

Wynter and I spoke about that at the ball. Being a hybrid, she understood. It was brilliant to have someone else who got it. Except, was I only kidding myself?

Wynter lunges at me with Midnight, and I sidestep her, staying out of reach of her blade. She regains her balance. Then she twists and dives to try and get closer to me, attacking with brutal thrusting motions. I fluidly block them with the handle of the ax, before sweeping the head of it in an arc. She gasps and dances backward, stumbling out of reach.

I raise my eyebrow.

She wants a fight, right?

She growls, and all the shadows, if it isn't the hottest thing I've ever heard.

My dick hardens, pressing against my tight jeans.

Nay, this is not the time to get excited, dick. Trying to concentrate here…

Distracted, I stumble back, and Wynter lunges forward with swift slashes like she was born to hold Midnight in her hands.

I swing Crown Breaker, holding Wynter back, at the same time, as I thrill at the way that she's determined to push toward me. The circle's scattering around us, as our fight becomes wilder; I hardly notice. There's no one in this but Wynter and I.

My inner wolf howls, struggling to burst free. I'm panting…shaking.

When Wynter slashes the knife at my chest and misses, she leaves herself open: too close with no defence.

She reeks of terror.

I snarl, sweeping her legs out from under her. When she slams to the floor with a yelp, I leap on top of her. My knees straddle her hips, and I push my fists into the dirt on either side of her head. Crown Breaker lies almost touching her cheek. She's pinned beneath me. Her hair's splayed out like a flower, which has opened to me, vulnerable. Her lips part, blowing out desperate puffs of air.

I still hold my ax, and she still holds her knife.

We could destroy each other.

We don't.

Yet.

"You could've easily beaten me," Wynter whispers. "Midnight feels like magic in my hand, but you've been training for years, right? But you didn't hurt me." She smiles, and her sudden warmth after her earlier coldness is like the sun. "I knew Hunter was wrong that you'd wiped out your pack in Ireland."

I freeze, stiff with shock and hurt.

She heard the rumors. Even if she didn't believe them before, *she had heard them.*

Did she seriously cold-shoulder me because she thought I'd murdered my own pack?

My mouth is dry. I want to hurl.

Don't go back there. I'm in Fable…I'm here…*with the feel of a woman beneath me who believed the rumors…*

"One of you needs to draw first blood," Thiago's voice sounds far away like I'm smothered. *Nay, not again, not like that night.* "The winner gets to choose the best rooms for their pack."

"Stab him," Ballard barks.

"What if we refuse?" Wynter asks.

"You don't," Thiago's voice is frostier than the snow. "Unless you wish your pack to spend their time in the academy's dungeons, instead."

"On the blessed sun, stab him," Ballard snarls.

I try to move my arm to defend with my axe, but I can't. I'm frozen. I'm lost to the night when my entire pack was murdered, and I took the blame.

Wynter casts me an apologetic look, before she nicks the blade as lightly as she can across the slight cut that was already almost healed. It's like she thinks if she reopens a wound that's already there, she's not hurting me.

But she is. She's hurting me more than she can possibly know.

I wince at the sudden sharp pain, and the light catches the blade.

A shiver runs through me. It no longer feels like a knife but a claw…the claws, which slashed me that night and left me scarred.

My wolf, which is already dominant this close to the full moon, growls his desperation to break out. I can't control him. I'm lost to the past.

Brey, I need you.

But I can't even open my mouth to call for her.

"The Sun Wolves win," Thiago announces. "What's wrong with you, Shadow? You're as pale as a ghost."

My eyes flash, and my teeth sharpen, as my nails become claws.

It's too late.

Triggered, all I can see is the smothering dark.

All I can smell is Irish linen.

And all I can hear are deafening screams.

My eyes are glazed, and I'm growling, low and dangerous.

I'm primal.

A shadow monster.

I rise up, towering above Wynter, who tries to scramble backward. I only see her and everyone else around me like specters, who are forcing their way into my past.

They're not real to me.

It's the memories that are: the wolves who crept into Da's castle at night and attacked my pack. The ones who left the scars raked across my back. The ones who left me with the nightmares that won't ever leave me.

Dark. Pain. Screams.

I throw my head back and roar. I hurl down my ax. I'm nothing but a flurry of claws and fangs.

Death.

Where am I? What's going on? Wild and confused, I twist in a circle, slashing and snarling.

Someone's calling my name. There's shouting. Cussing.

Then I holler, as a baton clubs me across the back of my head, and I tumble forward. I'm pressed to the floor by Thiago's powerful grip around the back of my neck and his knee in my lower back.

It's agonizing, and I can't breathe.

They're going to kill me. *Brey? Where's Brey?*

I blink like it'll help the pounding in my head. My mind clears just for a moment.

I'm not in Ireland. I'm in Fable. I'm safe.

Except, I'm not. I revealed my bad bastard primal side.

I'm screwed.

When I stop struggling, Thiago eases his hold on my neck. I raise my head and find myself staring into Wynter's horrified face.

I'll never forget the way she's looking at me now, and that's worse than any punishment.

What in the name of the shadows have I done?

CHAPTER 14

"Straight ahead," Thiago orders, pointing to an arched entryway into the enormous academy building at the end of the cobblestone path.

He wants the rest of us gone, while he's holding Ri back.

The eight of us initiates follow the stone path that leads us to the main entry. My pulse pounds, as the true magnitude of the academy's size hits me, the closer I get. Vines, trees, and shadows swallow the castle. When I tilt back my head, the sight of crenelations running between two towers makes me feel like I've stepped back in time.

Then I startle. There's someone up there: *a guard staring down at us*. He's dressed in a scarlet military style coat with an emblem, which I can't make out, on the left hand side of his chest.

Everything about this place reminds me of old ruins that time has worn away.

I always wanted to visit a castle but this is seriously not a vacation.

And if it is, then it sucks.

I slip my hand to the blade in the sheath that hangs low on my ass. What kind of vacation starts with a ritual weapon selection, followed by the psycho wolf breakdown?

The other initiates are whispering to each other about the attack, the fighting, and the weapons we'll all receive in the boxes. But I can't stop glancing over my shoulder at Thiago and Ri, who are still standing where we'd been minutes earlier.

They're talking in hushed words that I can't hear, and I so desperately want to know what they're saying.

What made Ri lose control?

He holds himself tall and keeps shaking his head, but Thiago has a tight grip on his arm like he doesn't trust Ri.

My chest tightens. Thiago backhanded Ballard just for having an attitude. What will he do to Ri for losing it like that? I don't want Ri hurt, even if his reaction scared the hell out of me.

One moment we were sparring, and the next, it was like he became someone else. It was like a switch had been flipped inside him. He became something that I didn't recognize, something dark.

What triggered him, meaning I could defeat him? In all honesty, I know he should've been the winner. It's scary how strong he is. I need to know tricks like that in battle because today's been a wake up call: I'm going to be faced with life or death here.

Is Ri capable of losing control and killing?

Killing me?

Yeah, I need to work out his Achilles Heel fast. Yet why is the churning in my gut warning me that Ri may mean so much more to me?

Ri's expression darkens, and his chin is tilted up, defiantly. He's arguing with the instructor now. He flings his free arm about, and I can hear snatches of his raised voice, which is wild and agitated.

Well, if he wants to get himself kicked out of the trials, then maybe it's best he does it now, before one of the other initiates gets to him first. He's just revealed his weakness in front of everyone. Sure, the trigger's unknown for the moment, but everyone will be pushing him until he breaks again.

Brey strolls behind us slowly, her head low. Her fists are clenched, and she keeps looking back to her brother, as shadows dance across her worried face.

I hesitate, unsure whether I should slow down and join her. Maybe I should ask her if she's okay?

Brey is alone and it must suck to see your brother hurting.

Yet before I can, a light touch grazes my elbow, making me jump. I glance to my side to meet Hunter's intense gaze.

"The Shadow Wolf's violent," Hunter's voice whispers from my side. "On the moon, if the smallest fight has Ri losing control, how long will he last in the actual games?"

I shrug but I also feel there's more to that situation than a simple loss of control. I looked into Ri's eyes when he turned, and the change came on from words not actions.

"Aren't we all capable of violence?" I say. "I'm guessing that every single initiate is here because we have something dominant in us that makes us no different to Ri."

The fallen expression on Hunter's face tells me that it's not the response he was hoping for. He opens his mouth and then closes it with a click, as Ri's sister marches right past us, and purposefully drives a shoulder into Hunter's. Then she storms ahead of the other initiates to reach the entryway first.

Instantly, I glance back to find that two guards are now dragging Ri roughly to the side of the academy. Thiago marches in my direction. His face is inscrutable.

My breathing is ragged, and my mouth is suddenly dry.

I hate that Ri's being separated from us by guards. I hate that I don't know what's going to be done to him. And I hate that I care so much, when I shouldn't.

"Where are they taking him?" I mutter.

Hunter's eyes become stormy. "Hopefully to a permanent holding cell or if they're smart, back into town. He's a monster, right?"

I tilt my head and stare into Hunter's sky-blue eyes. He always makes me feel safe and comfortable. He's beautiful and strong, but now I'm discovering he has a different side to him. He's a lot more ferocious than I imagined. Even the way he walks has changed: he moves with purpose, striding like a predator alongside me.

I sort of find it hot.

I cheer for him to finally have a chance to stand up for himself, to fight back, and to stop having to take others' bullshit. Sure, it goes against everything Mom instigated across Fable, but isn't that why we're all in these deranged games? To change our futures?

Out here in the trials, it looks like Hunter's decided not to play by the Alpha's rules anymore.

"Don't you want to know what really happened back there?" I bump my shoulder against Hunter's. "It's got to be more than just *he's a monster*. Think about it… the better you know the opponent, the easier it will be to defeat them."

Hunter gives me a deadpan look. "Thanks, Wise Wolf Wyn." I smother my smile, and cast him a stern glare, instead. "Trust me, don't fall for his Irish charm. The guy's unstable."

Hunter falls silent, as Thiago marches right past us. He watches Thiago walk into the building, then he turns to me.

"I'll always protect you." When Hunter cups the side of my face, his hand is surprisingly warm considering the chill in the air.

I lean against his touch, while my mind screams to remember how dangerous getting close to him is.

Am I prepared to give up my chance at the Alpha title for Hunter?

Do I want to give Mom the reason to strike against him?

She ensured her power remains after the games by promising me to the winner. That act of marriage, a bond between packs, offers her immunity from being dismissed from the role of co-rulership of Fable alongside whomever wins.

But if *I* win… I can change that and remove her from power.

I don't know yet *how* I'll win. If a plucky attitude and a super talent for eating Doritos helps, then I'm okay.

Probably not.

I do know, however, that I'm not going to lose.

All I can do is stare at Hunter, and remember our kiss at the Blossom Ball. He's always been one of the hottest guys I've known, and for a long time, I dreamed about going against Mom's command to be with him openly. Of course, I never acted on it out of pure fear of what she'd do to him. And now… I'm in the impossible situation where we're in these games together and Mom would find a way to destroy him if he won.

I can't tell him that, or maybe he already knows the risks but has thrown caution to the wind for the sake of freedom.

Something darkens behind his eyes. "Wyn, if Ri ever puts his hands on you, tell me because I'll cut them off." There's fury behind his voice, a brutal violence flashing in his gaze.

My breath catches. It's more ruthless than anything I'd expect him to say, but like I said, he's changed.

Hardened.

Grown dominant.

Gone is the meek Moon Wolf.

He's marking his territory for claiming the position of Alpha just like Ri and every other initiate.

Including me.

Only the strong survive these games, and the rest are killed off. Something Hunter seems to be prepared for.

I shiver.

Just how important is it for him to see a Moon Wolf as Alpha?

That scares me because what we have between us is complicated enough. And I need to find a way to put my emotions aside. I've been attracted to him for as long as I can remember. But when my thoughts swing to Ri, my stomach tightens into a knot. Except, I should be only focusing on winning.

I mean, my wolf hasn't come out in four years. And trust me, I've tried to coax her out.

"Hurry up," Thiago calls from the doorway.

"Guess that's our cue." Hunter grins.

Hunter and I enter the building side by side; our hands brush. We're the last of the initiates to enter, and I flush at the curious glances watching us.

I stop in the medieval-looking hallway and glance around. The place is cold and smells like turned soil. Wrought iron chandeliers hang from the impossibly high ceilings and flood the room with light. Their amber flames throw shadows across the black granite walls and paintings of great wolf battles.

War.

Blood.

Death.

The past engulfs me, and I start to better understand why the place is nicknamed Nightmare Academy. Walls that have laid witness to centuries of generations battling in the Wolf Games are reminders of our mission here.

The gruesome, bloody paintings send a shiver down my spine. Are they snapshots of other initiates in battle? One image shows a wolf as dark as midnight standing on a pile of three corpses.

I swallow hard, looking away.

In front of me, is a grand staircase, which sweeps up into the shadows, before splitting into three directions. A long banner dangles from the ceiling above each passage.

A bright golden banner with a brilliant white circle for the Sun Wolves hangs over the middle steps.

Deep blue with a sickle moon for the Moon Wolves on the right.

And a black banner with only the pale outline of a moon in full eclipse for the Shadow Wolves sits over the left wing.

The base of the stairs are flanked by two statue warriors in battle uniform, one male, one female. Each clutches a long sword with both hands and the tip points at the floor. Their expressions are fierce.

My mouth falls open. Whispered voices rise around me from the other initiates. Hunter looks around in awe; his eyes are wide with admiration.

And we're only in the hallway.

Everyone is murmuring. There might be just eight of us here, but our voices reverberating against the walls makes it sound like there are dozens of people in the hallway.

"Some of you will die," Thiago announces loudly.

Way to kill the mood.

Instantly, the voices flatline.

My gut clenches. Thiago appears to have a flair for the dramatic. Except, he means it.

The room is so silent, you could hear a pin drop.

"There are always casualties," he continues, standing on the third step, with his legs parted and his hands behind his back. "At Fable Academy, I want you to forget the rules from town. While here, the only ones you'll follow are mine. And they are easy for you to remember. Do everything I say. Follow the training schedule. And last, never leave the academy grounds."

He glances over his shoulder to the top of the staircase. Instantly, three uniformed men emerge from the shadows.

"Make an orderly line," Thiago commands, "and move toward your respective pack dormitory."

I try to remember to breathe. It's hard to stop feeling like I'm a fraud and that everyone will find out I don't belong.

I bite down on my lower lip and fall into formation with Ballard taking the lead, and Paige standing at my back. I take a quick look over to Hunter, who's leading the line of the Moon Wolves, while for the Shadow pack, it's Brey shoving herself first, and then Teo.

There's still no sign of Ri. What will happen to him?

The competition is only going to become fiercer, and that means I can't let my emotions show. I repeat that mantra, as we follow Ballard up the stairs straight ahead, as the other packs veer out of sight on either side of us.

My muscles tense with fear of the unknown.

At the top of the steps, us Sun Wolves are greeted by a dimly lit hallway flanked by two ostentatiously detailed pillars, which are painted in black with streaks of gold. We follow the guard, until we reach the end of the hall.

"To your right is the bathroom and showers," the guard barks, pointing to a single door with no signs on it. "All facilities are shared by each pack. Male and female alike."

Okay, that should be interesting. I'm not the biggest fan of Ballard, so I have no intention of stripping in front of him for a shower anytime soon.

"The women should have their own facilities," Ballard murmurs.

The guard shoots him a glare. "I don't recall anyone putting you in charge."

He turns to the door right at the end of the hall and with a snap of a lock, he pushes open the door.

We all stream inside after him.

The walls and ceiling are bright and decorated with designs to resemble sun rays. The floorboards are pale, and three beds swallow most of the space, along with a small round table and chairs. Windows allow in the light, but there are no curtains. They overlook a sloping mountain range, which is spectacular.

Well, at least we have a beautiful view.

"We're also sharing a room...?" Paige moans, which only gains her a hard, side glare from the guard.

Paige's cheeks pale, and her wide gaze sweeps the open room.

I would've thought she wanted to share with Ballard, unless she's never had to share anything in her privileged life before.

I glance around at the room. There are gleaming golden chandeliers with real lightbulbs and a rack of metal shelves against the wall, which are filled with folded clothes and towels, all in white. There's also a fireplace, so at least we won't freeze.

Each bed has a bedside table and drawers, and that's it. Way to strip a room of personality or warmth. Although, when I first saw the tumbledown fortress, I half expected us to be sleeping on straw in a cell riddled with mold.

I wince. I hope that's not where Ri's been thrown.

I take a careful sniff of the air. The walls might have been painted brightly, but it smells damp and abandoned here.

It could be a prison still.

I think Jex must be right that no one has made use of the dormitories since the last Wolf Games, which was over a century ago. I probably should've paid more attention to the local history lessons in school growing up. How many initiates have lived in these dormitories? Did any of them die here?

Geez, I hope not.

"Remain in the room, until you're summoned." The guard turns on his heel and marches out of the room, shutting the door behind him.

"Well, that was uneventful," I say.

"I claim this bed," Ballard calls out, flopping down on the first one, which is also the closest to the door.

It's obvious he has every intention of being the first out for every mission...even the mission to call first dibs on the beds.

Jerk.

Paige is already lingering around the second bed to be near him, so I walk past them and claim the last offering, which is tucked into the far corner with two walls of windows.

"Guess this is me then," I say as brightly as I can.

I settle down on my hard mattress. One glance over my shoulder shows Ballard has his back to me, taking off his coat, while Paige is peeling back the covers of her bed. I quickly empty the pockets of my meds, stuffing them into the bottom drawer, before they see me. I tuck my new blade in there too, then I also shrug off my coat.

"We need a plan," Ballard states. I twist around in my bed to see him standing at the end like a commanding officer. "The Sun Wolves must win the games. Do you want to even think what the Alpha will do to us if we don't? So, we support each other, protect one another, and destroy those asshole Moon and Shadow Wolves."

"Sounds like a plan to me," Paige agrees.

They both watch me closely, waiting for me to jump on board blindly.

I used to like Paige, but there's a distance between us now since I arrived back in Fable. But Ballard, I don't trust. I never did before, and nothing's changed. He's still as much a bully as he was back then.

There's an edge to him now though: he's driven.

A psycho.

When I don't respond, Ballard strides to the end of

my bed, his chest heaving in and out with fast breaths. As always, he gives me one of his haughty smirks that I hate. Coming from one of the richest families in town, his privileged background has him thinking he can act in any way he likes. His golden hair is short and perfectly styled off his face, and his mocha eyes are piercing.

His lip is swollen, and I wince at the memory of Thiago knocking him on his ass.

"What's wrong, Wynter?" Ballard's eyes narrow. "Are you too scared to stand up for yourself without your mom here? Or have you been spending too much time with those filthy Moon curs? They don't stand a chance of winning, especially if I have anything to do with it."

Anger churns in my gut, and I clench my teeth. But I refuse to play his games.

Instead, I ask, "What's your plan, if us three end up being the final contenders then?" I study his reaction carefully. "Let me take a guess. You'll stab us in the back to claim the position of Alpha for yourself, right?"

Ballard shrugs, as the corners of his mouth fight the urge to pull into a grin. That conceited look confirms I'm right.

Yeah, that's what you think, asshole.

I'll destroy Ballard myself, before I let him win. I won't be forced into a marriage with him.

"We'll work it out as a team," he insists, lying through his teeth.

I roll my eyes hard because I'll believe BigFoot exists, before I put any credibility in his words.

I mean, vampires, fae, and dragon shifters…but nope, not BigFoot.

Ballard huffs, grunting under his breath, before storming to the door.

"Where are you going?" Paige calls after him.

"To explore," he growls, slamming out of the room and banging shut the door.

"What a baby," I mutter.

Maybe pissing Ballard off isn't the right thing to do as he could literally kill me in my sleep seeing we're sharing a room. But I won't let him walk all over me.

Paige sits in the middle of her bed with her legs crossed in front of her. "I don't think he liked your response."

"And I'm not a fan of being manipulated."

"He's really not that bad," she tells me; her voice is sympathetic. "He's always looked out for me and even protected me from two Moon Wolves, who last year tried to hurt me in a revenge attack."

I cross my arms. "Moon Wolves wouldn't touch Sun Wolves."

Paige arches an eyebrow. "You've been away from Fable for too long, Wynter. There's a huge gap between how people behave when those in authority can see, and what happens in the shadows. The pack members hate each other worse than ever before, and Moon Wolves have changed. They're not all submissive like you remember."

I nod, thinking of Hunter. "I've noticed."

"Then be prepared to be stabbed in the back by any of *them*, rather than one of your own." She studies me for a long moment. "I know you're close with Hunter, but these are the Wolf Games. Only the fearless win. Look, Ballard's suggestion isn't as wild as it sounds."

Paige flops onto her back on the bed, stretching out her legs and crossing them at the ankles. "My plan is to let Ballard protect me…"

She doesn't finish her sentence.

Wow, I underestimated Paige. She's sneaky. At first, I assumed she was in over her head. Except, she's more cunning than I expected… maybe even more so than me.

"Hey Wynter, what's the deal with you and Hunter, anyway?" Paige asks. "Everyone knows he's got a huge crush on you, but you know your mom will murder their whole pack before allowing you to pair up with him."

Tell me something I don't know.

I sigh, climbing across my bed to sit on the side that faces Paige. It feels like a long time ago that we were friends at school, and things have changed. Plus, I won't forget that she snubbed me at the initiates' gathering.

Any friendship she shows me is a lie. She'll be using me like she's using Ballard. It *almost* makes me feel sorry for Ballard.

She comes from one of the Sun pack families who are positioned at the lowest rank of the Sun Wolves. Ever since her eldest sister took off to live in Romania, after falling in love with a dragon shifter, her family name has been tainted. Mom dislikes them, though she'll never show it in public. If she had it her way, she'd ship the whole family to Romania.

Fable wolves hate outsiders or other supernaturals. It's why Mom had such a hard time from locals when it came to Dad. And why I assume she pretends like he never existed now.

"Hunter's a friend, that's it," I say, not wanting her to think he may be my weakness.

"And Ri?" she queries, taking me off guard.

"He's the enemy. An arrogant ass. And most likely extremely broken, if today's performance is anything to go by."

She's still looking at me with that inquisitive look as though she doesn't believe me.

"You know every girl in Fable wants Ri...?" Paige presses. "They're all holding bets on who'll be the first to kiss him."

I lean forward, something in my chest squeezing.

"They do?" I find myself asking a bit too eagerly.

Paige bursts out laughing, pushing herself to sit up in bed. "I knew it. You're *so* into him."

Asshole.

I rear away, leaning back on my hands and trying my best to look as disinterested as possible. She's laughing, but I hate how bad I am at keeping a poker face instead of playing it cool.

"Under no circumstances am I interested in Ri," I insist.

Way too little too late.

"Sometimes, Wynter, it's the Big Bad Wolf who can turn out to be the true love of your life." Paige winks.

This time, I break out into a laugh. "I didn't realize

you still believed in fairy tales. Anyway, what's going on with you and Ballard? Are you two an actual item now?"

She shrugs and looks away. "It's complicated."

A light knock at the door steals my chance to ask more questions.

Paige jumps up and runs to the door, and I lean sideways to see who it is, half expecting it to be Ballard, as if he's suddenly learned some manners.

Instead, Paige backs up into the room, carrying a food tray. She takes it to the small table in the corner. "Looks like they aren't going to let us starve."

I stroll over to join Paige.

Paige paws at the variety of sandwiches, which are cut into triangles and lined up on the tray. There's a bottle of apple juice and three plastic tumblers.

"Looks so business-like," I tease.

"This doesn't give me hope for the meals here." Paige pulls out the only two egg sandwiches, before flopping down and eating them.

I eye her because the egg ones are always my favorite. So, I go for one with turkey and cranberries, then settle down to eat it, not realizing how hungry I am, until I'm reaching across for my fourth one.

"Ballard better return soon or he's going to miss out," I mumble around the sandwich.

"Tough luck for him, right?" Paige grins.

I really can't work out Paige. I thought she was here more or less as Ballard's reward for fighting. I expected her to support, comfort, even love him. Instead, he'd be wise to mistrust her as much as I do.

I take the time to enjoy the food as I have a feeling it's about to get crazy quickly.

Paige rubs her stomach and yawns. "That's it for me." She strolls back to her bed and lies down, closing her eyes without another word.

I get up and stare outside into the gorgeous woods, figuring I ought to enjoy the peace, before Ballard returns. Then I study the shelves, where every piece of clothing is white. I shudder. It's like joining a cult. I wander closer, and run my finger over the books on the bottom shelf. They're mostly about the animal kingdom, but I'm not going to be fussy. I randomly select one, climb into bed, and crack open the book.

Suddenly, the *thump* of the door opening makes my eyes snap open.

Wait, why's the room dimly lit? Outside the windows, it's pitch dark. It's night already? The book I was reading has fallen off onto the floor.

I must have fallen asleep.

Paige jolts out of her bed at the sight of Ballard darting into the room with dread on his face, tossing the blankets to the floor. Sleep clings to her.

"What the hell's going on?" she blurts.

Ballard lunges onto his bed, gasping for air, just as a loud knock comes on the door.

"What did you do?" Paige hisses. "Have you landed us all in trouble?"

"I almost got busted," Ballard whispers.

Paige looks more furious than concerned for Ballard.

Instantly, a guard stalks into the room.

I stiffen and jump to my feet, as does Paige.

With hands behind his back, the guard with short cropped black hair and the darkest eyes I've seen, marches across our bedroom, staring at our beds. Then he pauses besides Paige's but glares at both of us.

I'm kicking myself now for letting myself doze off.

"Your bed must be made at all times. The room is to be kept clean," he instructs. When no one responds, his brow furrows. "What are you waiting for?" he barks. "Make your bed now! You have until the count of five, or you'll be doing laps around the academy until dawn."

Nope, that's not happening.

While Paige gasps in shock, I turn and quickly straighten my blanket and pillow, which are mostly just scrunched up from my sleep.

"Five," the man begins.

Frantically, Paige jumps to fix her bed, shoving the edges of her untucked blanket under the mattress and folding it just below the pillow, which she fluffs.

The guard's counting down fast but before he reaches *two*, I'm already standing by my made bed.

Paige huffs but spins toward the guard with her bed done, just as he says, "One."

A single nod is all he offers. "There'll be random inspections, so never let your guard down. That is the only time I'll be soft on your team. Now, follow me."

I'd hate to see him being hard on us.

When the guard turns, I exchange confused looks with Paige. She shrugs.

Ballard has already fallen into formation behind the

guard. Paige and I scramble right after them, and my pulse thumps loudly in my ears.

"What's going on now?" Paige demands.

"The first Night Games are about to commence," the guard replies, over his shoulder.

Night Games? I mean, it could be fun...or sexy...right?

Yet why do I think it'll be more terrifying?

We prowl down the hall and grand stairs. At the base, we take fast steps to the right, down a dark passage, taking twists and turns. Soon, I'm completely lost.

We approach the glint of flickering light: fire torches sitting on metal brackets on the wall.

The guard leads us through a doorway. Ballard glances at us once over his shoulder, offering a confident smirk, which feels like it's meant to reassure us. Our pack enters an underground basement. It's musty, smelling old. Everything's made of cement: the floor, ceiling, and pillars. There are arched passageways all around us, and darkness yawns from within each one.

"What is this place?" I ask.

The guard stands tall before the three of us; his gaze weighs heavily on me, and his face is stoic. "Each pack has been given a different starting point in these tunnels. The first pack to escape the academy castle will win."

"What's the prize?" Ballard asks smugly, his chin lifted high.

Of course that's his only concern.

"The winners will get to choose their weapons to use next. If you're serious about becoming the next Alpha of

Fable, then you'll do anything to make sure Sun Wolves win."

He grins, meeting each of our gazes, and seeming to enjoy terrorizing us.

Ballard, on the other hand, is smirking. His eyes are filled with absolute resolution that he's going to win. Where he lacks humility, he embodies ambition and brutal determination. For a moment, I try to imagine what sort of Alpha he'll make.

Ruthless, reckless, and unapologetic.

Somehow, I fear he may be worse than Mom. Power has a funny way of corrupting people to their very core.

My heart sinks at the thought of him in a position of power, along with the knowledge that I'll be forced to take his side as his mate.

I'll die...or kill...before that happens.

Suddenly, the lights go out, and we're plunged into darkness.

Oh shit!

CHAPTER 15

RI

*I*n Ireland, my older cousin would whisper tales to Brey and me of a shadow monster. *Its claws and fangs are longer than any normal wolf,* he'd say with wide eyes, *and it's wild, bestial, and primal. Be careful, or if you're bad, you'll wake up one night and the shadow monster will be* you.

My cousin is dead now.

And it turns out that one night…he was right.

I howl, pulling at the shackles that bite into my wrists. I've been stripped to only my jeans, and I shiver in the freezing cold. My chest is purpled with aching bruises (Thiago truly loves his job). My back rubs against the rough stone of the cell that the bastard instructors locked me in, after chaining me up.

Fair play, Fable Academy have the whole dungeon vibe down.

My wolf fights hard against the panic of being chained, as I blink hard like that'll help me see in the black. How long will I be kept down here?

Dark. Alone. Dark.
The smell of Irish linen.
Screams and pain.

I bite the inside of my cheek to ground myself. It's like the assholes know that the dark is the worse punishment for me. It worms through me, threatening to drag me under, back to the worst night of my life, when I went from being prince to prey.

Darkest shadows, do they know how much it'll hurt me?

How could I've let myself lose control like that in front of all the other initiates? I may as well have presented my balls to them on a silver platter.

Have I blown my chance at becoming Alpha?

My breathing becomes ragged, and the web of scars across my back itch.

I howl again, rattling the chains. My wolf is desperate to break lose again, and I'm struggling to control him.

Is Brey okay? I could kick my own arse for being separated from her like this. Can I trust the Sun and Moon Wolves not to gang up against my pack, now that I'm in here?

I wince, as my cheek burns from the cut that Wynter nicked with her wolfsbane dagger. I close my eyes in resignation. What did I expect from a Sun Wolf, right? Did Thiago set up the entire fight to trigger me?

By the shadows, the thought of being Wynter's king crosses my mind. If I win, I'll place her on the throne. I was born to be an Alpha. Jack can bite my arse: I don't care anymore that she's a Sun Wolf, she'll share the throne alongside me.

But does a shadow monster even have a shadow?

I hiss a quick breath as memories assault me. Desperately, I try to hang onto good memories from my life, before I lost everything: the bracing sea salted air, Da drinking his favorite Irish whiskey after a long day with the Council, and the rain.

But I can't.

Dark. Alone. Dark.

The smell of Irish linen.

Screams and pain.

I bang the back of my head against the wall but even when I open my eyes, I'm still lost in the black...and then I'm lost in the black of that night a year ago in my home in Ireland.

And I can't escape the memory.

Gasping, I'm shocked out of sleep in my soft bed by the rake of claws down my back.

It's agonising and burning. The claws have been dipped in wolfsbane, and I scream, as I'm pressed into the bed. My face is smothered into my pillow, and all I can smell is Irish linen.

I can't breathe, I can't breathe, I can't...

I struggle, but there's a sudden growl, low and aggressive beside my ear. I freeze.

There's a huge wolf on my shredded and bleeding back, standing on me like I'm a conquered trophy. His puffs of breaths are hot against my skin, blowing my curls to the side. Then the wolf lowers his fangs to scrape along the back of my neck, preparing to bite.

Great Shadow Wolf, save me...

"Prince...our prince," the screams echo from the castle hallway, calling for me.

I thrash harder at the sound of my personal guards, yelling for me and struggling to save me. But then, I flinch at the howls and screams, which are suddenly cut off.

Silence.

Why would the Moon Wolves attack us? I smell their scent. We weren't at war with anyone. How could any wolf be cowardly enough to ambush another pack at night and kill them in human form in their beds?

The wolf pushes his claws more deeply into my back; blinding pain shoots through me. Then his teeth begin to bite...

Brey's scream rips through my consciousness from her room next to me. It's piercing, terrified.

I stiffen and something inside *snaps*.

I roar, and my eyes flash. My teeth sharpen as my nails become claws.

The wolf on my back flinches away like he can sense the change that's come over me — *fears it.*

I'm snarling, thrashing, *howling* my rage. Then I surge backward, throwing the wolf off me. I twist around and...

Everything is lost in a whirl of red, red, and red.

I don't remember anything that happens next in the haze, until I'm standing in front of Brey, coated in blood, and panting.

I taste tangy copper, as I run my tongue over my scarlet lips and fangs. Tufts of fur are caught in my claws, and all I feel is a fierce triumph.

Brey's staring at me like she doesn't even know who...or what...I am. She shoves a dead wolf off her bed. I can see the hilt of her favorite dagger, which she sleeps with under her bed, sticking out of its throat.

When Brey stalks warily to my side, we're two deadly creatures.

"I saw them drag Da past my door," she whispers; her voice is raspy with tears. "I'd guess to the throne room."

I nod.

Silently, we step out into the stone corridor, stepping over our murdered pack. Brey clings to my arm, and each time we see one more lost member...our cousin, tutor, friend...we whisper to the Great Shadow Wolf to accept their shadow, and the primal creature I've become, grows stronger.

The throne room is in darkness but the windows are high and arched; moonlight spears down across the vast stone chamber and the wolf carved throne. I love it in here; Da told me this would one day be my throne, unless someone challenged me for the right to sit on it.

Tonight, the Moon Wolves have mockingly dragged Da's savaged and bleeding body to sprawl in his throne.

Brey gasps, running to kneel next to him. She lays her head in his lap.

I shudder. Da looks so like me, it's as if I'm seeing my future, beaten self.

Inside, I howl. My world has been burned. Nothing

can ever be the same again. Outwardly, I prowl to Da and take his hand. To my shock, his fingers squeeze mine, and his blue eyes stare up at me with shattering intensity.

"You'll soon be king of a broken throne," he rasps. "Ruler over nothing but death. Promise me, you'll protect each other."

Brey and I nod.

I attempt to smile at Da around my fangs, but what must he think of me?

Why isn't he saying anything about what I've become?

"We'll get him to the healers." Brey's hands clutch Da's torn pajamas like she can hold him forever; tears stream down her cheeks. "He'll be fine."

"Healers are dead," Da wheezes. "Everybody's dead, apart from my clever son and daughter."

"Then we'll run and…" Brey bites her lip.

"*You'll* run." Da's wracked with a coughing fit; blood seeps down his chest. "The Moon Wolves are nothing but slaves. They're puppets to the Sun Wolves. Don't trust either pack. I tried…to create a compassionate and fair rule for our pack. And look where it led. I'm sorry…"

"Don't," Brey begs. "Don't, please, by the shadows, *please.*"

I don't know if she's pleading with him to not be sorry or not to slip into death and leave us, alone and in the dark, in a castle of the dead.

Either way, it doesn't work.

Da's hand falls out of mine.

I rest my hand on Brey's shoulder. "You have to leave."

Brey twists to me in shock. "And what about you, bro?"

My eyes blaze, and I snarl. "I'm going to *hunt*."

And I do...in a blaze of crimson death.

I shake my head, struggling to rise back to the present: shackled in a cell in Fable Academy. Why are my cheeks wet?

I should've become the next Shadow King but instead, I became the Shadow Monster.

I take desperate breaths and struggle to slow my heart. My temples throb.

I'm here, now, in the musty scented dungeon. And I have to get my arse in gear, if I'm going to become Fable's Alpha.

As a king without a kingdom, the Wolf Games are my only chance to make things right. But if I live in the past, then I'll mess things up. Yet Wynter doesn't understand the true dangers around her.

Can I be blamed for trying to get her not to enter the games? The thought of someone else close to me dying makes me want to rip out my own heart.

I've lost enough already, right?

My pack is dead. My castle and village burned to the ground. The blame was pinned on my sister and me.

I hate the other two packs: I don't trust or respect them.

Sun Wolves are ruthless schemers.

Moon Wolves are cowardly slaves.

I wish that Wynter could see it. Except, I can't share my past with her. Perhaps, I can't hide my scars, but that night is like a shard of glass lodged in my heart.

I'm damaged, broken.

Cursed shadows, I know it.

I can't break Wynter as well.

But I will take Fable as my new kingdom, and finally as Alpha, I'll avenge the murder of my pack.

My eyes flash, and I tip my head back and howl my rage into the black.

The packs are already turning on themselves in Fable. It's happening with supes everywhere. The weather is becoming more extreme; we turned against nature, and now it's turning against us.

This is the end of the world. My inner wolf feels it. What matters now is how we face our fate.

Do we hide or bite back?

I startle, as suddenly, the heavy cell door bangs open.

I squint against the light, which streams through, as my retina's burn. I struggle to make out Thiago's silhouette.

"You're lucky, Shadow pup, that you're being let out after your pathetic display," Thiago says, coldly. "But it's the first Night Games, and every initiate must take part. At least you know the punishment if you lose control again. Only next time, I may just forget to let you out. Do you want to battle to become Alpha or be locked forever in the dark?"

A scream rings through the darkness.

Who the hell was that?

I flinch, raising my hands in defense... but it's not like I can see a thing, not even my hands in front of my face.

Goosebumps dance over my skin at the eerie feeling.

Of course, it sucks balls. I'm stumbling in the dark in this room with my poor hybrid vision, while those around me are full breed wolves and can make out some shadows in the night. At least, Hunter once told me that about his pack.

So, I'm at a huge disadvantage.

Exhaling loudly, I slide a foot forward along the cement floor, then another.

We've been at the academy less than a full day, and we're being thrown head-first into danger after danger. If I knew, I would have at least kept my blade on me. I don't even have my coat.

I don't know if I'm in more of a hurry to get out of here because of the screams or because I'm freezing my ass off.

Guess the lesson to learn is mine. *Get your shit together, Wynter.*

Rubbing the chill from my arms, I call out, "Paige, Ballard, are you here, guys?"

Footfalls slapping the concrete floor are my only response, and they're fading away like they're running in the opposite direction.

"Hey," I move forward in slow motion in the same direction, my hands out in front of me to avoid face-planting into a wall or pillar, "wait for me."

Midnight Goddess, it reeks in this basement. I scrunch my nose at the pungent stink.

"Paige," I try again, but there's no response. *Nothing.* "Guys, you do remember this is a *team* effort," I say louder, putting emphasis on the word, *team.*

Silence.

I glance around, as if that's going to make any difference. "You know, assuming you're both okay and not the ones screaming," and weirdly, I feel a twinge of concern for my pack mates who've left me on my own, "then you both really suck!"

Why am I surprised that Ballard took off and left me? Of course, Paige is just following him.

Frustrated, I keep edging through the room. Sure, I may be blind in this mission, but I sure as hell am not going to lose.

The toe of my shoe hits something, and the next thing I know, I'm falling forward.

"Shit!" I gasp.

My arms pinwheel. I hit the hard floor with my knees, then hands, and wince. The ache shoots up my legs, and involuntarily, tears spring into my eyes at the pain.

By the sun, for all I know, the guard is watching me with infrared goggles and laughing to himself. The thought alone has me pushing myself to my feet once more. I dust my knees, ignoring the pain, and straighten my back.

I stick my hand out and raise my middle finger just in case he's watching.

Flipping off the dark is a great way to reduce frustration.

Then I take a deep breath and push my way on again but more carefully this time. I use my hands, swaying them outward for anything in my way. The moment my fingers brush against the cold stone wall, I nearly cheer.

"I've got this," I mumble to myself, sliding my flat palm along the rough wall.

The wall abruptly turns right, and I'm hit by an icy breeze.

A tunnel.

Okay, now I *do* cheer.

A breeze can only mean a way out, right?

It seems I'm in this alone, as Ballard has zero clue what teamwork means.

I cuss under my breath, clenching my jaw, as I work my way through the pitch black. I tap along the bumpy surface of the stone wall.

When suddenly voices sound from up ahead, I rush, praying that I've gone down the right tunnel.

The wall goes abruptly left this time, and again, I follow it. The heavy stink of freshly dug earth grows stronger, but it comes with a swoosh of air like someone's left a window open.

I must be close to an exit.

Please, Goddess...

Another scream pierces the silence, and I almost jump out of my skin. Whoever that was sounds like they're only feet from me.

I shudder and plaster my back to the wall. My breaths are lodged in my lungs.

"What the hell is going on?" I mutter.

My heartbeat pounds in my ears, as I try to take deep breaths to calm down.

For a split second, I have a terrifying thought that something's hunting us down here. The instructors wouldn't do that to us... would they?

Tightening my grip on the wall, I start shuffling sideways. I have no idea how long I've been following this wall, but it's definitely taking me in a circle. If I somehow end up back in the basement, I'll be so pissed.

When something sharp jabs me in the shoulder, it's *me* who screams.

Snarling, I whip around with my fists raised. "Who's there?"

"Wynter, it's me, Parker," a deep voice whispers.

I exhale loudly.

I'm desperate to hug Parker madly, the charming Moon Wolf who's Hunter's foster brother, and not something *hunting* me in the black, but I'm worried that I'll end up leaning forward and hugging the air or worse, smacking my face into his.

"Crap, Parker, you scared me."

"I am a scary wolf."

I pat the air in front of me, and my hand hits Parker square in the face.

There, see, called it.

"*Ouch*," Parker groans. He reaches out and calmly takes hold of my hand. "You can't see anything in here, can you?"

"Is it that obvious?"

"Well, only *after* you slapped me in the face," he teases. I wince. "But it's really dark here, and I can barely make out a few shadows myself. You're going the wrong way."

"I am?" *Of course I am.* "Can you point me in the right direction?" I plead. I smile at him, although I doubt he can see me. "It's more than my own team has done to help me."

"No one said we can't help each other, right? Plus, Hunter would kick my ass, if I didn't." Parker drags me closer to him. We're now shoulder to shoulder, and I feel his warm breath on my cheek, as he says, "Now, the next step is tricky."

"Okay, I'm listening." I stare into darkness, gripping onto Parker's arm tightly; my fingers curl around a strong bicep, which when flexed is super distracting.

I had no idea he was this chiseled. When did this happen?

Hunter asked his pack to look out for me, and it

does funny things to my insides that he always has my back. I'll take the Moon Wolves' help any day of the week over the Sun Wolves'.

Mind you, Parker has always been sweet to me. He has a way of giving me this adorable smile, and it's how I'm picturing him now. He has the kind of smile that lights up a room... It's something I used to find cute about him.

"We need to move to the center of the room; there's a passage there from what the others have been saying. But the killer is that there's a dip, which can cause us to fall down. At least, that's my guess from the screams and shouts. I think it's a game of luck, whether you fall down...or whether you land in the right place."

"Then we go slowly." I hold onto his muscles even harder now.

"I've got you," he reassures.

I seriously could hug Parker right now... and it has nothing to do with finding out if he's as built all over as his arm.

"On one," Parker instructs, nudging me forward.

We take a step forward.

Instantly, I feel the sharp decline of the floor beneath my foot.

I grit my teeth. Parker's warm and steady next to me. I force myself forward.

The moment I take another step, there's a hard shove of a hand in the middle of my back. "Who…?"

Instantly, my feet slip out from under me, and I cry out.

Then I'm falling, while I'm simultaneously sliding furiously fast downward, feet first.

My hand's ripped away from Parker, who's shouting something at me, but I can't hear him.The slope is as steep as a slippery slide. Air buffets against my face, tearing at my hair and clothes. I'm screaming like all the others have done, then I hear Parker yelp.

Is he okay?

Next thing I know, I'm flying right off an edge and am dropping straight down.

My yells echo around me. My throat is raw, and I fling my arms and legs out, attempting to find anything to catch myself.

I'm going to die here.

All I know is that if I end up dying, I'm coming back as an angry ghost and haunting Ballard for eternity for rushing off without me.

An angry ghost who may just accidentally cut his neat hair and suits that he's so proud of, at the same time as making sure that he never becomes Alpha.

I hit the ground, landing on my hip and on something soft. Still, I groan, especially when something wet soaks through the back of my pants.

"Well, this sucks." I rapidly push myself to my feet, my hands pushing against the moist moss beneath me.

Where the hell am I?

There's another scream, which sounds so far away. But there's no grunt of Parker crashing to land next to me.

Were these traps built in as part of the game and do they deliberately separate the packs?

Who the heck shoved me up there to make me fall?

"Parker," I call out; my voice echoes around me.

No response.

If some of these holes lead out of the tunnels and some don't, please don't let me have fallen down the wrong one.

I scramble to my feet and squint, desperate to see something. But still, nothing surrounds me but blackness. Slowly, I take a step forward and then another. I hold my arms out in front of me, as I search for something to hold onto and gain my bearings. My knees shake on each step.

It's deathly silent in here, and my skin pricks with the freezing cold.

I'm not weak. I won't fail these games. Yet I also can't deny that this test is freaking me out. Do the instructors know that they're playing to my *weakness*?

When I hear a scraping sound behind me, I freeze.

That's not the kind of noise I want to hear.

Come on universe, give me a break.

The scratchy noise fills the void again, and it's growing louder, as if it's coming toward me.

Don't let me be right about us being hunted.

I glance over my shoulder to stare into the darkness; a shiver races up my spine. "Hello?" My voice comes out shaky.

Nothing.

A swoosh of air rushes past me. I might've just yelped.

"This isn't funny," I growl.

It has to be one of the other initiates, right? *Please, let it be them.*

I whip around, seeing nothing, of course. I'm getting really sick of being unable to see.

"Who are you?" When no response comes, I continue, "That's fine. Really, you've done enough. You've shown me the way out."

Reverse psychology always used to work when Dad did it on me.

A deep chuckle filters through the darkness. It's male, that much I can tell and in human form. At least the academy isn't using other supes to hunt us then.

Yet.

After today, I wouldn't put anything past them.

Footsteps approach me, and I stand tall, trying my best to look his way and appear like I can see in the dark.

"So, you're lost," he says.

His voice is deep, gravelly, *and Irish.*

Why in the name of the wild wolves does it have to be Ri? Last time we were together, he lost control and could have easily sliced my head off with his ax or by the way he'd lost himself to his primal side, savaged my throat with his fangs.

Now, I'm stuck with this crazed, supposed murdering wolf. Just great.

Maybe being alone was a better option.

"Ri," is the only word I seem capable of voicing, as warmth spreads over my body, while a shiver curls around my spine. Even my body can't decide how it wants to react around him.

"Not who you were expecting? Did your boyfriend, Hunter, abandon you?"

"He's not my boyfriend," I snap back a bit too quickly; mentally, I kick myself.

"Aye, right."

"Anyway, what are you doing here? I saw the guards drag you away for going all…crazy."

I hear the hitch in Ri's breath, and I regret that I've touched a sore nerve.

"It's like this, see, no one gets to miss out on these fun missions. Are you going to stir yourself and move or are you hiding down in this cellar tunnel for some reason?"

"Wait, you know where we are?" I step forward and bump right into him, chest to chest, also stepping on his feet in the same move, and I instantly bounce backward.

"Careful." His hand snatches my wrist, holding me close.

I may just die of embarrassment. I want the earth to open up and swallow me. When that doesn't happen, I embrace the darkness for once. This way he can't see me burning as red as a tomato.

"I'm sorry," I murmur..

"You're blind in here, right?"

I swear I hear mirth in his voice and huff, while wrenching my hand from his grasp. "I'm fine on my own."

"Well, I'll be impressed to watch you fall on your arse...on your own."

"You can't see me right now, but I'm narrowing my eyes really hard at you."

He laughs and grabs my arm again, then pulls me alongside him. "I'll help you."

"Why?" I stumble to keep up with him. He's practically running, and I'm holding my free hand in front of me to avoid bumping into anything else. "And if you're trying to so-called accidentally get me to slam into a wall, you won't even see my revenge coming."

He's laughing again. Why does it have to be the most perfect sound I've ever heard?

I get now why Ri has the females in the packs forgetting just how dangerous he is.

It's a neat trick.

"Will you stop fussing?" He says. "I'm helping because I scared you earlier today and I want to make it up to you."

"You do?" I snort. "Are you sure you didn't hit your head when the guards took you away?"

He pauses, and suddenly we're facing each other. His hot breath gusts across my face, and I feel the heat of his body in front of me. We aren't touching, but we may as well be.

My heart is doing that crazy thing where it's beating too fast with excitement. For a ludicrous moment, I think Ri's going to kiss me.

He moves with deliberate slowness closer, until I feel the faint graze of his lips against my ear. Instantly, my heartbeat jackhammers into hyper mode.

Ri sniffs me. "By the shadows, I almost get the impression you want to lose this mission. Self sabotage is a real thing. I just can't work out why you'd want that."

I stiffen and pull away from him, startled by his brazen accusation. "Maybe the real reason is because I don't know who *you* really are. Why should I trust you blindly?"

I give a bitter laugh at my own pun.

"Who I am?" How is it possible to hear someone smirking? "Rumors say I'm dangerous. But the Great Shadow Wolf knows that I won't harm you, if I can help it."

"Wow, way to instill confidence."

"Take my hand," Ri demands.

"*Hmm.* Remain alone in a musty cellar or whatever this place is, or go with a self-proclaimed dangerous wolf. Let me think..."

"Nay, *I never* said I was dangerous." He clutches onto my hand without warning. "Come on, let's go. You're stubborn enough to stay here and you know the instructor will leave you here all night to teach you a lesson."

"I don't trust you," I say but don't pull my hand back because dammit he's right, and that fear of being left down here all night has me walking faster.

I lean against him to help keep my footing steady.

"Fine," Ri snarls, but I can hear the anguish underneath that he's trying to mask, and it surprises me, "I don't need your trust."

We don't stop, not even when the faint tingle of what can only be cobwebs clings to my face. I flinch and frantically wipe it away, running my hands across my face.

Abruptly we swing left, and I trip over my own feet,

but Ri's got his hand snapping around my waist, steadying me.

"Hey, give a girl some warning," I growl.

Ri's arm tightens around my waist, holding me closer. Is it suddenly hot in here? And why is his touch like fire?

Except, I can't quiet the unease: I've needed Parker and Ri's help tonight. Both the Moon and Shadow pack have helped me in the first Night Games: *rival packs*. I was abandoned by my Sun Wolves. What will happen, when things become more serious and the other packs no longer look out for me?

How am I going to win these games, when as a hybrid, I don't have all the wolf attributes? I may have won the first mission earlier by turning my weaknesses into strengths, but I'm floundering on this one.

Did Thiago set this up to make a point?

"I think this is the way. Can you hear the voices?" Ri asks.

I try to listen, but right now, my ears are flooded with the banging of my out-of-control heartbeat.

Just then, however, a faint voice reaches me too.

"Yeah, I hear it," I say, excitedly.

Immediately, we begin to sprint. Up ahead, a faint light flickers around the outline of a door.

"And you say you don't trust me," Ri pants. "That's our exit."

Next thing I know, we're at the door, and he's pushing it, but it won't open.

"Stay back," he orders.

Thump. Thump.

A creak of wood sounds, and I can only imagine he's either kicking the thing or ramming his shoulder into the door.

"The bastard thing's locked and not opening," he growls.

"Okay, do you have anything small and sharp on you?" I pat my pockets, checking them as well.

Just as he says, "Nay, nothing," my fingers graze one of the diamante hairpins in my back pocket. Mom has these all over the house and in my room with the hope that I'll make it my thing to wear them. How they got into my pocket is anyone's guess, but right now it's a lifesaver.

"I've got a bobby pin. Let me try." I shuffle forward, until I find the door, then run my fingers over an old fashioned keyhole. I kneel down and pry open the pin. Slowly, I jab it inside and pray this works.

"So, I'm learning new things about you all the time," Ri says. "Like the fact that the Alpha's daughter is an expert at breaking and entering."

"Ha, I'm far from being an expert, but I had a friend at high school who often got locked out of her own home, as she had asshole parents, so she taught me a few things. It's a handy trick to have. I'm sure you have a bunch of secrets no one knows about."

"Don't we all," he replies, mockingly.

Part of me wants to keep pushing and see if he'll open up about the rumors I've heard about him.

"I shared one of my secrets, your turn."

It's worth a try, right?

I jiggle the pin, and when nothing happens, I fold the pin back and try again.

After a pause, Ri replies, "I hate broccoli."

"Are you kidding me?" I twist around toward him, even though I can't see him. "There's no way that's equivalent to my secret. Try again."

He huffs. "Fine, if it'll make you get this door open faster. I have brilliant sight, and I'm not just bragging."

I roll my eyes at him.

"You just rolled your eyes."

I gasp because that's crazy. It's pitch black in here.

"Can I help it if you're a wee doubter? Everything I say isn't a lie, right? The dark doesn't pose a problem for me, unlike most other wolves."

"That's kind of impressive, but don't get a big head or anything. It's not a compliment." I turn back to the door.

Finally, when that click sound comes, I give a *whoop*. "Now, that's how it's done."

I leap to my feet and pry open the door to a yard outside where tiki torches pepper the grounds, their glow glinting against the fresh snow.

"We made it." *I'm* bragging now.

"Aye, we made it together." It makes something squirm inside me at how amused Ri sounds.

Ri hurries out right behind me, and we swagger forward side by side.

Eight pairs of eyes are glancing our way.

Damn, so everyone is out already...? *That means we're last.*

I can't deny that I'm upset. But at least we made it

out, right? The thing is, I won the last test, so it's not like I'm a loser on both. Unlike…

I glance over guiltily to Ri because would he have come last again, if he hadn't stayed to help me?

For the first time, I see the bruises on his face and the tears across his clothes. My gaze skates over how truly built he is, when he stands next to me, how much larger he is with his broad chest and sculpted biceps. *But he's hurt…*

An ache forms in my heart at his pain and what the guards must've done to him.

Why didn't I ask if he was okay?

Why didn't he tell me that he'd been hurt? Did I make it worse, when I held onto his arm?

Yet he doesn't seem phased. Even now, he holds his head high regardless, not seeming to let cuts and bruises stop him; his eyes gleam with fire. With his wild appearance, it looks like he's just returned from forging across the harsh mountain slopes after battling a bear.

There's almost something alluring about him looking so rugged.

Most of the initiates are scowling at us… Well, except Ballard and Hunter, who are giving us death stares.

Brey's huge eyes match her smile at seeing her brother return. No one looks at me that way on my return, not even Parker, who's too busy chatting with Jex.

"Finally, our last two missing pups have arrived," Thiago calls out with a mocking tone.

He's standing stiffly, with his arms by his side, and he's frowning.

Okay, someone isn't happy.

Ri leaves my side without a word and joins his sister, while I stumble toward the crowd. No one comes near me. Not even Paige who's frowning at me too, and not Hunter who hasn't taken his eyes off Ri.

Thiago gives a loud clap, drawing our attention. "The first person to escape from the academy building was Brey, followed by Teo, later followed by Ballard in third place. While your determination is admirable, each of you has failed the core of this mission: Teamwork."

There's distaste in Thiago's voice.

I knew that us Sun Wolves should have stayed together.

Ballard looks sulky; his lips curl like a pouty kid, yet his gaze is on me. He's going to hurt me because he failed, isn't he? I'm going to sleep with my new dagger under my pillow tonight.

Teo groans loudly enough to draw everyone's attention, as frustration flares across his face. There was no way that the Shadow Wolves ever had a chance to win, since Thiago kept Ri locked up and released him late to the games.

That's when I catch Ri staring at me with a strange expression I can't work out, while Hunter is still watching him. Talk about awkward.

"The first group to arrive back as a team and win the first Night Games are the Moon Wolves," Thiago's cool gaze sweeps across Hunter, Parker, and Jex. "You may not be fast, but you're at least capable of obeying and listening to instructions."

Parker and Jex cheer, punching their fists into the air. Hunter smiles but doesn't seem as excited as his pack. In fact, he winces at Thiago's words.

Parker darts a glance at me, as if checking that I'm okay, and when our gazes meet, we exchange a smile.

"Take what you learned from your lesson today and head back to your dorms," Thiago commands. "We start at six in the morning. Seeing as most of you ignored orders on the task and most of you were downright pathetic, you can all take part in a punishment ten laps around the castle at the crack of dawn. Now, in silence, head inside."

I groan, as does everyone else. Then we trudge toward the front of the castle. There's no talking, as guards wait to take us to our rooms. The only voices are Parker's and Jex's; I love seeing how close they are as friends, but they never stop bantering, and it'll bite them in the ass under Fable Academy's tyranny.

Still, good on them for winning, even if it puts everyone else in a pissy mood.

Personally, I'm just glad I made it out. It's weird I have Ri to thank for that. I never expected him to help me. The guy surprises me, or is that his thing? Make people lower their guard, while he plays them?

I shake my head, too exhausted to think straight.

The moment I'm back in the Sun Wolves' dormitory and the door shuts, Ballard is on me. He shoves me up against the wall. I gasp, as the back of my head smacks into the wall.

My pulse is on fire just as fast.

Ballard pushes his face into mine. He's pale with rage.

"You made us a laughing stock out there," he growls, "and cost us the win. And fuck, you partnered up with a Shadow Wolf to complete your mission...? Just drop out of the games already, before you make the Sun Wolves a real embarrassment."

"Get out of my face," I hiss, shaking with anger. I shove my hands into his chest, pushing him back a few steps. "Don't you dare blame me. You left me alone and completely ignored the instructions that we needed to work as a team. If you want someone to blame, then look at yourself for being a selfish asshole."

My breaths are coming fast now. *Of course he'd blame me.*

Ballard's nostrils flare, and his hands curl into fists. "You think I left you behind on purpose...? Don't you understand why I had to try to come first or would caring about anyone but yourself and your precious toy wolves be too hard? Do you have any loyalty to your own pack?"

"Hey, let's not do this," Paige says, her voice too cool and calm. Why does she sound like she's the one in control? "This is what they want. For us to turn against one another."

"Too late, looks like Wynter's already done that." Ballard never lifts his gaze from mine. "What did our win cost you, Wynter? Did the Shadow Wolf ask you to suck his cock, and you couldn't resist?"

"Fuck you!" I lunge at Ballard; my breathing is

ragged. He dodges to the side. "At least I'd be able to find his dick. I bet yours is so tiny that if it'd been you, I'd still be stuck in those tunnels, searching for it."

Ballard snarls, baring his teeth. "So, you did get on your knees for that psycho?"

"Ballard, please," Paige yells, shoving herself between us and facing him. "Think about what you're doing."

What the hell is she talking about?

"Fuck!" Ballard roars and throws his hands into the air.

He turns away from me, breathing hard and pacing from his bed to the table. Paige doesn't even look at me but stands there, watching him.

I'm so mad now, and my eyes are pricking with tears.

How dare they shame me for working with the other packs? If Ri is dangerous, then so are these prejudiced Sun Wolves.

I want to scream, but Ballard's a snake. If I push him further, then he'll strike viciously when I least expect it. It's obvious that he has his sights set on winning at any cost and taking me as his prize. Yet if he has to destroy me to become Alpha, he will.

Clenching my teeth, I march to my bed at the far end of the room and know that I won't be getting any sleep tonight. Not when I'm sharing a room with a ruthless wolf, who thinks that he has the right to own or ruin me.

CHAPTER 17

WYNTER

I gasp for air, convinced I'm going to pass out and die. Every inch of me hurts, including my pinkie toe, which is impossible, but there you have it. Doing laps around the castle in the crazy early hours of the morning is the single most painful sports activity I've ever been forced to endure.

On purpose, I dosed up on my meds this morning to give myself the best chance not to fail this mission from exhaustion. And so far, it's worked.

I drag myself into the mess hall with everyone else. Despite being sweaty, we've been instructed to go straight to breakfast first, then shower. After which, it's a day of theoretical lessons.

And I'm ready to take on anything thrown my way.

The moment I step foot into the vast room, my mouth drops and some form of unintelligible sound tumbles out.

I honestly feel like I've stepped back in time: the iron brackets cradling flaming torches on the black stone castle walls, the tapestries of wolves in battle, the arched ceiling, and the ornate architecture.

I breathe out, before a slow smile spreads across my face. Everything here is so cool.

Long wooden tables and benches line the mess hall, which is made to fit at least a hundred people. At the far end sits a stone staircase that's closed off by a rope.

What's upstairs?

This hall had been designed with the purpose of entertaining a large group of people, not just us nine initiates. So, how did they run the Wolf Games in the past with so many people?

I trail behind Teo to the cafeteria style counter across the room and collect the pre-plated tray of food, as it's shoved into my hands by one of the guards.

"Take a seat," the guard instructs.

Gladly, as my legs are still wobbly from all that running in the snow.

Each pack seems to be sitting on their own house pack table — Sun, Moon, and Shadow — under a banner that bears a symbol of each. It still freaks me out that Shadow Wolves are represented by dark banners with no marking like their true face is veiled even here.

When I glance at the Sun Wolf table, my guts churn. My hands tighten around my tray. As much as my mind tells me that I need to join Ballard and Paige, after last night, I can't stand to be in their company. I barely slept thanks to Ballard, and I don't want to deal with them right now. I feel Paige glancing my way, but I pretend I don't see them and walk past them.

On the table to my right, Ri has his back to me. He's in deep conversation with Brey, and her hand's clasped tightly with his. Teo is ignoring them both, as he eats. The next table over, Hunter doesn't even notice me and has his head down, while Parker and Jex are chatting.

Part of me contemplates going over there, but then what? Make the Sun Wolves hate me even more? I want to say, *screw them*, but that's not how this works.

So, I drag myself to a free table over to the far left of the others.

This is a game to win and everyone in this room is my rival. I'm alone in my pack in the Wolf Games. And while Parker and Ri helped me, I don't know how long it'll last.

I'm bringing my A-game from now on.

I keep my head low and dig into my breakfast of eggs, bacon, and toast. The food is warm and fills me. When I glance up, I catch Ri's gaze. Even from my distance, I see his pupils dilating. What is he thinking?

I look away and pick up the glass of juice and drink half of it, before returning to my meal.

"Had a fight with your team?" Parker asks, as he flops down across the table from me.

Instinctually, I want to tell him to leave, but another part of me is grateful that he cares. Except, I need to remember this is a game to the end, not about making friendships.

"Just needed some time alone after that run," I admit, which is partially the truth. "Anyway, thanks for your help last night."

He shrugs, nonchalantly. "Always got your back, you

know that, but not sure how much I did seeing I lost you shortly after." He gives me a lopsided grin, which has me smirking. He leans forward across the table. "Hey, there's an initiates party out in the woods tonight. You should come too. We're sneaking out after nine tonight to celebrate the TriWolf moon and the Wolf Games."

I haven't heard the word TriWolf in years. It's a phenomenon not too different from a blue moon: a rare type of full moon that has the power for an hour or so to channel the sun as well. After all, we only see the moon because light from the sun falls on it. And that means it's the only night when all three types of wolf can transform freely: Moon, Sun, and Shadow.

Mom always warned that TriWolf was the most dangerous time for us. That's why she banned anyone from going into the woods on those nights. She said that the event made wolves lose control,

Who knows if she's right?

Day and night are separated for a reason, Mom taught me. *And if you're taken over by shadows, then you'll be blinded. What's more dangerous than the three wolf packs coming together unnaturally?*

Plus, haven't we been ordered not to leave Fable Academy?

"Is the party a good idea?" I ask. "I mean, I seriously could do with a good party after all the freaky, but the instructors have big, *big* sticks."

I can't believe I'm the one preaching this to a Moon Wolf. I've never seen one of those break a Sun Wolf's rule in my life. Well, unless you count Hunter, and even then, he's only ever broken them out of love for me.

Why does that make my heart clench?

"Shit's gonna get serious fast at the academy, and this may be our last chance to just have fun." Parker shrugs and reaches over to my plate, stealing a slice of my toast. "I mean, if we get busted, what are they going to do? Send all the initiates home?" He bites into the buttery bread and smirks, finishing it in two more bites. "We're holding it on the other side of the mountain at Demon's Den. We're going to have a huge fire, drinks, and music."

"That place is forbidden." I glance around us, in case the guards are eavesdropping.

Parker's talking about the other side of the mountain where Mom's given strict rules that *no one* is to travel. Where three wolves were found butchered and the killer has never been found. So, it's off limits, though part of me wonders how much of the story is an exaggeration. After all, Mom uses fear to keep pack members under her thumb and close to Fable.

"Well, that makes it more exciting." Parker's practically bouncing in his seat with adrenaline. "There are so many rumors about the Demon's Den. Some say you can hear the screams of the pack members who've died up there."

He's grinning now.

"You seem more excited about that than the party," I tease.

"You know I love horror books, so this is my very own ghost hunting trip. I've always wanted to be the first Moon Wolf to catch a spook. Hey, don't take this away from me."

I roll my eyes, and he chuckles. Evidently, tonight Parker has every intention of hunting ghosts. This should be interesting.

"And everyone's going...?" I find myself leaning forward too, a tingle of excitement surging through me at doing something both forbidden and fun.

Breaking Mom's orders.

Parker's eyes light up. "Yep, Ballard will be there too, unfortunately. So, you're in? We can head off together tonight."

Ballard's going? So, even *he's* breaking Mom's rules.

I half wonder if he'll take the chance to barbecue me over the fire to get his revenge for losing the first team mission. Part of me wants to say *no* to the party instantly at that thought, while the other half insists I'm automatically going.

"Count me in. I don't want to be left out," I say, before I can back out.

I glance over at Ri. Has he been staring at me this morning because he wanted to ask me if I was going to the party? Or wanted to be the one to ask me?

My attention snaps to Hunter, however, who trudges over to my table. He has shadows under his eyes, and his golden hair hangs over his face. His expression is carefully blank.

He sits down across from me too.

"Hey, Wyn," Hunter's voice is darker than normal.

"What's with the doom and gloom?" I ask, lightheartedly and instantly regret it, seeing the way that Hunter glances up at me with that haunted look. "I-I mean, the Moon Wolves won, right? That's fantastic."

"Heck yeah, we've been on a high all night," Parker answers and howls, throwing punches into the air, and drawing everyone's attention.

Yet Hunter turns his attention over to Ri; he doesn't look the slightest bit enthusiastic about the win.

I shouldn't care about Hunter's jealousy, but deep inside, I do. He's a close friend, a guy I've always admired and dreamed about, but I'm starting to see how much harder things between us are going to become, if we let emotions get in the way.

"Give us some space," Hunter orders Parker.

"Tonight, we're on," Parker whispers to me, then strolls back to the Moon Wolves' table.

"What's going on?" I ask Hunter, pushing my plate aside.

Hunter hesitates, before clasping his hands together on the table; his nails are biting into his skin so hard that I think he'll make himself bleed.

"I'm worried about you," he finally says.

My shoulders rear back, and I'm unsure where he's going with his confession. "Why? Did someone say something about me?"

But the voice in my head tells me this has everything to do with Ri, with the darkness in Hunter's gaze last night.

"First, are you safe?"

"What do you mean?"

"The assholes put you in a room with Ballard. Seriously, what the hell is that about? I know he's your pack, and you're the Alpha's daughter, but he's a dick and...it's been killing me that I'm not there to protect you."

I avoid his gaze. "I'm fine."

Hunter studies me; I both hate and love that he knows me too well to believe me. "Look, you know that I care about you and..."

I nod. "Hunter, maybe this—"

"Let me finish," he insists, looking almost astonished that I'd try to stop him. "I don't want you to get hurt, right? So, trust me like when we were kids."

"This isn't just about Ballard, it's also about Ri, isn't it? And what you told me about him."

"Just be cautious, that's all." There's a heartfelt look in his sky-blue eyes.

It used to calm me and remind me that he has my best interests at heart.

But my inner wolf is snarling at Hunter issuing commands like he's Alpha, and I'm *his* already. Is all of this just to get rid of Ri, the competition?

"*Trust me*, Hunter, I've got my eyes wide open. But thanks for always looking out for me," I reply with a smile.

Does it come across as sincere? I hope so because it's not. Inside, I'm freaking out about how this is going to play out. And how I want to desperately tell Hunter that we should just focus on the games, while we're at the academy.

"You know you don't have to ask me to trust you. And I'll always have your back." His expression softens. I must've come across as sincere because he's believed me, and it's chased the haunted look away. Why does that hurt so much? "But how about avoiding that dickish Shadow Wolf to be on the safe side?"

I stare at him, incredulously. Pulling back in my seat, I bite my tongue not wanting to say something I'll regret.

Hunter notices my reaction and leans his forearms on the table. "I'm sorry. Please, don't take this the wrong way, Wyn. But you haven't been in Fable for a few years and things have changed. I'm trying to help."

We're silent for a moment.

But then I can't help myself. "You know, you're right. I'm still catching up on what's going on here, but I also don't need to be told what to do. I get enough of that at home," I say harshly; my heart beats faster.

I hate the paleness sliding over Hunter's face.

He closes his eyes and pulls back as if I've hurt him. "Did you seriously just compare me to your mom after everything...? I'm your friend, concerned, and doing my best to do the right thing. But why am I risking everything, when you don't even want my help?"

Instantly, he's on his feet and stalking away from me, toward the exit.

Flushed, I almost call out to him.

Guilt churns in my gut about what I've said. He was only looking out for me, right? I want to go after him, but perhaps, it's for the best that he's walked away.

He's my rival.

A different pack.

The competition.

And he's a complication I can't deal with at the moment. Just like Ri.

*T*here's a chill in the air.

I've been walking with Hunter and Parker for over an hour through the mountain… Maybe it's two hours. It's hard to tell, when it's only darkness surrounding us. Hunter takes the lead, holding a flashlight and guiding our path along the rough, ascending terrain. My thighs are burning from the cardio workout.

Parker is alongside me, and Teo I'm told is already at Demon's Den setting things up with help from the others. Parker looks smarter than I've seen him yet. Why do I get the feeling he's dressed up for this? Hunter and I haven't exchanged more than a few words since breakfast, and the awkwardness between us makes me regret coming to the party.

I step over a log and pull the collar tightly around my throat. With the cold, I've rugged up in jeans, heavy boots, and two layers of shirts, all under my massive winter coat. It's not normal party attire, but to be fair, I did style my hair in waves around my face and did my best with the makeup Paige brought with her to Fable Academy.

"How do you know where you're going?" I call out to Hunter to break the stifling silence.

"We scoped the place out the day after the initiation gathering," Parker answers instead. "I've heard lots of stories about this spot, and Jex told us about the deaths. That's when I knew we'd be coming here."

He's wearing that excited expression again, and I

can't help but smile at seeing how much he's enjoying himself.

"And you thought, *what a great place for a party?*" I say, sarcastically.

"Exactly!" He smiles to himself. "Look, you don't mind turning up with the Moon Wolves? Ballard's not going to give you a tough time, right?"

"He can try." I shrug.

Hunter remains silent, sweeping the beam of his light across the thick pine trunks, and the snow around us that glistens beneath the light. Each time I look over at him, my gut tightens. Perhaps, tonight I'll be able to set things straight with him and not feel like the worst person in the world. I'll come clean and tell him it's better we focus on the games during our time here. For that matter, I'll stick to myself and focus on the training because I'll need all the help I can get.

"Almost there," Hunter says.

Eventually we leave behind the woods and walk into an oversized clearing that's half the size of a football field. Farther in the distance, the landscape slips away on a sharp rim. Only darkness glances back from its gaping openness, and instantly, I know we're on an enormous cliff's edge. Several crates have been set up along the perimeter to make it clear where we can't walk past for our own safety.

A blazing pit fire roars and crackles in the middle of the area, and I'm drawn to its heat. I have my hands out, chasing away the chill. Up ahead, crates set up in a make-shift bar, lined with red, plastic cups, and a keg. Who'd been the sucker to carry that thing up here?

Ballard's serving himself a drink, while Paige lines up behind him for her chance.

Teo and Brey are mock fighting, sparring with pretend punches, while nearby Jex is setting up a small stereo. Moments later, a fast-beat song is cranked up, and everyone's cheering. I can't help myself and join in as the excitement is contagious.

As much as I had doubts about attending, now that I'm here, I'm smiling because even I deserve time out from the stress. I wasted a lot of time back in New York not attending parties or doing much besides school and staying home. But what's funny is that I haven't felt as sick in Fable as I had back in New York. Maybe it's all the fresh air...or the extra meds I'm pumping into me.

"Wynter, you're getting a drink." Parker pokes me in the arm. He waves for me to follow him, and we pass right past Hunter. My heartbeat jacks up at having him look at me for a change, and I offer him a smile. "Cool party."

He grins back, and that softens the ache in my chest. But Hunter keeps on strolling past me regardless, and I go to collect my drink, which Parker is handing out to me. I glance back to Hunter to notice he's not coming after us. It feels strange, as I'm used to him always being where I am.

Is he coming to the same realization that we're better off apart right now?

Even if my mind knows it's the safest option for us both, my heart still feels like it's been savaged.

I look down at the plastic cup in my hand and swirl

around the cola. When I sniff the contents, a strong hit of sweet alcohol fills my nostrils. "What is it?"

"Coke and bourbon. Figured you'd like it better than the beer," Parker replies.

"And you thought right." I tip my cup at him.

Though in truth, I've only ever tasted alcohol once before, and that's when Dad let me try his whiskey. It was horrible, so I'm hoping this tastes better.

"Here's to a night of partying and ghost hunting!" Parker hollers and knocks his plastic cup into mine. "Now, chug!"

He swings his back and gulps down his drink in seconds.

I take a small sip of mine and surprisingly, it's not disgusting. So, I do as Parker did and drink it all down. Only then does the heat burn across my throat and I'm coughing.

Of course, it's exactly the moment Ballard rocks past us, bumping his shoulder into mine purposefully. I stumble a few steps.

Ballard blurts, "Careful there, *princess*, so that you don't accidentally fall off the cliff in your drunken state."

My mouth falls open at his comment, as he struts away.

"What the fuck did you say?" Parker lifts his chin.

Ballard laughs and throws over his shoulder, "Keep on drinking, little Moon cur, then come and ask me that later."

Parker looks at me with huge, silvery eyes. "I think he just threatened to throw me off the cliff too!"

"He may be crazy enough to do it."

I wiggle my cup at Parker, who takes it and refills it.

"Then we keep an eye on him," Parker says.

I'm nodding and also burning up. "Why do I feel like there's a fire in my chest?"

I laugh at the lopsided look Parker gives me.

"You haven't even tried my infamous tequila shots yet." Parker's eyebrows are wiggling up and down, and his silliness is just perfect.

I've always considered Parker cute, with his dark hair that he always runs his hands through, the sharp cheekbones that might be made of marble, and then there's the way he stands like he's posing for the camera.

"Why don't you have a girlfriend yet?" I tease.

"Who said I don't?" He shrugs and grabs himself another drink. "Want one?"

I shake my head.

He looks uncertain just for a moment. "This isn't you *picking a toy* for the night, right?"

My brow furrows. "What does that mean? Anyway, if you did have a girlfriend, I'd never hear the end of it."

When he returns, he's looking almost sheepish. "Just haven't found my shadowmate yet, I suppose. And yeah, I'm romantic enough to believe in that."

He's sipping his beer now, which I take as him not wanting to talk about girls or shadowmates anymore.

Back by the fire, I notice Hunter standing across the clearing and watching me, while Paige chats to him. Should I join them? He's holding himself stiffly and looks like he wants to be rescued from the other Sun Wolf. After all, I want to enjoy what I'm now deeming my last night of letting loose with him as well.

But as I watch Paige shuffle out of her coat, I can't get my legs to move. She's wearing her slinky black dress. Even though it has long sleeves, it's so thin, it reveals every curve and grabs all the guys' attention. The girl has always been curvy and beautiful, but against the blazing fire, the fabric of her dress gives a sheen like it's transparent.

Suddenly, I feel like I'm wearing a potato sack in jeans, underneath my big coat.

Why would Hunter choose to spend time with me, after I've rejected him...? After I was mean enough to compare him to my mom, who's spent her life tormenting him?

Karma's a bitch.

Hunter looks like he's working hard to only focus on Paige. She says something, and he laughs.

What the hell?

I roll my eyes. "Talk about fake. Why's he pretending to be nice to her, when he hates her guts?"

"She's not that hot," Parker whispers alongside me.

I huff. "W-what? I don't know what you're talking about."

Except, a burning jealousy slides across my chest, when I see Hunter and Paige flirting.

Is that what they're doing?

My inner wolf howls and paces, furious to burst out and savage Paige. My eyes widen. Is this how Hunter feels when he sees me with Ri...or Ri, with Hunter?

Wow, this taste of my own medicine is seriously horrid.

Plus, I'd been the one to push Hunter away, and now look at my reaction. What is wrong with me? I can't deny that I've had a crush on him for as long as I can remember, but coming back to Fable, things feel different. He's not the same wolf, but then, neither am I.

"You know, Hunter and Paige have a tiny history," Parker says, distracting my thoughts.

His words strike me hard.

"What does that mean?" I study Parker, as he finishes another beer, then wipes his mouth with the back of his hand.

"I shouldn't be telling you this. I mean, my bro would kill me if he knew but...whatever happened between them doesn't mean anything. He's got eyes only for you and always has. Plus, Paige has kissed half the guys in town."

My breath hitches. "He kissed her?" My voice may have climbed a bit too high, but thank the Midnight Goddess for the crackling fire, which conceals my words.

"Things have changed in Fable. No one's exactly as you remember them."

An involuntary snarl rolls past my lips. "I wish people would stop telling me that."

"It was a crazy night at one of the banned parties in the woods." Parker waves his hands in the air like he can conjure that night for me. "It'd been a seriously rough day for Hunter and...everyone was kissing everyone.

Paige more or less threw herself at him. *She* kissed *him.* He regretted it big time the next day."

I narrow my eyes, turning my attention back to Hunter and Paige.

Hunter doesn't look like he's regretting the kiss that much now.

Then someone's calling Parker and he leaves my side. Soon, I lose sight of him as he heads into the woods.

I keep telling myself I shouldn't care about Hunter talking to Paige...or having once kissed her.

Perhaps, Ballard knows and cares though. Is that why he's such an asshole to Hunter? I mean, even more of an asshole than normal?

Yet if I don't care, why can't I look away? My heart's pounding so hard that I feel like I may pass out.

When Hunter suddenly touches Paige's hair and leans in close to whisper something to her, I feel like I'm going to hurl. I can picture him kissing her, his hands all over her body, telling her how much he wants her...

When Paige reaches over to place her hand on his chest, Hunter flinches like he's uncomfortable. His expression becomes shuttered, and for the first time, he draws back. Then they walk away from each other.

I watch, as Hunter prowls toward the edges of the party and further into the woods, but not before his gaze darts to me. It's dark and searching.

It's like he's asking me something. But I don't understand.

What was that about? Making sure that I'd seen his

show with Paige? An attempt to incite my wolf to jealousy, after how I'd treated him at breakfast?

Or him honoring my wishes, keeping his distance, and moving on like I'd demanded that he do with every word and action?

I'm an idiot.

Paige strolls away from Hunter with a horrendously gleeful look on her face, as she comes around the fire and toward me.

"Careful, your green scales are showing," she mocks, turning to the drinks table behind me.

I can't move.

My inner wolf scrabbles inside, desperate to escape and rake her claws down Paige's face. Paige, that bitch, knew the whole time that I'd been watching Hunter and her, and how much it'd hurt me. So, she'd flirted with him to spite me. And I'd thought she was being nice to me by letting me use her makeup.

I'm never going to underestimate her again.

The games were in full swing from the moment we stepped foot into this place, and it doesn't matter if it's a party or a mission, they never stop.

Stupid. Stupid. Stupid.

I begin to back away from the blaze a bit too quickly, as my head starts to spin from the bourbon.

It was a mistake to come to this party...to drink alcohol...around others who want to hurt me and see me as the enemy.

How many times have others warned me that I no longer know anyone here in Fable? Not even Hunter, who once told me he'd never treat me differently because I was a Sun Wolf.

But I don't know what to think now.

Quickly, I retreat, leaving behind the fire. Once I reach the woods, I glance back.

Has anyone noticed me leaving?

I turn but stumble right into something, which is as solid as a mountain. I let out a startled *oomph*.

"Watch yourself, pretty wolf," a familiar Irish voice mutters, as I bounce backward from the person I bumped into. "Is there something I should know? You keep walking into me."

Ri's licking the side of his mouth like he's just finished eating ice cream.

"S-sorry." I tilt my head to meet his gaze. He's tall and strong, and I'm desperate to lose myself in his wicked green eyes. But before I can do anything crazy like that, I clear my throat and do the right thing. "I was leaving."

I sidestep past him, when he snatches my hand. "The party's only just begun."

A strange sensation slides over me, and I'm breathing deeply, unable to focus on anything but the way Ri's holding my hand and how his thumb makes small circles on the inside of my wrist.

A strange déjà vu crosses my mind, and when I turn back to him, something deliciously playful flares over his expression. Maybe I'm not the only one who's been drinking tonight, especially when his smile makes me gasp.

One moment, my heart is on fire at seeing Hunter

with Paige, and now it's beating ferociously for Ri. An ache digs into my chest. Is it wrong of me to feel this way and find myself attracted to two guys?

Are wolves only meant to find a single shadowmate?

Yet these two guys are both from rival packs, fighting to become Alpha. Only one of us can win, right?

The moon hangs full and bulbous in the night sky. I can feel the tug to transform. Mom was right about the wildness of the TriWolf moon. I can sense it in all the initiates tonight.

I need to leave this party, before our savage sides burst out into violence.

"Here's the thing of it, see, I owe you an explanation," Ri mutters, before reaching over and pushing a loose strand of hair out of my face.

The tenderness of his touch surprises me.

"What do you mean?"

"I scared you during our training yesterday." He's searching my face for my reaction.

"Oh that! You didn't scare me," I say like he didn't scare me half to death. "But you know, what happened?"

Ri licks his lips again, and I'm left staring at his mouth: it's inviting and kissable.

We're silent for a moment, until he finally speaks again.

"Sometimes my memories haunt me; then they're all I can see. It's like I'm no longer in the present...my mind's lost. But I never intended to harm you and I didn't mean to ruin our first training session."

"You didn't ruin anything," I answer, quickly. "It just took me off guard."

I want to ask him about his memories. What's happened to him that's so traumatic he gets flashbacks? Do they have anything to do with the rumors Hunter told me about?

"Aye, I did." His lips quirk. "It's brilliant of you to pretend it was nothing."

"Well, there's the little fact that you helped me in the mission last night. So, I guess we're even."

I can't look away from Ri, but I pull my hand away from his, needing to leave the party before I do something I'll regret.

The dominant thrum of my wolf, combined with the warmth of the alcohol, is making me bold.

Ballard strolls right past us at that moment like the stalker that he is. He glares at me, then pushes his tongue on the inside of his cheek, his curled hand at his mouth, moving it back and forth to imitate giving head.

Fire scorches across my cheeks. "Asshole."

"Want me to take him out for you? I can toss the bastard over the cliff and into the gorge. No one will know," Ri asks like it's no big deal.

I ice over. *What the hell?* I snap my attention up to Ri, which has him bursting out into a loud chuckle.

"Would you take it easy?" His grin is sharp. "Wynter, you should see your face. Did you think I was serious?"

My muscles untangle, and I nudge his elbow. "Haha, so funny."

Ri's expression darkens. "But I swear on the Great

Shadow Wolf, if that idiot Sun Wolf ever touches you, I'll hurt him. I can become that monster you think I am."

This time, he means every word. Is it wrong that I'm turned on by his offer?

"I can take care of myself." Yet I can't hide my smile. "And why would you say that? You're not a monster... are you?"

Ri ducks his head, and his expression becomes anguished. "The way you looked at me at the training still haunts me like my memories. I felt like the beast I saw in your eyes."

"I-I'm sorry."

"Don't be. I just want you to know I wouldn't hurt you."

He doesn't pull away. Simply having him stand so close to me, as he rests his hand on my arm, fills me with a strange burning sensation. I keep telling myself it's the bourbon; except, it reminds me of the surging adrenaline I used to experience when I called to my inner wolf.

"You're beautiful, you know that?" Ri murmurs.

Wait, he called me beautiful?

"You don't need to say that." I turn away my head.

We're standing by the woods. Shadows dance around Ri, and behind me, the music and voices blare.

I really should go now. But something holds me here.

"Aye, I do." He leans forward, pulling my chin up.

My heart races.

Suddenly, Ri's mouth grazes mine, softly. Then he's kissing me with raw, primal hunger. Our lips crush together like they were always meant to be touching. The taste of beer is on his tongue, as it tangles with mine, and my hands press flat against his rock-hard chest.

Everything falls away into the background, my head spinning with the way he tastes so delicious, how he seems to be wrapping himself against me, how he kisses like nothing else in the world exists but me.

My entire body shivers, and my pulse is racing. His muscles clench under my touch, and a groan slips past my throat.

With it comes the similar sensation from earlier, rising through me once more, the one where I swear I can feel my wolf rising. Except, she's been dormant for the past four years.

But now, she's awakening, being drawn to Ri's wolf.

A snarl rolls through Ri's chest, as if responding to my wolf, and I'm drawn to him in ways I've never experienced before: a desperate need to kiss him harder, to have him sweep me away so we're alone.

I'm trembling with an unbearable need I don't understand, when another growl rolls from my throat.

Ri breaks away, leaving me breathless. "Wynter, I'm loving your dominance. Fair play to you, it's making me hot, but you're shaking something fierce. Are you okay?"

I try to shake my head, but instead, a deep ache pinches in my chest, and I wince, clutching my solar plexus, where the pain burns.

Tremors wrack me, until my knees give out. I hit the

ground, and Ri is there to pick me up, but I push him away.

"Don't—" Another growl tears past my throat, deeper and louder.

Next thing I know, I'm convulsing. I gasp in agony and fear.

What the hell is happening?

My vision blurs in and out; my body hums with the magic of the moon. It strikes me so fast, I can't think beyond the panic gripping me.

I force myself to stumble back up to my feet, needing to get back to the academy and take my meds. But I can't tell what direction I'm staggering, and somehow find myself closer to the fire and the party.

Strong arms reach for me, but I leap back from Ri. Instead, I turn on the spot. My vision sharpens; colors grow vivid. The wave of adrenaline brings a terror that I'm about to pass out from my sickness.

I've never felt this kind of pain before.

Everyone at the party is staring at me. Even Hunter, whose eyes are huge with shock and hurt, as he glares at Ri and then me.

He was in the woods. Did he see the kiss?

Then I notice Ballard's smug expression, and I just know that he's told everyone at the party that he saw us together. Did he hide and watch the kiss as well?

Ri steels himself, before giving me a shaky smile. He holds out his hand to me reassuringly, and I stumble toward him on wobbly legs. That's when I look down at my front white paws. They are huge and so beautiful.

My whole world stills.

I've finally shifted into my wolf after all this time.

My first ever shift has happened on the night of the TriWolf moon. Does that mean something?

My heart beats with harmony because for too long, I assumed that my wolf would be trapped inside forever because I was a hybrid.

That I was broken.

But I'm not.

"Wynter." Ri steps toward me, startling me back to reality.

Someone nearby is laughing. Then another person snickers.

They're laughing at me.

I whimper, ducking my head.

I crave to run through the woods, hunt, and howl at the moon. I'm desperate for the rest of my pack to transform as well and run at my side like the wolves we are.

Instead, they're laughing at the girl who thinks she can win these games but has no control over her wolf. The Sun Wolf who kissed a Shadow Wolf, and had her first ever shift in front of everyone.

This should've been a magical moment between the two of us or only pack.

It's ruined.

A desperate howl is wrenched from me.

Ri lifts his head, baring his teeth at the others. His growls rumble through the air...at the same time as Hunter's.

My two protectors look set to tear out the throats of the other initiates.

But it's too late… the damage is done.

I keep turning on the spot, the world tilting, and breaths coming too fast.

My heart leaps with confusion and the terror that I don't have any control over my wolf.

And everyone's just seen my weakness.

I never should've come to this party in Demon's Den.

I dart my gaze between Ri and Hunter, desperate to weave between both of them. What would it be like to prowl through these woods with both a transformed Moon and Shadow Wolf at my shoulder: not one dominant wolf but *three* under the bright moonlight?

But I can't. Everything is wrecked.

I turn and run.

Ri calls after me, but I don't stop.

My paws hit the snowy ground, and I don't even know where I'm going. All my wolf knows is that if you've shown your belly to a predador, you must escape, before you're savaged.

I thought that once I reached the Wolf Trials, I'd no longer be expected to *know my place.* At last, my shadow would be able to howl as an Alpha.

Wow, was I wrong.

Because the other packs are smart. They don't need to use you as a servant to make you feel like you're on your knees: they can reject, mock, or *kiss another wolf.*

In my run, I kick a snowbank, while my hands ball into fists. I'm burning up with fury. With jealousy. With utter shock. It seriously killed me to see Wynter in his arms. Kissing him! How many days has it been since she kissed me?

Fuck!

Here I thought we had something, that I was special, but I'd been an idiot to believe that. Or to even think Wynter would come back to where we'd left off.

I dart deeper into the forest away from Demon's Den and the party before I explode. Quickly, the path leads me down the mountain. The dark here is smothering. The branches are thick overhead, and moonlight struggles to break through. I shiver, pulling my long coat around me.

Rage simmers like the constant growl rumbling in my throat.

I sniff, struggling to make out Wynter's scent from the overpowering one of pine. There's a sharp breeze through the trees, which cuts across my cheeks and makes it hard to catch her scent, but I can just follow the trail.

It turns out that even when Wynter wrecks me, I'll still dash after her into a wood to protect her. I'd say that's me being smitten by her, completely lost. Except, Ri ran with me into the woods, searching for her, snarling just as loudly as he had done with me back at the party at Ballard.

The asshole Sun Wolf had been laughing at her.

I want to rip him apart.

My thoughts are racing just as fast as I am, swerving around trees and under branches, needing to find her. *Let's have a party on the forbidden side of the mountain with ghosts and freak transformations and heartbreak...*

I grit my teeth.

Tonight sucks. Scratch that, the entire day can go to hell. And how did I screw up so badly with Wyn at breakfast?

Once, we used to understand each other so easily. We even had a secret code that only the other knew. Does she even remember it? I haven't forgotten a thing about her but...since she went to the human world... she's forgotten me, right?

We were each other's worlds, and now to her, I'm a toy to be picked up and used when she needs me and dropped when she doesn't.

Still, I'm the asshole because my pain meant I let Paige manipulate me again. There was a time, when Flint trained me so hard that my body ached, bruised and bloodied, and I was half dead from exhaustion. Then I slipped back into believing that Sun Wolves could use me as a toy because I'd never get a chance to be a weapon.

Paige took advantage of that.

It's the only time Sun Wolves don't mind mixing socially with Moon Wolves because they call it: *picking a toy*.

Does Wynter even know that or is she too innocent?

And tonight, I'm the moron for letting Paige do it again because I was hurt at Wyn's rejection.

And Wyn saw.

Is that why she kissed Ri?

I bare my teeth, and my inner wolf paces angrily, desperate to be let out into the night. But if I transform, I won't be able to control him. I thrum with such rage that my skin itches.

Ballard announced to the party that Ri was *screwing* Wyn. Is it weird that the fact I saw Ri and Wyn *kissing* was somehow worse?

I catch my foot on a log that's hidden under the snow and stumble to my knees. I catch myself. I hiss, and for a moment, I close my eyes and take a steadying breath.

If Wyn had chosen anyone else but Ri to kiss…I

mean, I've had some kinky wank fantasies. I'm not a prude. Despite what I bet she thinks, I'm not a jealous asshole like the Shadow Wolf. Moon Wolves learn that they have to share when they're young or they go without.

But with Ri, it burns me up from the inside out.

I know that Wynter can't be mine. At least, not unless I win the Wolf Games. We can't be together publicly. But in private...in secret...under the moonlight at the Blossom Ball, she was mine.

We kissed.

And I was hers.

She *chose* me as her Blossom Prince.

It was the best moment of my life. But was it a lie? Because she's spent so long amongst the humans that she's forgotten what it means to be a wolf. What she did was as good as holding me down and biting a mating mark into my neck...or at least, pressing her fangs into the imprint of a bite like a promise of one.

In my heart, she's my mate.

But then, she kissed Ri and transformed. The stories say that in the past, your first kiss (or even first meeting) with your shadowmate, would pull out your wolf completely.

But that's bullshit, right?

We all saw at training that Ri's the monster amongst us: primal and feral.

My eyes narrow. I have to save Wynter from that killer, just like I've spent my life protecting my pack.

Up ahead, the trees are thinning. I can catch a

glimpse through it of a glade, which backs against the dark cliffs and gaping mouths of caves.

Wait, are we at the infamous spot of the murders?

Once I find Wynter, I'm bringing Parker here. He'll explode with excitement at the ghost hunting possibilities. I tilt up my chin. And from now on, I can be a good pack member: nobody's going to stop Moon Wolves from howling again.

I scrunch up my nose, as I sniff, and am flooded by Wynter's scent.

She's close.

Despite the breeze, I can make out something else in the air as well, which shouldn't be there: coppery and wrong. It makes the hair stand up on the back of my neck.

I rush forward, weaving through the trees.

In my mind, I picture the terror in Wynter's eyes when she transformed, and remember how beautiful she was as a wolf; I always knew that she would be. She was elegant in her white fur but powerful.

Okay, her eyes had been a shock: midnight black.

They'd transfixed me, shockingly dark against the white of her fur. I've never seen a wolf with eyes like that.

They're not the same as other Sun Wolves'.

My own wolf stirs at the memory, desperate to run to join her. I lift my head and sniff the air, but her scent has vanished.

Shit!

I turn on the spot, needing to find her. How could I lose her?

I snarl, slamming my fist into a tree trunk. "Asshole...Dick... Jerk." I punch the tree again, and it's weirdly satisfying when my knuckles bleed, even though I'm numb. I can't feel anything but cold, and I can't get the kiss out of my mind. "Why did it have to be Ri?"

A chuckle in the dark. "*Aww, you're talking about me...? You sweet flatterer.*"

I jump backward. Okay, *I'm* the *asshole, dick*, and *jerk* to have allowed myself to be too distracted to miss the other wolf hunting *me*.

Ri is scarily good at it.

Ri is at my side in seconds and snatches me by the neck. My feet scrabble on the slippery ground, as he swings me around and smashes me against the tree. I groan, as the back of my head thuds into the trunk, and I black out for a second, before my vision blurs, and I struggle to refocus on Ri.

I try to say something, but my brain's still too scrambled.

Ri pats my cheek; his nails are claws, and I wince, as they nick me. "Lost for words now, are you?"

I shove my hands into his shoulder. "Get the hell off me!"

Barely affected by my strikes, Ri leans one muscled arm over my throat, and I choke. I curl my hands over his arm, trying to wrench him away, but he only presses closer, putting on more pressure. My eyes roll back.

Ri's grin is sharp, and his gaze predatory. "What was that? Well, since you've come over all shy in my presence, why don't I talk? It's like this, see, I admire your spirit, but you're only a Moon Wolf and the son of a housekeeper too. So, tuck your tail between your legs, get back to the party, and stop sniffing around my mate, before I have to really hurt you."

"She's not your mate," I rasp. My neck is bruising; my temples throb. Yet fury courses through my blood. "She's *my Wyn*."

I can't hold back. I'm seconds from transforming into my wolf, as I did with Ballard. I've been hiding who I am for too long. I need to become the warrior I've been trained to be – the Alpha.

If I want to win the games and Wyn, then I must fight.

All those years taking the beatings from Flint weren't for nothing. It's time Ri found that out.

Ri blinks at me in shock, as I smile. Then I grip his elbow with the strength of my wolf with both my hands and in a quick, learned move, force his arm away and above my head, before ducking under and away from him. Then I turn and kick him in the back. He lets out a surprised holler, as he's slammed face first into the same tree that I'd just been pinned against.

I grin, as I crouch in a fighting stance. Ri may be bigger than me and think he's the king of everything when he's holding his shiny ax, but I'm quick and know how to fight.

And right now, I want to kick his ass.

I'm shocked that Ri's grinning, as he turns back to me. Lazily, he licks the blood off his lip.

"So, it's a fight you want?" Ri asks.

Why's he eying me with amused respect? I expected a flurry of fangs and claws. *I need it.*

I merely growl in response.

Ri's lips quirk. "Like I of all the initiates wouldn't like to see a wolf letting out his Alpha. Fair play to you, at least not all Moon Wolves are cowards."

In a sudden blur of movement, almost faster than I can see, Ri rushes me. I snarl, but it's too late, he's knocked me off my feet, crashing me into the snow and knocking the breath out of me.

He kneels above me, pressing his knees into my chest. Bruises deepen, and I pant, punching at his thighs, but he only grins an infuriatingly slow smile, flashing his fangs.

My heart is thudding too fast, my pulse is loud in my ears. All wolves are taught not to show their bellies, unless they're prepared to submit. Ballard bared his neck, when I held him down like this.

I'll never bare mine to Ri.

I snarl and fight harder.

Ri's eyes darken, glowing emerald in the black, as he leans down and snatches my wrists, gripping painfully, holding them by my side.

"But you see," Ri whispers into my ear; I shudder, kicking my legs, "you may be more than a Moon Wolf, but you're still less than *me*."

When Ri draws back, our noses are almost touching.

My eyes glint, dangerously, and just for a moment, Ri's expression sparks with fear. "You don't know what I am, asshole. No one does. But by the time we're done in these games, you'll be calling *me* Alpha."

Ri scrutinizes me, cold and serious. "Mind yourself, you're starting to sound like *me*."

I swallow. I'm nothing like Ri, right?

My temples are throbbing worse. A spear of moonlight breaks through the branches and across Ri and me; my wolf is about to burst free.

I can't stop it.

But then, a howl rises from the glade, close and desperate.

"*Wyn*," I gasp.

At the same time, Ri pulls back from me, alert and tense. He leaps up and dashes toward the sound. I'm on my feet in seconds and sprint after him through the snow for the glade up ahead.

Is Wynter hurt?

The world is in sharp focus at the thought that she needs me. My throbbing temples, neck, knuckles, chest...they don't matter. They've faded into the background. Yet Wynter's scent winds around me, calling to me.

Let me be in time...

Ri's growling next to me when I catch up. I can sense that he feels the same draw. But he's faster than me and bursts out into the glade first.

He suddenly freezes, however, and I skid on the icy ground, sliding into his strong back and tumbling over onto my knees.

What the hell...?

"Wyn?" I whisper, hardly daring to look up. "Parker...?"

I'm shaking. Lost. Sick with it.

Ri's at my shoulder, but I don't look round at him. I can't.

My cheeks are wet. Why are they wet?

My hands are stained red; they're tacky with it. The snow is soaked, as if a frozen crimson puddle; the moonlight glistens on it like crushed rubies.

It stinks; coppery and tangy. That is the scent... something is very wrong.

All of a sudden, my head is too heavy, as I force myself to raise it.

I don't want to see.

I can't...

Please, don't make me see...

I stare into Parker's silver eyes.

He's lying so close that our fingers are almost touching but not quite. They're frozen in the cold. His best shirt that he insisted on wearing for this party is shredded, hanging off him.

He's been mauled. His throat has been torn out. The river of red is running from him, and I'm stained in it.

I keen, scrambling back in horror from my dead foster brother.

"*No, no, no...*" I huddle back, my chest heaving for breath but I can't draw enough into my lungs. "Great Shadow Wolf, don't take my brother..."

I raise my head and stare into Wynter's black gaze. She's standing over Parker; her white paws are dyed red.

Ri stalks to her side, before kneeling next to Parker and checking his pulse. Dazed, I notice that his fingers become as stained as mine.

"Save him…you're a healer…you can still save him," I beg Ri.

Ri shakes his head with a deflated expression. Is he sincere? Why isn't he trying…something, *anything*?

I howl from deep within my shadow, desperate and despairing, fills the night. Wynter tips back her head and lets out a mournful howl to join me.

But it's too late. I know it. But I can't believe it.

Parker is dead.

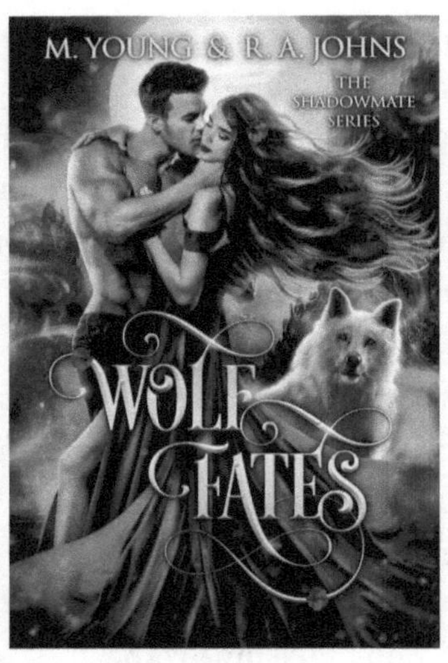

Start Reading Book 2, Wolf Fates!

Sun Pack

The Alpha, Wynter's mom and leader of all the packs in Fable

Wynter, hybrid and initiate

Addison, Alpha's mate and Wynter's step-dad

Hades, Wynter's dog

Iris, Wynter's friend

Ballard, initiate from elite family

Paige, initiate

Sun House, Alpha's mansion

Shadow Pack

Jack, Healer, leader of the Shadow Wolves, and Ryan and Brey's uncle

Ryan -- Ri, initiate and Irish Shadow King

Brey, Ri's sister, Irish princess and initiate

Teo, initiate

Moon Pack

Flint, leader of the Moon Wolves

Hunter, initiate and secretly trained warrior

Tala, Hunter's younger sister

Faith, Hunter's mom and housekeeper at Sun House

Parker, initiate and Hunter's adopted brother

Dex, Hunter's friend

Jex, initiate and Dex's twin

Initiates in the Wolf Games

Wynter

Ballard

Paige

Ryan

Brey

Teo

Hunter

Parker

Jex

ABOUT M. YOUNG

M. Young is an Aussie girl who loves all things wolves and vampires. She grew up listening to dark fairy tales, so it's no wonder mythology so often creeps into her writing.

When she's not writing Young Adult romance, she writes under Mila Young, a USA Today bestselling author of paranormal romance.

By day she rocks a keyboard as a marketing extraordinaire. At night she battles with her mighty pen-sword, creating fairytale retellings, and sexy ever after tales. In her spare time, she loves spends time with her husband and cuddling up with her cats, and dreams of her next vacation to Hawaii.

For more information...
www.milayoungbooks.com

ABOUT R.A. JOHNS

R. A. Johns makes her home in the English countryside with her swoonworthy husband, son, and mischievous cat. In the rare moments that she's not writing paranormal romance or fantasy, she's reading, listening to music, or devouring chocolate.

R. A. Johns also writes as USA Today bestselling author Rosemary A Johns. You know with Rosemary's books that there'll be enemies-to-lovers, swoonworthy book boyfriends, and shifters! She loves music, vampires, and of course, her cat.

Get ready for unique twists, fantasy worldbuilding, and lovers you'll never forget. The magical rebel worlds lie in front of you: laugh-out-funny, action-packed, and likely to hook your heart and never let go.

For more information...
https://rosemaryajohns.com

www.ingramcontent.com/pod-product-compliance
Lightning Source LLC
Chambersburg PA
CBHW050752190726
48285CB00005B/1624